Committed to Her Enemy

B. Heather Mantler

Mantler Publishing Prince George

Library and Archives Canada Cataloguing in Publication

Mantler, B. Heather, 1987-
Committed to her enemy / B. Heather Mantler.

ISBN 978-0-9868759-2-2

I. Title.

PS8626.A676C65 2011 C813'.6 C2011-906516-9

ISBN: 0986875929
ISBN-13:9780986875922

I want to dedicate this book to all those who helped me get through high school. In order of appearance: Penny Roze, Glen Monteith, Kristi Smith, Kathi Hughes, Dan Poulin, Tammy Livingstone, Judy Addie, and Mauri Bell. Thank you all for your support in my life.

Committed to Her Enemy

CHAPTER 1
RECOVERY

Emily's fingers lost their hold and the gun clattered to the ground. She slumped down and slid to the floor. Her eyes saw the puddle of blood around her, as it seemed to grow. Listening to her own breathing Emily thought it sounded shallow.

"Emily?" Brett moved Emily's head so she could see him. His red hair was soaked with sweat and there was blood smeared across one cheek. There was a worried look on his face.

"Emily?" Brett repeated.

"Get help," Emily said, her voice sounding raspy to her own ears, "If I lose much more blood there won't be any chance of saving me." Brett let go and Emily's head fell to one side. She watched Brett's feet leave.

What he was doing here? Emily wondered before passing out.

"Emily," a naggingly familiar voice called her back from the dark depths. Emily fought to get to the voice, but something paralysed her. The darkness wrapped itself around her and everything went black.

"The surgery to remove the bullet was successful and she has been given blood to replace what was lost," the voice was compassionate but professional, "The other injuries will have to heal on their own. She has yet to regain consciousness."

"How soon can I move her?" Grace's voice asked.

"I do not know, the doctor is one to determine that," the nurse answered.

"Then I need to see the doctor," Grace said.

"He is in surgery at the moment but I will let him know the minute he gets out," the nurse replied. The door shut and someone sat down in a nearby chair.

"I died and am now in hell, right?" Emily asked.

"I hope not," Grace answered, "If you're in hell then I'm dead and don't know it."

"Then how come I'm too hot and in a lot of pain?" Emily asked.

"How much pain?" Grace asked.

Emily opened her eyes and turned to look at Grace. Grace's medium brown hair was tied back and her grey eyes showed professional objectivity.

"I was wrong, this isn't hell, this is where they put the insane and mentally unstable that's why the walls are white and it smells like disinfectant," Emily said closing her eyes.

"Obviously you didn't injure yourself enough, the snide remarks are still coming. You are in a hospital because you tried to get yourself killed," Grace said.

"Is that what happened?" Emily asked.

"That is my guess," Grace answered.

"How many days ago was that?"

"That was this morning."

"Explains the pain, as well as the feeling of fresh stitches."

"I can call a nurse if you need something for the pain."

"Nah, I'll just sleep it off."

Grace didn't say anything. The room was quiet for a few minutes. Emily opened her eyes ready to ask Grace something. Grace was gone and it was dark in the room. Emily closed her eyes again and went to sleep.

"The doctor has informed me that she has woken up," Benjamin's voice filtered in through the fog.

"For short periods of time, yes," Grace's voice answered.

"Has she said anything about what happened?" Benjamin asked.

"No," Grace answered, "Even if she does remember it she won't discuss it with anyone but you, and only during the debriefing."

"When can she be moved back to the department?" Benjamin asked.

"I don't know. It has been a week, but the doctor doesn't think she should be moved yet," Grace answered, "And he has final say."

"Bring her back as soon as possible," Benjamin said.

"What about the other two bodies?" Grace asked.

"Were claimed before we could investigate them," Benjamin answered.

"But usually bodies have to be kept until after the autopsy," Grace said.

"A few pockets have some more money than before, I suspect," Benjamin said, "The police aren't going to launch an official investigation either. Which works in our favour, but also means the scene was scrubbed clean before we got there."

"That doesn't sound right," Grace said.

"I'll find out more once Emily debriefs," Benjamin said. The door shut and Emily drifted off again.

When Emily woke up again she felt the bed moving. She opened her eyes. Emily recognized the walls going passed her as those of department H and closed her eyes again.

The next time Emily woke up she was lying on the bed in the part of the medical lab that Grace referred to as Emily's office. The door was closed but

Emily could hear noise coming from the main room. Emily pulled the IV out of her arm. After the bleeding stopped Emily slowly got out of bed. Putting on her lab coat she left the office. There were three bleeding agents lying on examining tables and four with less major injuries sitting in chairs. Grace was trying to stop one of the three from bleeding to death. Emily went over to the next one and looked at the injuries.

The guy had taken a bullet in the stomach, had a broken arm, and there was a deep cut across his forehead. Emily went to the next person, whose wounds were still bloody, but there was no pulse or breath.

Emily went back to the guy. After making the preparations she started to fix him up.

By the time she was done Grace has finished and was taking care of the other agents. Emily went into Grace's office and started up the computer.

She had finished and had sent off her report when Grace came into the room and sat down in the other chair.

"Glad to see that you are finally up," Grace said.

"My muscles are complaining," Emily said, "But as long as I don't try to do too much I should be fine."

"Benjamin wants to talk to you," Grace said.

"I'll get there eventually," Emily said, "Where was the shooting gallery?"

"The group was coming back from a mission when a gang attacked them. They were caught by surprise," Grace said, "Benjamin believes that the gang had nothing to do with the mission."

"What do you think?" Emily asked.

"I'm willing to believe they are unrelated," Grace said, "I'm just concerned about the number of agents that are coming in here hurt. I'm one person, I don't need two dead bodies and one live one because all three arrived in the same condition."

"Benjamin won't let me go out again until he is positive that I'm better," Emily said, "I can help until then."

"That'll be good for now," Grace said before getting up and checking on her patients.

Two days later Emily showed up at Benjamin's office. Cynthia was sitting at her desk working. Emily leaned on the opposite side on the desk.

"Is Ben in?" Emily asked.

"He is talking to Mara, but I'm sure if you knock he'll be willing to interrupt the discussion," Cynthia answered.

"How long do you think they will talk?" Emily asked.

"Until the supper buzzer goes," Cynthia answered

"Will I interrupt anything other than talking?" Emily asked.

"I don't know, I don't interrupt them," Cynthia answered, "But if you do interrupt them remind Benjamin that he has a three foot pile of work he has to get done."

"Got my debriefing file in there?" Emily asked.

"No, it is right here," Cynthia answered handing Emily a file on the top of a pile on her desk, "It came in this morning."

"Thank you," Emily said taking the file.

"You're welcome," Cynthia said before going back to work. Emily went over to Benjamin's office door and opened it. Benjamin was sitting behind his desk and Mara was sitting in the chair opposite him. They both looked over at Emily.

"You wanted to talk to me?" Emily asked.

"Knock before coming in," Benjamin said.

"I can go away, I have better things to do," Emily replied.

"No, we'll deal with it now," Benjamin said.

"Then I will see you at supper," Mara told Benjamin as she got up. Emily entered the office and Mara left closing the door behind her. Emily sat down. Benjamin started searching his desk for something. Emily tossed the file on to his forearms. Benjamin stopped.

"Cynthia asked me to remind you that you have three foot pile of work that needs to be done," Emily said. Benjamin ignored her as he opened the file and looked through it.

"You've already filed your report?" Benjamin asked.

"Yes," Emily answered.

"Did you finish the mission?"

"Yes."

"It says here that you were attacked on the way back to the department."

"That's true."

"Why?"

"I think I walked into a secret meeting and they thought I heard something or saw something I wasn't supposed to."

"Did you?"

"No."

"Did you recognize either of the two men?"

"No."

"There appeared to have been a third person at the scene, but you only report two attacking you and only two corpses were found."

"The third guy didn't attack me. I don't even remember seeing him after the fight started."

"There are a few other things that seem inconsistent."

"Yeah, you are getting the side of the story from the person who was trying to stay conscious. There are bound to be some inconsistencies."

"Mr. Penn may have some further questions, but that is all for now."

Emily got up and left the office.

"I reminded him, but I don't think he was listening," Emily told Cynthia.

"Thanks for trying," Cynthia said, "I'll just hope that Benjamin gets in trouble when Mr. Penn shows up to find out what the hold up on the files are, and not me."

"I hope so too," Emily said before heading to her room.

A month later, Emily worked her way through an intensive training session. When Travis had finally given up on her for the day Emily staggered into the locker room. Stephanie was sitting on the bench.

"You're doing better," Stephanie commented.

"Thanks, but I feel like a beginner doing professional work. My muscles haven't hurt this much since basic training," Emily replied.

"You'll get it back, it'll just take a little while," Stephanie said, "Though it does put you out of the running for the competition."

"Competition between agents in the department, now there is a good reason to be injured on a mission," Emily said.

"What's your schedule for the rest of today?" Stephanie asked.

"I'm not sure. I probably should talk to Ben."

"He'll probably tell you to go see Mara. That's why he asked for a psychiatrist. And they were discussing you over breakfast, he wants to know that the mission didn't affect you mentally."

"It didn't affect me any worse than any other mission."

"Ben made a comment about agents needing to be fine mentally."

"If we were 'fine mentally' we wouldn't be agents."

"Just don't see how many times you can stare death in the face and live. That does funny things to the mind."

"Not in the plans." Emily went to the shower.

Benjamin was waiting for her when Emily left the locker room.

"Do you have a minute?" Benjamin asked.

"Probably," Emily answered.

"Yes or no would be the preferred answer," Benjamin said.

"Then no, unless you have something to say that I want to hear," Emily replied.

"You have an appointment with Dr. Mara in two hours," Benjamin said handing Emily an appointment card. Emily took the card.

"Make sure you are there," Benjamin walked away.

"Whatever," Emily ripped up the card before heading to her room.

Four hours later Mara entered Benjamin's office. Benjamin stopped and looked up as she sat down.

"How was your appointment with Emily?" Benjamin asked.

"It could have gone better," Mara answered.

"How so?"

"She could have shown up."

"She didn't show up?"

"She must not think it is important to talk about her experience. But from my observations people who go through a near death encounter have to talk about it or it has negative consequences."

"I'm not going to give her another mission until she has talked to you."

"I'll try talking to her tomorrow."

"Okay."

Mara got up and left Benjamin's office. Walking down the hall to her office Mara saw Stephanie.

"Stephanie," Mara called. Stephanie stopped and turned around.

"I was wondering if you had a minute," Mara said catching up to Stephanie.

"Only a few then I have to go talk to Logan," Stephanie said.

"You're a friend of Emily's, aren't you?" Mara asked.

"We know each other and talk to each other, but I'm not sure friends is the correct term," Stephanie said, "More like colleague."

"Have you talked to her lately?" Mara asked.

"This morning," Stephanie answered.

"How do you think she is doing?"

"About usual, logically insane and trying to out do herself. In a little bit of pain still but she doesn't want to admit it."

"Why not?"

"That's Emily."

"It seems to me that she doesn't want to talk about what happened."

"Emily is a trained agent, unless ordered otherwise she isn't going to tell anyone, except for maybe Dr. Grace, what happened. That is procedure."

"Why would she tell Dr. Grace?"

"If you don't know I don't have time to explain it. I have to go see Logan now." Stephanie walked away.

Mara watched her walk away before going to her office.

Emily sat down on Grace's examining table. Grace entered the office.

"How are you today?" Grace asked.

"Sore, tired, and starting to get bored," Emily answered.

"How tired and sore?"

"Travis worked me over this morning, all my muscles are screaming at me. The salve helps somewhat."

"Take it easy, you won't be back to your normal level of activity overnight."

"I know."

"Anything else bugging you?"

"Do you think Mara and Ben are sleeping together?"

"That is their business if they are."

"But if it affects their objectivity then people above them should be told."

"Yes, I think they are sleeping together. But I think Mr. Penn will figure it all out for himself," Grace responded, "Now can we get back to your medical check?"

"Yeah," Emily laid down. Grace took out the hand held medical scanner. Running it slowly, five inches above Emily, Grace ran passed it along Emily's body. Once finished Grace placed the medical scanner into its slot in the computer and brought the results up on the monitor. Emily sat up. Grace studied the results.

"Need any help around here?"

"Not at the moment," Grace looked up from the computer, "The scan shows that everything is normal. One piece of advice though."

"What's that?" Emily asked as she got off the table.

"Take it slow," Grace answered as Emily opened the door.

"I am," Emily said then left. Grace closed down the scan's results.

"And don't do anything stupid," she said under her breath.

The next day Mara knocked on Emily's door and then waited for an answer. After a minute Mara knocked again, receiving no answer she opened the door. Emily was lying on the floor reading a magazine. Mara noticed the bed was unmade, magazines were scattered all over the floor and shelves. Emily did not look up as Mara stepped into the room.

"Emily, you missed your appointment yesterday," Mara said.

"Must have slipped my mind," Emily's voice was cold.

"So, why don't we talk now?" Mara suggested.

"Because I'm busy at the moment and you are disturbing me," Emily's voice got colder.

"Emily, you just about died, most people need to talk that through before they are better," Mara said.

"Getting killed is a hazard of my job, I knew that when I took it. That and the contract I signed states that I only discuss my missions with my superior. As you do not fit that description I would rather you leave me alone and let me deal with my problems on my own," Emily said.

"I am here if you need to talk," Mara said.

"Whatever, now get out," Emily told her. Mara turned around and left. The door slid shut behind her.

Grace was shutting her computer off for the night when Emily walked into the medical lab.

"What's up?" Grace asked.

"Not much, besides Mara believing that I might talk to her," Emily answered.

"Some people are more delusional than others."

"I tried to explain the contract to her, but I don't think she quite understood."

"Most doctors have a similar contract, I don't know about psychiatrists."

"I doubt it matters, she probably tells Ben everything anyway."

"So you told her that you couldn't talk about it. What are you going to tell Mr. Penn?"

"The same story I told Ben. Brett was on a mission, I don't plan to get him in trouble if I can help it."

"I'm surprised he didn't call the department rather than the hospital."

"I'm glad, I know you are a good doctor, but the hospital is better equipped to deal with life or death situations."

"That is true. Anything else up?"

"I keep wondering how I ended up where I am."

"I wonder how you got to this point too, but it doesn't keep me up at night. I usually don't need to think further than you are you and you don't get into situations like the rest of us do."

"I guess that is as good an answer as I'll get right now."

"You're bored, aren't you?"

"What was your first clue?"

"Then why don't you do the night shift, so I can get some rest. I'm pretty sure someone has come in injured every day this week."

"Sure."

Grace got up and left the medical lab. Emily sat down and rebooted the computer.

One thirty in the morning the door opened and Jerry dragged one of his crew inside.

"Where's Dr. Grace?" Jerry demanded as he dumped the guy onto the table.

"Asleep," Emily answered as she got up. She pulled the medical scanner out of its slot.

"Aren't you going to wake her?" Jerry asked.

"No, you're stuck with me. Though I'm not sure why you're worried, you aren't the patient," Emily replied.

"You're an agent," Jerry said as Emily started the scan.

"Yes, but I also moonlight as a doctor," Emily said. Finishing the scan she put the scanner back in its slot, "What happened?"

"Shouldn't that have been your first question?" Jerry asked.

"That is my first question. Now answer it," Emily brought up the results on the computer.

"We were doing a training run, he complained of being tired then he collapsed," Jerry answered.

"That it?"

"Yeah."

"Did he hit something when he collapsed?"

"The ground."

"Did he hit anything that would give a viable reason for the internal bleeding?"

"He might of, it was dark and I wasn't really paying that much attention. When can I get him back?"

"When he is done healing, which will be at least several days."

"Have someone call me." Jerry left the medical lab. Emily did what she could for the guy and then went back to the computer.

Grace arrived at six thirty.

"You okay?" Grace asked.

"I'm fine," Emily answered.

"Fall asleep?"

"No, I'm in the middle of a bout of insomnia."

"Nightmares?"

"Inability to fall asleep or stay asleep."

"Anything happen?"

"Jerry brought one of his guys in. He should be okay in a couple of days."

"Sounds about usual. How long do you think this bout of insomnia will last?"

"Not sure, why?"

"Might as well make use of it while it lasts."

"I can do night shift until the insomnia goes away."

"Thank you."

"But since you are here I'll go see if I can get enough sleep to function.""

"See you later."

Emily got up and left the medical lab.

Warner showed up at seven o'clock at Benjamin's office. Cynthia was at her desk when he arrived.

"Where is Benjamin?" Warner asked Cynthia.

"As far as I know in his room," Cynthia answered, "I can page him if you would like."

"No, just direct me to where I can find," Warner paused to look into the file he was holding, "Emily."

"I don't know where Emily is currently but I would suggest the cafeteria," Cynthia replied.

"Thank you," Warner said then turned around and went down the hallway.

After failing to go to sleep Emily ended up in the assignment lab. She was typing on a project she was working on when Jeff wandered over to her.

"How are you doing?" he asked as he sat down in the chair at the next console.

"Bored," Emily answered not looking up from what she was doing.

"I heard Benjamin had another mission for you. He wouldn't give it to you because Mara hasn't okayed you mentally. I think it is a rumour though."

"Doubt it, he seems to have forgotten the rules of the contract."

"Anyway, I was wondering if you could do me a favour since you're bored."

Emily stopped working and looked at Jeff.

"What's the favour?"

"I have a problem and I don't want anything on my medical record."

"That's simple enough to do depending on the problem. Jerry and crew are supposed to have their pre-mission medical checks today just before lunch, so I'll meet you there just after breakfast."

"Thanks." Jeff got up and left. Emily went back to what she was doing.

The cafeteria was not yet open when Warner got there. Noticing no one around he headed back to Benjamin's office. Warner was half way there when he found Benjamin and Mara standing in the hallway talking.

"Good morning, Mr. Penn," Benjamin said when he saw Warner.

"Good morning, Benjamin, Dr. Mara," Warner replied.

"Good morning," Mara said.

"Benjamin, I'm looking for one of your agents," Warner said.

"Which one?" Benjamin asked.

"Emily."

"She could be anywhere, but she is most likely to be in her room."

"And where would that be?"

"It's near the gym."

"I think you better show me."

"Alright. I'll talk to you later. Dr. Mara," Benjamin said.

"Okay. Good-bye, Mr. Penn," Mara left them and headed for her office. Benjamin led the way to Emily's room.

"Thank you, Benjamin, You can go to work now," Warner told Benjamin when they got there.

"You're welcome," Benjamin replied then went off to his office. Warner knocked on Emily's door. Getting no response Warner knocked louder. Stephanie came out of her room next to Emily's as Warner knocked a third time.

"Emily isn't in her room, if that's who you're looking for," Stephanie said.

"You wouldn't happen to know where she is, would you?" Warner asked.

"I doubt she would be in the medical lab, so she's probably in the assignment lab until the cafeteria opens," Stephanie answered.

"Where is the assignment lab?" Warner asked.

"You go back the way you came until you can see Benjamin's office, then you take the first left, and it's easy to find from there," Stephanie told him.

"Thank you," Warner said.

"No problem," Stephanie replied before heading in the opposite direction. Warner followed Stephanie's directions and found himself in a hallway with three rooms going off it. Each had the name of the room beside the doorframe. Upon entering the room marked assignment lab Warner found three people sitting at different consoles, only one female. Warner went up to her.

"Excuse me, but are you Emily?" he asked.

"Could be, who's asking?" she asked without looking up.

"Mr. Penn, Benjamin's superior," Warner answered.

"Then I'm Emily," Emily answered.

"Good, I would like to talk to you about the report you sent in on your last mission, if there's a place to talk privately around here," Warner said.

"Benjamin's office is the most private room in the building," Emily said as she shut down the program on the computer and got up. Warner and Emily headed for Benjamin's office. Cynthia was sitting at her desk typing when they walked up.

"Where's Benjamin?" Warner asked.

"Talking to Mara in the cafeteria," Cynthia answered.

"So, which do you think good friends or sleeping together?" Emily asked.

"Definitely sleeping together. I just didn't think he would get over Jessica so quickly," Cynthia answered.

"She's only been dead, what three months?" Emily asked.

"Two, it just feels longer," Cynthia replied.

"We are going to use Benjamin's office, and I ask that we're not disturbed. That means Benjamin as well," Warner told Cynthia.

"Okay," Cynthia responded. Warner and Emily went into the office. Emily sat down in the chair in front of the desk and put her feet up on the edge of the desk. Warner shut the door and sat down in the chair behind the desk.

"Sleeping together?" Warner asked Emily.

"Benjamin and Mara," Emily answered, "Though no confirmation on that, but everyone thinks so."

"Two months after his wife died?" Warner asked.

"Not entirely uncommon, but I would think that Mara would know better," Emily replied.

"May I ask why the rumours?" Warner asked.

"It seems to be affecting Ben's ability to do his job," Emily said, "Jessica used to set him straight if this happened, but now there isn't anyone who is able to."

"Did he ask about your report?"

"A little bit, but he didn't go into any detail."

"Did he mention that there have been ten incidents of agents or groups of agents being attacked after they have completed their missions and are headed back?"

"No," Emily answered.

"It all happened in a two week period. According to Benjamin's note you thought you walked into a secret meeting, is that correct?"

"Yes, that was my guess."

"Did you recognize any of the three men that were there?"

"No."

"Did they say anything to you?"

"Directly, no," Emily answered, "But two of them decided they should 'take me out' so that I wouldn't repeat anything I had heard."

"And did you hear anything?"

"No, my mind was on something else."

"The police cleaned up the scene and did not investigate what happened," Warner said.

"Why?"

"According to Benjamin's theory in the initial report he figured that there were a few lined pockets and the whole incident was covered up."

"You don't believe it?"

"There was no money exchanged, or if there was there is no trace of the money," Warner said, "The next theory was that the Black Company was involved, since they like to get nasty. This has been true in eight of the nine incidents. On each of those the agents were doing a mission given to us from the Carbrat institute."

"But two weren't."

"Your incident and one other."

"Given the neighbourhood I was in I could have stumbled into a gang meeting," Emily said, "They have their wars, secret meetings and such too."

"Yes, they do. And there have been some gang activity."

"But there is no way to figure out?"

"Whoever attacked you had police well enough in hand to get both bodies before autopsies were performed and get the case dropped."

"Which sticks us back to not knowing who or what," Emily sighed.

"There has been talk of another player, but that is still unverified," Warner said, "Since the third man got away I would advise you to be careful, they may still be searching for you."

"Does that mean I'll get a mission sometime soon?"

"Benjamin hasn't given you one?" Warner was surprised.

"He wants me to spill my guts out to Mara first, just in case I went insane from my near death experience."

"You are a voluntary agent, are you not?"

"If you want to call it that."

Warner opened the file to the last page and started writing.

Mara and Benjamin finished breakfast and headed to his office.

"I'm not sure why you want to push it, you know the rules better than I do and Emily won't talk about what happened because of the rules," Mara said.

"I don't feel safe sending her out on a mission until you have made sure nothing from her experience is going to affect her later," Benjamin said, "Rules or not."

"I understand that but I don't think Emily is going to talk about it," Mara said as they got to Benjamin's office. Benjamin put his hand on the doorknob.

"Mr. Penn is using your office," Cynthia said from her desk. Benjamin dropped his hand. "He asked not to be disturbed."

"Why?" Benjamin asked.

"I don't know," Cynthia answered.

"I have to get back to my work," Mara said then left.

"If he is using my office how am I supposed to work?" Benjamin asked.

"I have no idea," Cynthia said as she went back to her own work. Benjamin stood there looking lost for a minute before sitting down on the floor.

Grace was surprised when Jeff entered the medical lab.

"Something I can do for you?" Grace asked.

"No, I asked Emily if she'd do me a favour and she said to meet her here after breakfast," Jeff answered.

"Well, she isn't here right now," Grace told Jeff, "When did you talk to her?"

"This morning while she was working in the assignment lab."

"She usually keeps her word, unless there is a good reason. Maybe she's a little late."

"Maybe. I'll wait a few minutes, but I have to meet Jonathan to discuss my next mission in half an hour."

"Well, you can wait until then. She'll be here for Jerry and crew," Grace said.

Silence settled over the room as Warner wrote in Emily's file. Emily sat in the chair across from him. He finally looked up.

"My advice to Benjamin is to let you have another mission as soon as Travis says it is okay. As far as your sanity, Mara isn't going to help you regain that. And as far as your near death experience, as Benjamin keeps calling it, I can't see any ill effects," Warner told Emily. She nodded. "On your way out tell Benjamin I want to speak with him."

"Okay," Emily said as she got up. She left the office.

"Warner wants to talk to you," Emily told Benjamin. Benjamin got up and went into his office. Once the door was closed Emily went over to Cynthia. "Can I use your computer for a minute?"

"Sure," Cynthia shut down what she was doing and got out of her chair. Emily sat down and started typing. Cynthia tried looking over Emily's shoulder but Emily was going too fast for her. Then suddenly the monitor went red and asked for an ID number.

Emily pulled a card out of her pocket and swiped it though the ID reader. The computer processed the information then the screen came up in a program Cynthia had never seen.

"Where are you?" Cynthia asked, as Emily started typing quickly again.

"The security system," Emily answered without pausing. Half a minute later the screen again went red, this time Emily typed a number in. The computer screen changed almost immediately and Emily went on typing. Cynthia could barely keep up with what Emily was doing. In less than three minutes Emily finished what she was doing.

"Thanks," Emily said as she got up.

"You're welcome," Cynthia replied as she sat down and went back to work. Emily headed to the medical lab.

Benjamin entered his office and shut the door behind him. Warner sat in the chair behind his desk, so Benjamin took the other chair in the room.

"You wanted to talk to me?" he asked.

"Yes. Why do you insist that Emily talk to Dr. Mara?" Warner asked.

"I feel it would be better for her to talk about what happened," Benjamin answered.

"You feel? What happened to objectivity? What happened to the clearly stated rules? You know it is against the rules to talk about the details to someone other than the person's superior."

"Yes, but no one has had a near death experience like that without it affecting their performance on other missions."

"I have two suggestions. One: give Emily another mission as soon as Travis says she is ready. The second: quit mooning over Dr. Mara. It doesn't help anyone." Warner got up, gathered his papers and left.

Grace was sitting at her computer and Jeff was nowhere in sight when Emily arrived at the Medical lab.

"Welcome back. What have you been up to?"

"Ended up talking to Warner most of the morning. Did Jeff come in?" Emily asked.

"Yeah, came, waited and left. Not five minutes ago he decided you weren't coming and left."

"Oh well, I'll have to see him later."

"Doesn't sound like he'll be here long. He said he had a meeting with Jonathon today."

"I know I'll see him before he leaves."

"How is your private practice doing?"

"Business is slow at the moment."

"You going to stick around a play referee for Jerry's goons?"

"Sure."

"Good."

Jerry's crew were finished their medical checks in three hours. Grace was relieved when the last one left.

"The energy level of a five-year-old on sugar and the manners of a cave man, each and every member of that crew is a handful," Grace commented, "How does Jerry handle them?"

"His fists and having the energy of a five-year-old on a couple pots of coffee," Emily answered from where she was working on the computer.

"How do you know?"

"Reports posted in the security system."

"I don't even want to know how you get into there."

"Like I'll ever tell."

"What did Mr. Penn want?"

"To ask a few questions about my report. Mine is one of two that didn't connect to a pattern they were following. Warner said that I get a mission once Travis has okayed it."

"Travis came by the other day to check on your progress."

"He can see most of my progress for himself."

"He thinks you need more time."

"And you think?"

"I agreed with him."

"Okay. Warner figured I didn't need to talk about my problems to Mara."

"How'd he figure that?"

"He figured I am beyond Mara's help."

"He's right. Benjamin in on the discussion?"

"No, he was forced to sit on the floor outside his office while we talked."

"That would have been funny."

Jeff entered the medical lab; he had a file in his hand.

"I'm supposed to be here for my medical check before Jonathon sends me out on my next mission," Jeff said handing the file to Grace.

"Why don't you do this one? I'm tired," Grace said handing the file to Emily. Emily took it before standing up.

"After you," Emily said gesturing to her office. Jeff entered the office and Emily followed him in. Grace sat down and finished Emily's game of solitaire before getting to her own work.

Twenty minutes later Jeff left Emily's office and then the medical lab. Five minutes after that Emily came out and sat down on the other chair.

"So?" Grace asked.

"He's fine, as per his medical check," Emily said.

"And the problem he wanted to talk to you about?"

"Dealt with that first."

"I'm sure he's happy about that."

"Yeah."

Neither said anything for a few minutes.

"I'm gonna go try to get some sleep before I have to do the night shift," Emily said standing up.

"See you later," Grace said. Emily left the medical lab.

Emily showed up at the medical lab just before Grace was going to head for bed.

"Have a good night," Grace said as they passed.

"I'll settle for a quiet night," Emily replied. Once Grace was gone Emily sat down at the computer and started working on her project. Two guys came in shortly after, one with a broken nose and the other with a broken arm. Emily dealt with them and sent them to bed before going back to work. The rest of the night was quiet.

Mara entered the medical lab about six in the morning.

"Where is Dr. Grace?" she asked Emily.

"In bed asleep or just getting up, it's hard to tell from here," Emily answered.

"When will she be in?" Mara asked.

"Probably within the hour, unless she has decided to sleep in, which is doubtful," Emily answered.

"Is there any reason why you are being so general?" Mara asked.

"Because I don't know exacts, she left last night and I haven't seen her since."

"She leaves the medical lab in your hands at night?"

"Only while I'm dealing with my current bout of insomnia. If it is necessary for you to see Grace, you can sit and wait."

"You have no respect for people and their stations. You call Benjamin Ben and now you forget the proper address for Dr. Grace."

"Sorry, old habit. I'm used to talking to Grace rather than talking about her."

"I'll wait for Dr. Grace," Mara sat down. Emily went back to her project.

Grace entered the medical lab half an hour later.

"Can I help you, Dr. Mara?" Grace asked seeing her.

"I have been feeling sick lately and I would like to know why," Mara said.

"Well, if you get up on the table I can do a medical check," Grace said. Mara got up on the table and lay down. Grace took out the scanner and did the check. Mara sat up. Grace put the scanner back into the computer and brought the results.

"Well?" Mara asked.

"Emily, will you come here," Grace said. Emily got up and went over to look over Grace's shoulder.

"What is wrong?" Mara asked looking at Grace and then Emily.

"You are developing a serious departmental problem," Emily answered.

"I'm what?" Mara asked.

"You're pregnant," Grace replied.

"That's impossible, how could I get pregnant?" Mara asked.

"I hope that's a rhetorical question," Emily commented as she went back to what she was doing, "I really don't want to have to explain those facts of life."

"Emily," Grace said.

"The scan looks healthy, as long as you don't do anything stupid you should be fine. Though I wouldn't suggest telling Ben."

"How would you know all this?" Mara asked.

"Agent and M.D.," Emily answered, "That and experience. Though at the moment sleep sounds good," Emily got up and left the medical lab.

"M.D.?" Mara asked.

"Why not? They allow other things that are worse," Grace said, sitting down in the seat Emily just vacated.

"Why did she suggest I not tell Benjamin?"

"He is the head of a department that does not recognize children born within it."

"Oh," Mara sat and thought for a couple minutes before getting up and leaving the medical lab.

Travis was waiting for Emily that morning, when she arrived in the gym.

"What took you so long?" Travis asked when he saw her.

"I was sleeping until five minutes ago," Emily answered.

"Benjamin asked whether you were ready for another mission. I talked to Dr. Grace, she agreed with me that you need some more time before going out on another mission," Travis said. Emily shrugged.

"What woke you up?" Travis asked.

"Not sure exactly, the dream faded before I could pin it down," Emily answered.

"You pass out on me and I'll get Dr. Grace to put you under for two days," Travis said.

"Whatever," Emily said. Travis got her to start.

Emily entered the medical lab that evening and immediately sat down at the computer without saying anything to Grace. Grace finished up what she was doing and headed for the door.

"Have a good night," Grace said to Emily. Emily nodded and Grace left.

At two in the morning, the door of the medical lab opened and a stretcher was rolled in. Emily got up and went over. The young man on the stretcher had blood pumping out of a hole in his chest.

"Why is he here? Why wasn't he taken to the hospital?" Emily demanded, turning to the guy who had brought the stretcher in before she started grabbing what she needed.

"I was told to bring him here," the guy answered.

"Well, then you better get Dr. Grace and get the hospital to send a helicopter," Emily said starting to work, "And do it now." The guy left.

Grace entered the medical lab, followed by the man that had woken her up. Grace took in the scene. A young man that looked familiar was lying covered in blood on a stretcher. Emily was sitting against a back cupboard hugging her knees to her chest and staring into space.

"Call the hospital back," Grace told the man behind her, "Tell them to send a coroner's van instead of a helicopter." The man left the medical lab. Grace went over to where Emily sat and crouched down.

"Emily," Grace said. Emily looked up at her. Grace shivered at the coldness in Emily's green eyes, "Are you okay?"

"I will be," Emily answered after a moment.

"What happened?"

"Someone, somewhere decided to send the guy here instead of the hospital. I did what I could but he had already lost a lot of blood. If they had been that much quicker and sent him to the hospital he might still be alive."

"I'll talk to Benjamin about it. It won't bring the guy back but it might save the next person."

Emily nodded.

"Go try to get some sleep, I'll take the rest of the night shift."

"I can finish it, I doubt I'll sleep tonight anyway."

"You sure?"

"Yes."

Grace opened the cupboard next to Emily and pulled out a sheet. After closing the cupboard she went over to the stretcher. She unfolded the sheet and placed it over the corpse. Grace started toward the door then stopped.

"Are you sure you'll be okay?" Grace asked Emily.

"I will be fine," Emily answered. Grace left the medical lab. Ten minutes later the coroner showed up and took the body away.

When Grace entered the medical lab the next morning it appeared to be empty.

"Emily," Grace called. There was no response. Grace looked around the medical lab. She found Emily asleep on the bed in her office. Grace went over and pulled the covers over Emily. Emily didn't stir. Leaving the office Grace closed the door and sat down at the computer.

A month later Benjamin went looking for Emily to give her the next mission. He found her in the assignment lab working on the computer.

"Doing anything important?" he asked.

"Yes," Emily answered.

"What?"

"A personal project, one you don't need to know about."

"Do you have a few minutes to hear about your next mission?"

"Yes, in about five minutes."

'Then I'll see you in my office in five minutes." Benjamin left.

Cynthia was working at her desk when Emily came up to her.

"Ben in?"

"Yes, and he's waiting for you," Cynthia answered.

"Thanks," Emily entered Benjamin's office.

"What is my mission?" she asked sitting down in the chair across from Benjamin and put her feet up on Benjamin's desk. Benjamin looked up from his work.

"You took ten minutes," Benjamin stated.

"I got stopped in the hallway. Now what's my mission, I've waited two months to get it," Emily said.

"Because this is the first one since your accident I have chosen an easy mission for you. For the mission you will have to pick up a briefcase and deliver it."

"That's what you call a mission?"

"Do you want a mission or not?"

"I guess it's better than sitting around here."

"Here are the specifics of the mission," Benjamin handed Emily a file. Emily took it and stood up.

"You gonna sit there and watch every damn thing I do as well?"

"No, Travis is."

Emily left the office. Cynthia was sitting at her desk talking to a tall guy with shoulder-length red hair. Cynthia was talking to the guy like he was the last man on earth. Emily walked the short distance over to the desk. The guy looked up and smiled at her.

"Long time no see," he said.

"Gotta be at least six or seven years," Emily answered.

"You two know each other?" Cynthia seemed surprised.

"Yeah, Brett and I grew up together, or at least since we were three," Emily answered.

"Oh."

"What are you up to?" Brett asked Emily, "Getting into trouble?"

"Nope, got handed an errand to run," Emily answered, "What are you doing here?"

"For some reason this department is asking for outside help."

"And you're the help? This department is in trouble."

"I'm the top agent from my department."

"So was I, then I went and tried to get myself killed."

"Was it a fun experience?"

"Not really, it was more frustrating."

"Oh well, you survived it."

"Yeah, anyway I gotta go meet Travis. I'll probably see you around depending on how long you stay."

"See you."

Emily headed for the assignment lab and Brett went back to talking to Cynthia.

Travis was waiting for Emily when she arrived.

"Took you long enough," he said.

"What do I need to do?" Emily asked.

"You will go see Matt, the inventor, in his office. He will give you a metal briefcase with a laptop that has the blue prints to his latest invention on it. You will deliver it directly to Caden Carbrat."

"So, I've been demoted to errand girl now. When do I head out?"

"Tomorrow morning."

"Why tomorrow?"

"Because Grace should do the before mission medical check."

"If Grace does another check of my health I'll guarantee the scanner finds something. I'll see you after I run my errand." Emily turned and stalked out of the room.

Entering her room Emily threw the file folder on her bed. Still annoyed, she slumped into the oversized chair. Emily closed her eyes and focused on calming down. She didn't need to see Grace again, what she needed was to get out of here before the walls finished closing in and crushed her. Emily smiled at the thought of the look on Travis and Benjamin's faces if they saw her really go nuts. Slowly relaxing, Emily realized how tired she was. Trying not to go to sleep, Emily picked up the file folder off the bed and started to read.

Emily woke to the door of her room being opened. Keeping her eyes closed Emily sensed someone step into the room and then heard the door close.

"You asleep?" Brett asked. Emily opened her eyes to look at him.

"Not anymore," she answered.

"Sorry if I disturbed you," Brett said sitting down on the bed.

"I shouldn't have gone to sleep anyway."

"I know you're probably tired of being asked this, but how are you?"

"Doing better than when you last saw me. Just about dying isn't half as bad as people make it out to be. It's the people afterwards that drive you nuts. They haven't let me out for months, now they hand me an errand and call it a mission."

"Stir crazy?"

"Something like that."

"And these people think they know you? How could they be that wrong?"

"Don't ask. Speaking of my near death experience, I've been meaning to thank you."

"You're welcome. I was just glad you didn't break my cover. Your mission was over, while I was in the middle of mine."

"I figured you had some reason for being there, so I didn't say anything. What do you think about this place?"

"Benjamin is not the brightest bulb."

"I call him Ben, because it is disrespectful if you don't call people by their proper name and or title."

"Like what?"

"Benjamin Ben, Dr. Mara, just Mara. I call Dr. Grace just Grace because every time I call her Dr. Grace I get Dr. Emily in return."

"Ah. You got your degree?"

"Yeah, I even get to use it occasionally."

"Cool and congratulations."

"Thanks, that was a while back."

"You weren't in much of a talking mood when we last met and before that we hadn't talked since you went off to school."

"We were twelve, you went off to get military training and I went off to become a doctor."

"A while back."

"How are you getting along with Cynthia?"

"Was it that obvious?"

"Your face wasn't but hers was."

"I met her when she showed up with Ben for a conference with Mr. Penn and the other department heads. No shoulders included. Anyway, we met and we got to know each other. I like her and she's really pretty."

A buzzer went off somewhere outside in the hallway.

"What is that?"

"Lunch or supper, probably supper."

"This department has a buzzer to call people for meals?"

"Yeah, what did you guys in the other department use to call people for meals?"

"We don't, you eat when you're hungry."

"Well, the cook wouldn't go for that so we have designated meal times."

"Then we'd better go for supper." Brett got up. Emily followed suit and they headed for the cafeteria.

Travis accompanied Ryan to the medical lab. When they got there Grace had already gone for supper.

"Now if you hadn't broken your arm we would be eating instead of waiting," Travis told Ryan.

"It's not my fault," Ryan whined as he cradled his right arm. Travis was close to banging his head on the wall when he saw Emily coming down the hall with the young man Benjamin had introduced to him earlier. Neither seemed to notice Travis and Ryan.

"Emily," Travis called. Emily looked at him. Travis saw no trace of the anger that was there this morning.

"What?" she asked.

"Do you know where Dr. Grace is?" Travis asked.

"Nope, why are you looking for her?" Emily asked.

"Ryan did something stupid and broke his arm," Travis answered.

"Doesn't sound too serious. Grace is probably eating supper, you'll have to wait for her," Emily said.

"Can you help?" Travis asked.

"Nope," Emily answered.

"Why not?"

"Because I don't have a key into the medical lab, only Grace does. You have to either find her or wait." Emily and the young man continued on. Travis sighed and leaned his back against the wall.

Grace came down the hallway five minutes later.

"Emily said you needed help," Grace said.

"Ryan broke his arm," Travis replied. Grace swiped her ID through the ID reader and opened the door.

"You can go have something to eat," Grace told Travis, "I'll take care of the rest of this."

"Thanks. I don't suppose Emily has come in?" Travis asked.

"No, but I expect her this evening," Grace answered.

"I want to know that she is fine before she leaves," Travis said, then he walked away. Grace led Ryan inside the medical lab.

Shortly after nine Emily came into the medical lab. Grace was sitting at the computer.

"So, you have a mission," Grace said.

"More like an errand," Emily responded.

"Well, you get out of here for a while."

"Two hours max, if that."

"Travis is asking for another medical check before you go."

"He said something about that, I told him no."

"Since I gave you a medical check at the beginning of the week you should be fine, unless you have done something that would affect your health.

"No. Brett has moved to this department on a temporary basis."

"Why?"

"Someone, somewhere feels that the department needs help. He's apparently the best from his department."

"Well, if the department needs help then he is the one to help."

"There is something else, but I don't know what it is."

"Something else?"

"Yeah, he didn't mention it but I can tell there is another reason he is here. That and he said something about being on a mission when he helped me."

"How would being on a mission be unusual?"

"I don't know, my gut says there is more to this than he is telling me."

"Hopefully it isn't anything serious."

"I haven't seen Mara since she showed up here in the medical lab. What happened to her?"

"She disappeared from the department, but is safe and healthy wherever destiny has placed her."

"I'm sure the departments aren't that interested in one pregnant woman who isn't all that useful."

"No, but from the sounds of it Benjamin is looking and Mara got scared."

"I'm not sure whether I should be cheering for one or the other or ignore it completely."

"Easier to ignore it completely."

"True, I just hope the baby is okay."

"Some days I think you care more about children than adults."

"I have to go to bed, I'll see you tomorrow."

"Good night."

Emily left the lab.

Emily woke to the sound of her alarm. As she rolled over the alarm stopped. Slowly Emily got out of bed and headed for the shower.

"Six o'clock ante meridian, why'd my alarm have to go off now?" Emily muttered to herself. Emily tossed her pyjamas at her bed before she stepped into the shower. Twenty minutes later she stepped out, dried off and got dressed. Once dressed Emily started to look for her toothbrush, then caught a look at herself in the mirror.

"You look like hell," she said to herself. Her brown hair was dripping, her clothes looked like they hadn't been washed in a week and she looked like she hadn't slept at all. Finding her toothbrush Emily brushed her teeth. After that she washed her face, then brushed and dried her hair. Going through her drawers Emily realized that she had to do laundry soon, but she found clothes that were clean and mostly wrinkle free. After she changed Emily left her room and headed for Benjamin's office. Cynthia was already sitting there working when Emily got there.

"What time do you get up?" Emily asked Cynthia.

"Five usually, unless someone is coming or going earlier than that," Cynthia answered without looking up.

"You're nuts," Emily said.

"Someone has to be here, Benjamin doesn't get up before eight unless someone kicks him out of bed," Cynthia said. Both ladies heard footsteps coming down the hall. An older man came around the corner. He walked briskly toward Cynthia and Emily.

"Would either of you two ladies know where Benjamin's office is?" the man asked, he had a slight accent that Emily didn't recognize.

"This is Benjamin's office. What do you need?" Cynthia asked.

"I am Alfred, I am here to replace Benjamin," Alfred said pulling out some papers and handing them to Cynthia. Cynthia looked them over and then handed the papers back.

"Welcome to department H, I'm Cynthia."

"Pleased to meet you," Alfred said, "And you would be?"

"Emily, an agent."

"Ah, I have heard many things about you. I hope some of them are not true," Alfred said.

"Depends on who's telling the stories," Emily replied, "Why are they replacing Ben?"

"They feel Benjamin is not doing his job appropriately," Alfred answered. Emily nodded.

"Anyway, nice to meet you. I've got a mission to do. I came to get my ID and head out," Emily said. Cynthia went through one of her drawers and pulled out Emily's ID.

"Do you usually keep agent's IDs?" Alfred asked.

"No, just anyone that has been recovering from an injury," Cynthia answered as she handed Emily's ID to her.

"I'll probably be back in time for lunch, but if I'm not back by supper send a search party," Emily said then headed off.

"That was a joke," Cynthia explained. Alfred nodded before entering the office. Sitting down at the desk, his mind went back to Emily. Alfred looked over the messy desk. He carefully went through the piles and then went through the filing cabinet until he found her file.

"Emily Jackson, M.D., agent," Alfred read to himself, "Could you be the right person?" He sat back down at the desk and read through the file. Finally closing it Alfred stared at the cover.

"The future just got very interesting," he said.

CHAPTER 2
MEMORIES

Emily watched as Matt got the briefcase out of his safe. He turned around and handed the briefcase and a set of handcuffs to Emily. Emily took them and handcuffed the briefcase to her left wrist.

"Make sure this gets to the Carbrat Institute," Matt said, "Caden has the key to the handcuffs."

"The sooner I get back, the better," Emily said, "The last thing I need is a briefcase permanently attached to my wrist."

"I haven't seen anything more from you since the last time I was at the institute," Matt commented.

"The handheld medical scanner is more than enough inventing for my lifetime," Emily said.

"You haven't had time, have you?" Matt laughed.

"Putting out inventions every five years is more than fine with me, it isn't like we need a whole lot more things in this world," Emily said with a shrug. Matt shook his head.

"See you another time," Matt said.

"Bye," Emily turned around and left Matt's office. She walked down the hall to the door of the office building. The secretary stopped her at the front desk to sign out. Emily showed the secretary her ID and signed the paper handed to her. Then she left the building.

It being only six blocks to the Carbrat Institute and not raining, Emily decided to walk it. Having been raised in this town Emily took the short cut through the alleyways.

She was about a block from the Institute when something smashed her on the back of the head and Emily blacked out.

Two guys stepped out of the shadows.

"Good job," one commented to the other, "Now, get what Black is paying us to get and let's get out of here."

The other man grabbed the briefcase and raised Emily's left arm.

"Damn, it's handcuffed to her wrist," the man said.

"Maybe she's got the key on her," the other man said. The other man went through Emily's pockets, dropping anything on the ground that wasn't want he wanted. Finally he pulled out a set of keys.

"Here we go," the other man said. He tried every key in the handcuffs, none of them worked.

"Well?" the man said impatiently.

"Gimme a second," the other man said as he tried all the keys in the briefcase lock. Again none of them worked. "None of the keys fit either lock, we need a hacksaw."

"Don't tell me we need to go all the way back to get your hacksaw," the man said.

"No, I'll see if one of the neighbours would be kind enough to let me borrow one, shouldn't be long," the other man said.

"What if she wakes up?"

"Hit her again," the man left the alleyway.

"I'm the brains and he's the muscle and he says to just hit her again," the man muttered. A black-gloved hand clamped itself over the man's mouth. The man struggled for a moment before he passed out. Brett dragged the man to the far end of the alleyway from Emily. Pulling his glove off so that it was inside out Brett stuffed it in his pocket. He went back to where Emily lay.

"Emily," Brett called quietly. Emily didn't move. Brett stuffed everything back into her pockets, before remembering to check if she was breathing. She was, but there was a large lump on the back of her head.

"Emily," Brett tried again. Hearing voices near the end of the alley Brett stepped into the shadows. A couple walked passed, but didn't look into the alleyway. Once he was certain that they were gone he went back to Emily's side.

"Emily." He shook her shoulder a little. Emily didn't respond. Brett pulled a piece of paper out of his pocket, scribbled something on it and put it in Emily's pocket before stepping back into the shadows and pulling his glove on again.

The man that had hit Emily over the head came back into the alleyway.

"Earl, I found..." the man stopped and looked around, "Earl?"

Brett stepped up behind him and clamped the gloved hand over the man's mouth. The man struggled a full minute before succumbing to what was on the glove. Brett dragged the man over to where Earl lay. Then he dragged both of them to a car that was sitting on the curb and dumped them in the trunk. Getting in, he drove off.

Emily groaned and slowly sat up. Her head was throbbing. She lifted her right hand to the back of her head, and feeling a lump there, Emily groaned again.

"What the hell happened?" she asked herself out loud, "Better question who am I? And why do I have a briefcase attached to my wrist?" Looking around Emily saw no clues as to what could have happened. Sitting there Emily went through her pockets. She found a money card, twenty dollar bill, an ID card, a computer ID card, a set of keys and a piece of paper with the words 'don't go back' written on it. Emily looked at the ID.

"Emily Jackson, 109735880," Emily read off the ID. The name didn't sound familiar. The computer ID had the same number on it, except a few more digits. Emily tried the keys in the handcuffs and none of them worked. She tried them in the briefcase lock, but none of them worked in there either. Emily put everything back in her pockets and stood up. She was unsteady on her feet, but she didn't collapse. Slowly moving to the wall she used it for support. Once she reached the street Emily looked around. There were different specialty shops along the street. Emily wandered down the street trying to figure out where to go.

Emily wasn't sure how long she'd wandered around, but she felt tired and thirsty. It was getting dark. Seeing a lit up sign above the door of a bar Emily decided to go in and have a drink. The interior was dimly lit. Most of the tables scattered around the room were full and a jukebox played some classic rock. The bartender looked up as Emily approached the bar.

"Beer," Emily told him. The bartender handed Emily a bottle after taking the cap off. She took the beer and went to a table away from everyone else.

Trent came out of the back room.

"How's everything going?" he asked Tyler.

"No trouble so far," Tyler answered.

"That's good," Trent said. He looked around the bar, his gaze stopped on a woman sitting alone at one of the back tables. Her back was to the wall, but she stared into her beer bottle. She had light brown, almost dirty blonde, hair that was tied back in a ponytail with loose bits framing her face. The jeans and shirt she was wearing would have fit in anywhere. If Trent hadn't noticed that she was sitting alone his eyes probably would have slid passed her.

"Who's that?" Trent asked Tyler.

"Don't know, she came in maybe five minutes ago, asked for a beer and sat down," Tyler answered, "She looked a little lost."

Trent nodded before going over to where the woman was sitting. She looked up at him as he sat down at the table. Her deep green eyes held no expression.

"Trent," Trent said holding his hand out above the table.

"Emily, I think," the woman said shaking his hand.

"You think?" Trent asked.

"That's what the ID in my pocket says," the woman said, "So I'm assuming that is my name."

"What happened?" Trent asked.

"I'm not exactly sure. But I have a lump on the back of my head," Emily said.

"Have you seen a doctor or talked to the police?" Trent asked.

"No."

"Maybe you should."

"I don't know where to find a doctor."

"I know a doctor, I can call him for you."

"Thank you."

Trent got up and went into the back room. He came out a few minutes later and went directly to the table.

"The doctor said he would come by in the morning. I have a room that you can stay in for tonight," Trent told Emily

"Thank you," Emily said.

"What all do you remember?" Trent asked.

"I know world events, history, politics, but I can't remember anything about myself. Who I am, what I do or that stuff," Emily said. Emily was quiet for a few minutes as she stared into space. Then she seemed to snap out of it.

"I know you've been very helpful so far, but can I ask you another favour," Emily said.

"Sure," Trent said.

"Did you have any way to remove handcuffs?" Emily asked.

"Handcuffs?" Trent asked. Emily lifted her wrist enough that Trent could see that it was handcuffed to a briefcase.

"I should have a hacksaw in the back, if you follow me," Trent got up and headed for the back room. Emily grabbed her beer and followed him. The back room was a work area and storage space with stairs leading to space above the bar. Emily sat watching Trent searching for the hacksaw for about five minutes, sipping her beer.

"You know your hacksaw is hanging on the wall above you, right?" Emily asked at the end of five minutes. Trent stood up and looked at where his hacksaw was hanging on the wall.

"Actually, I hadn't noticed," Trent said taking it down. He went over and started sawing at the handcuffs. Emily finished the beer and put the bottle down. It took Trent a few minutes longer to cut through the handcuffs.

"Thank you," Emily said.

"You're welcome," Trent said. Emily left the briefcase there and went back into the bar.

"How long overdue is she?" Warner asked Alfred.

"Fifteen hours," Alfred answered.

"This is an agent, the routine is to wait twenty-four hours," Warner said.

"Yes, I read that, but her mission was delivering of a briefcase. The other thing is that on her way out she said that if she was not back by supper to send a search party," Alfred said.

"She was probably joking," Warner said.

"That does not matter, does it? This department is short on agents. She was out for a while, Ryan broke his arm, and Brett is merely on loan. If we find her we will have a good agent back who can work and take on different missions," Alfred said.

"Okay, I'll get a team out looking for Emily," Warner sighed.

"Thank you, Mr. Penn," Alfred said and left Warner's office.

"You and Emily will get along very well, when you get to know each other," Warner muttered.

Emily had drank three more beer and already gone to bed when two o'clock came around. Trent sent Tyler home and was about to lock the doors when a small elderly woman stepped inside.

"A word from an invisible friend," the elderly woman said, "Schultz put out his list."

"Another to die list?" Trent asked.

"We have taken three more people, but some are unknown and others we can't help," the woman said.

"I understand," Trent said. The woman nodded and left. Trent locked up and went to the back room. Trent put his hacksaw away and wondered where he was going to sleep. Turning around Trent saw Emily standing at the bottom of the stairs.

"I thought you had gone to sleep," Trent said to Emily.

"I was, but my head is bothering me," Emily said sitting down on the stairs.

"Need some painkillers?"

"No, I don't think they would help."

"How is your head bothering you?"

"Ever had the feeling that you know something, but you try to remember and it's gone?"

"Once or twice, I usually don't worry about it."

"I'm trying to remember who I am."

"Maybe if you relax it will come to you."

"What do you think the beer was for? Getting drunk?"

"So let's play detective and see what we can find." Trent sat down on the stair next to Emily.

"Detective?"

"We know you are used to alcohol, because you drank four beers and aren't tipsy."

"Yeah."

"But you also stopped at four beers, which means you aren't likely to be an alcoholic."

"Makes sense."

"What is in the briefcase?"

"I don't know, none of the keys I have fit it."

"Okay, that probably means it isn't your briefcase."

"Means I was probably delivering it somewhere."

"But without knowing what is inside it could mean you delivering something to a jewellery store, for the Carbrat Institute or the Black Company."

"Or any other organization of that nature."

"Which means that you could work especially for those organizations, or be a hired mercenary, or even a CEO."

"Given what I'm wearing I think CEO is unlikely."

"Probably."

"What else?"

"Well, after listening to you speak I would guess that you have lived in this town most of your life."

"How do you get that?"

"I travelled at lot as a child and teenager, and I've noticed some differences in the way people speak in various towns."

"I'm used to alcohol, I could be a deliver person or a hired mercenary and I grew up here. Not a lot to go on."

"Given that you had the briefcase handcuffed to your wrist, I would guess that someone will be looking for you by tomorrow, if they aren't already."

"Yeah," Emily stood up, "I think I'll go try to sleep again."

"Good night," Trent said as Emily headed up the stairs. Trent didn't move until the bedroom door closed. Getting up, he unburied the couch with all the legs busted off. As soon as Trent lay down he was asleep.

The doctor arrived at eight the next morning. Emily was wide-awake, but Trent was sleepy and half awake. The doctor examined the back of Emily's head.

"Does it hurt?" the doctor asked.

"A little," Emily answered.

"How much is a little?"

"I know there's a lump there without reaching back and touching it."

"You have a very high pain threshold. You have a concussion to go along with the memory loss. For the concussion, I usually prescribe painkillers, but in your case the only advice I have is if anything seems familiar, check it out and try to remember why."

Emily nodded.

Trent went back to sleep after the doctor left. Emily found the newspaper and read it. There weren't any stories about missing people. There were murders, break-ins, medical discoveries and comics. Emily read the medical discoveries and the comics, but skipped the other stories. Putting the newspaper on the table Emily looked for something else to do until Trent woke up. In the corner of the back room she found a pile of magazines. She started with the one on top.

Cynthia was trying to get some work done before everyone else got up when Alfred came out of his office.

"Anything?" he asked Cynthia.

"I haven't heard a thing," Cynthia said looking up from her typing.

"I am going over to talk with Warner again," Alfred said.

"Okay," Cynthia replied then went back to typing. Alfred headed for the door.

An hour later Brett arrived at Cynthia's desk.

"I'm supposed to get a mission from Alfred," he said.

"Alfred isn't here at the moment, but Travis should have all the information on the mission," Cynthia replied.

"Travis?"

"He is the other person that hands out missions. You're more likely to be directed to him by Alfred anyway."

"Isn't he also supposed to keep track of the agents while on missions?"

"Yes, but Emily was never one that they could keep track of, otherwise she would be back here already."

"Sounds like Emily. So, where do I find Travis?"

"The gym, the assignment lab or the cafeteria. But he might not remember much about missions at the moment."

"Emily missing seems to throw a wrench in things."

"It's Alfred's reaction that is causing this."

"Well, I'll go find Travis and remind him about my mission." Brett turned around and went back down the hallway.

Fifteen minutes later Travis came jogging down the hallway.

"Is Alfred in his office?" he asked Cynthia.

"No, he went to see Mr. Penn," Cynthia answered.

"Damn, I need to speak with him," Travis said. At that moment Alfred came around the corner.

"Something happening?" he asked Travis.

"Yeah, I think I have something on where Emily might be," Travis answered.

"Really, where?" Alfred asked.

"I don't have an exact location, but," Travis turned to Cynthia, "May I use your computer for a moment?"

"Sure," Cynthia shut down what she was working on and moved away from her desk. Travis moved in front of the computer and brought up what the program he wanted. It was a map of the city. Travis highlighted an area and zoomed in.

"This is the main route from Matt's office to the Carbrat Institute, but Emily grew up in this city. She knows every route and every short cut. There are actually three routes," Travis pointed them out as

Alfred looked over his shoulder, "These two are on main roads, and since no one remembers seeing her, we can assume she took the third route. Which is through back alleys and not somewhere most of us stray."

"So she should be around there somewhere?"

"Yes."

"Then that is where we should be looking."

Trent woke up about eleven o'clock to find Emily sitting on the floor reading through a pile of magazines.

"Bored?" Trent asked.

"No, I found something to read," Emily answered looking up from her magazine. Trent looked at the cover.

"Medical Journal?"

"It has some interesting articles," Emily shrugged.

"Whatever. I'm gonna go over to the store and get some breakfast, want some?"

"Sure."

Trent put on his coat and shoes on and went out the front door of the bar. Trent stopped and sniffed the air. The air was supposed to be clear and fresh since the city put in the new clean air policy, instead the air was worse than ever. Trent wandered down the street to the grocery store. Entering Trent picked up four sandwiches and a two-litre bottle of pop.

"Hey, Trent, how are you today?" John asked as Trent set down his stuff on the counter.

"Tired, but good," Trent answered.

"Seen anything strange lately?" John asked pointing his thumb at the guy who had been talking to John when Trent came. John punched up Trent's purchases on the ancient cash register.

"Nope, not even the air is unusual," Trent answered. John laughed.

"Five bucks total as usual," John said as the empty drawer slid open. Trent handed John a five-dollar bill, when John finished bagging the sandwiches and pop. John shut the drawer and put the money in his pocket.

"Have a good day," John said as Trent picked up the bag.

"You too," Trent said then left the store. The sunlight was filtering through the haze making the day bright and Trent slowed down to enjoy it. He enjoyed it for a full minute before he realized that Alex and two goons were entering the bar. Trent quickened his pace.

When he entered the bar Trent found them sitting at a table by the bar. Emily was nowhere to be seen.

"Ah, you were out. We called and were wondering what was taking so long," Alex said standing up as Trent came in.

"I stepped out to get some breakfast," Trent replied, "Since thanks to you I can eat."

"Well, these loans are better than some gifts I've given," Alex said fishing an envelope out of his jacket pocket. Alex handed the envelope to Trent. "How's business?"

"Still have most of the regulars, but only a few new people come in and they don't stay long," Trent answered.

"As long as people are coming in, this place should stay open," Alex said signaling his goons to get up. As they stood up the door to the back room opened. Alex and his goons turned at the sound of the creak, the goons reaching into their jacket pockets. Emily stood there with the door open. She looked at Alex and his goons and stepped the rest of the way into the bar, letting the door close behind her.

"Emily?" Alex asked in a voice almost bordering on fear.

"Do we know each other?" Emily asked.

"You're a hard person to forget," Alex said, "And we've met a few times."

"Well, you weren't quite so memorable," Emily replied.

"How could you forget?"

"The doctor suggested that it was probably a blunt instrument to the back of my head."

"That may be a good thing."

"What do you know about me?"

"Your name is Emily Jackson, you were a pain in my ass before disappearing with three thousand dollars of my money."

"How long since you last saw me?"

"Six or seven years."

"And you don't want your money back?"

"I considered it a small price to pay for getting rid of you."

"Nice to know."

"I don't know what you do now, or whether anything has changed, but you used to be a trouble magnet."

"Thanks for that little bit of information."

"You're welcome. Anyway, see you another time Trent," Alex said before he and his goons left.

"Well, that's some more information to add to what little you already know," Trent said.

"That was Alex Johnston, the leader of the local mob," Emily said, "And he gave me four thousand dollars to get rid of me."

"You remember that?"

"Just that."

"Why did he want to get rid of you?"

"Blackmail, that's all I can remember."

"I brought breakfast," Trent put the bag on the table.

"You brought lunch."

"Lunch for you, breakfast for me." Trent went into the back to put the envelope away while Emily took the sandwiches and pop out of the bag. Coming back Trent took two glasses from under the bar and filled them from the bottle of pop. Both sat down and started to eat.

"There weren't any stories of missing people in the newspaper," Emily said.

"Police don't like searching for people until they've been missing twenty-four hours," Trent said, "They may not have started to search for you."

"Or no one is searching for me," Emily said. Trent didn't respond. "Maybe I am trouble like Alex suggested."

"No trouble has come around here since you showed up," Trent said, "Alex said he didn't know what you were doing now. You can stay here until you figure that out."

"Thank you."

Travis took off his gloves and dropped them on the desk, before removing his glasses and placing them there. Slouching in the chair he put his hands through his hair. Alfred paced the room, not standing still for even half a second. Warner sat calmly across from Travis.

"Have you two given up yet?" Warner asked.

"I've read her file, she always comes back," Alfred said.

"We could do a citywide search, it might yield more clues," Travis suggested.

"You could search the whole country, but would you find anything?" Warner asked.

"We are more likely to find her if we are actively searching, then if we sit on our asses doing nothing," Travis said.

"This department doesn't have the man power to be searching for one agent, even if it's Emily," Warner said.

"You knew when you chose me that no one gets left behind, forgotten or remains missing. I am going to do everything I can to find Emily, for no other reason than she is an agent of this department," Alfred said then left the room.

"He doesn't have time for that," Warner said standing up.

"I suspect he'll make time," Travis said. Warner left.

Brett was waiting in Alfred's office when Alfred arrived.

"I have established myself as a factory worker," Brett reported once Alfred had closed the door.

"And with Schultz?" Alfred asked.

"No one can hide the fact that I'm an agent in department H," Brett said, "Schultz thinks he needs ears in here."

"Does he have others?" Alfred asked.

"As far as I know he does," Brett answered.

"Did you tell Emily?"

"No, why would I tell her?"

"You were the one who helped her when she stumbled into the meeting, were you not?"

"Yeah, but she doesn't know what she stumbled into and all I told her was that I was on a mission."

"Schultz put out his latest to die list and her name is on it."

"He is paranoid, no one is going to take out Emily."

"I've got a week to find her before Warner gets tired of the search."

"I'm sure she'll come back."

"I hope so."

"Is she of any other importance than just being a missing agent?"

"I do not like my agents missing. Go play Shultz's game, report back when you can."

"I will." Brett got up and left the office.

Trent opened the bar at five. Tyler arrived ten minutes later. Emily bought three beers and disappeared into the upstairs bedroom. People started to come in at five thirty. Shortly before six, Rob, one of the regulars, brought in a new guy.

"Tyler, Trent, this is the new guy from work. Says it's bad for your health to drink, but I think the beer you serve will change his mind," Rob said with a huge smile. Tyler filled two glasses with beer and set them in front of Rob and the new guy. Rob drank his down, the new guy looked at his.

"I didn't catch your name," Trent extended his hand over the bar.

"Brett," the guy answered shaking Trent's hand.

"Nice to meet you," Trent said.

"You're Trent?" Brett asked.

"Yup," Trent answered. Brett took a sip of beer. He made a face as it went down.

"Ugh," Brett said.

"That's beer," Rob said.

"Then why do you drink it?" Brett asked.

"To forget, to break the monetary of the day, to relieve pain," Trent said, "Even to relax."

"How can a terrible drink do all that?" Brett asked.

"You get used to the taste," Rob said. Brett took another sip.

"Still doesn't taste good to me," Brett said.

Emily sat on the floor in the bedroom drinking beer and listening to the conversation going on downstairs. She recognized Brett's voice and she could see flashes of memories. But one instant they were there the next they were gone. Memories of pain and a young man leaning over her kept coming back over and over again. Slowly the whole memory came back. Two men beating her, Brett killing one, her killing the other and Brett making sure she was alive. I've got to be found, Emily thought. If I'm found I might remember, but the paper said 'don't go back'. What did the paper mean and who wrote it? Finishing the third beer, Emily fell asleep.

She found herself in an emergency ward that was in complete chaos. She was bandaging a bullet wound; people were yelling at each other but she couldn't do anything else. The bandaging was finished, people were yelling at her to do things, a little girl appeared.

"Take me home, Mommy," the little girl said holding out her hand to Emily. Emily took the girl's hand and the girl pulled her through the chaos. The girl stopped in front of a doctor. The girl disappeared. The doctor took Emily's hands.

"Adriana is dead, Emily," the doctor said leading Emily to a bed. Emily realized she was in a hospital gown.

"Why did she die?" Emily heard herself say.

"She died before you gave birth to her, now you need to sleep," Grace said.

"No, I can't sleep, people need me. People are dying, I need to stop it," Emily said.

"You're the only patient, no one needs you but you. Rest," Grace said. Emily lay down, Grace left. Emily sat up, stared at a man holding a gun in front of him.

"Time to die, bitch," he said then fired the gun; the bullet buried itself in Emily's chest. Grace came over and put her hands on Emily's shoulders.

"Emily, Emily," a male voice said. Emily slowly became aware of the throbbing sensation in her head and Trent shaking her.

"I'm awake," Emily mumbled. Trent stopped shaking her.

"You were having a bad dream," Trent explained.

"What time is it?" Emily asked.

"Three," Trent replied.

"Sorry, I woke you up."

"That's okay, these things happen," Trent sat down next to Emily.

"I'm trying to figure out whether it was memories or imagination."

"Could be both?"

"Probably, it was just eerie."

"You're awake now, it shouldn't be as bad. Any memories coming?"

"A few before I went to sleep. I could hear you talking to someone that sounded familiar. Brett was the name that came to mind."

"One of the regulars brought a guy named Brett in with him. Is that it?"

"I've known him a while, but a recent memory of him saving my life came up."

"Saving your life?"

"I don't understand it I just know they were beating me up and he stopped them. Something didn't sit right about his explanation, but I don't know what." Emily pulled her knees to her chest and wrapped her arms around them.

"Maybe you should go to bed and try to sleep," Trent suggested.

"Yeah," Emily slowly stood up. Trent stood up. Emily crawled into bed and closed her eyes. She fell asleep almost immediately. Trent left the bedroom and went back downstairs to the couch.

Emily opened her eyes. The room was dark. She got out of the bed and put on her lab coat before leaving the office. The medical lab was dark. There were three stretchers with bodies covered in sheets. Emily went to the first one and pulled the sheet back. It was a male agent with a hole in his chest. Emily went to the next one and pulled the sheet back. The charred left hand of what was left of this agent tried to reach out for help. Emily stepped back and went to the third stretcher. She pulled the sheet back. Brett lay there. Emily stared at the two electrical burns on his chest.

"Don't go back," Brett's blue eyes opened to look at Emily.

Emily jerked awake. Trent was sitting on the bed, just about to shake her. Emily sat up.

"You were screaming in your sleep," Trent explained.

"That was a nightmare," Emily said catching her breath, "I'm not sure sleeping is a good idea."

"You're awake, it will be okay," Trent said wrapping an arm around Emily. She laid her head against his shoulder.

"I'm sorry to keep waking you up," Emily mumbled into his shirt.

"It's okay, I'm used to staying up all night and sleeping until opening," Trent said. Emily was quiet. Trent didn't interrupt her thoughts and soon he realized that she had gone back to sleep.

"Why my bar?" Trent asked quietly, "Emily Jackson, what did you do to Schultz? Who are you? Why am I being pulled in? I can't be part of that fight." Emily's face was relaxed. "I guess you don't know either, do you?"

Cynthia found Grace in her office.

"Travis and Alfred are looking for you," Cynthia said.

"Why?" Grace asked.

"They are hoping you can tell them how Emily's mind works," Cynthia answered.

"I'm a medical doctor, not psychiatrist. The only thing I know is that Emily will come back when she wants to," Grace said.

"They still want to talk to you," Cynthia said.

"Yeah, yeah," Grace got up from her desk. Cynthia left. Grace closed the medical lab and headed for the conference room. Alfred was sitting on one side of the table and Travis sat on the other with map between them.

"Do you have any ideas where she would have gone?" Alfred asked when she entered.

"Not without knowing what happened," Grace answered.

"If we knew that this search would be a lot easier," Travis said.

"Then she could be anywhere. If she was injured she might have been found and is now in the hospital. If she is angry at us, she might have found a place to hide for a few days," Grace said as she sat down in an empty chair.

"I do not understand why she would be angry, but where would she hide?" Alfred asked.

"Probably a hotel or place similar, near a bar," Grace said.

"No money has been taken off her card," Travis said.

"She isn't likely to use the money card, Emily is smarter than that, she would use cash," Grace replied.

"Where is she going to get cash?" Travis asked.

"I have no idea, all I know is she has more than enough to pay for anything she wants," Grace answered.

"Then we have somewhere new to search," Alfred said, "Which brings me back to why would Emily be mad. She seemed to be in a good mood when she left. And she said something about sending a search party if she went missing."

"Emily felt that it took too long for her to be given another mission after she recovered from the last one. Grace and I felt she should be in good physical condition, but Benjamin wasn't willing to give her another mission until she was mentally ready. Mr. Penn told Benjamin where to go, but she still had to wait a while for the mission. When she got it she felt that it was too simple," Travis explained.

"What exactly did Emily say on her way out?" Grace asked.

"She said that if she was not back by dinner to send a search party," Alfred answered.

"We may be off base then," Grace said.

"What do you mean?" Travis asked.

"We are assuming that Emily's mind would go to revenge," Grace said.

"That's where her mind usually goes when she's angry," Travis replied.

"What if that isn't where her mind went? She told Alfred to send a search party not because she expected to be gone for a couple days, but she felt the mission was too easy. She knows if she isn't back in a certain amount of time it will take longer to get another mission. Why would she jeopardize the possibility of getting a harder mission by disappearing for a few days?" Grace said.

"That makes sense, but if that is the case then where is she?" Alfred asked as he stood up and started pacing the room.

"I think we are running around in circles," Travis said.

"Have you tried the hospital or any medical clinics around?" Grace asked.

"Not yet, but what could've happened to her on an easy mission like taking a briefcase from one place to another?" Travis asked.

"What was in the briefcase?" Grace asked.

"A delivery for the Carbrat Institute," Travis answered.

"That means something that is one of a kind and wanted desperately by the Black company," Grace said.

"Which means Emily could be anywhere," Alfred said.

Grace went up the steps of an old office building. Going in the front door Grace headed for the second floor. Reaching the first office she knocked on the door. A muffled response came from within. Grace opened the door and stepped into the office. A man sat in a wheelchair near the bookshelf along one wall with a book in his hands.

"Grace, what a pleasant surprise," the man said putting the book back.

"I don't have anything to report, Edmund," Grace said.

"Then may I ask why you're here?" Edmund asked.

"I need a favour from the invisible friends," Grace said.

"Consider what you have done for them I'm sure they wouldn't mind," Edmund said, "What is it that you need?"

"Help finding a friend," Grace answered, "Her name is Emily Jackson and she has been missing about two days."

"You think she is in trouble?" Edmund said.

"She's been known to get into more than her fair share of trouble," Grace said.

"I'll pass you message along," Edmund said.

"Thank you," Grace said as she turned around and then left.

Emily woke up to the noise of Trent moving around downstairs. Sitting up she looked at the electric clock; it said two post meridian. Emily got out of bed and went downstairs. Trent was busy preparing the bar for opening.

"Good afternoon, lunch is in the 'frigerator in the back," Trent said seeing her.

"Thanks," Emily said then went in search of the refrigerator. She found it in one of the back corners of the room, barely recognizable as the ancient bar refrigerator that it was. Inside were three sandwiches and a litre of pop. Emily took one of the sandwiches and went into the bar where she sat down to eat.

"Was there anything in the newspaper?" Emily asked.

"Fires, robberies and politics, but nothing about missing people," Trent answered.

"I guess no one is looking for me," Emily said.

"Give your memory a few days, maybe it will come back and you'll be able to go home."

"Yeah." Emily didn't say anything more as she ate. When she was finished she went into the back room. Going over to where she left the briefcase and ID cards Emily picked up the ID cards. Suddenly a memory came of a lady handing her the card, then it was gone. Emily shook her head. Sitting on the couch Emily looked around the back room. Her eyes landed on the pile of medical magazines. Emily went over and picked up the top one, she had read it yesterday but now there was something about it that tugged at the back of her mind. Loud voices and clamouring coming from the bar broke her reverie. Dropping the magazine back on the pile Emily went over and opened the door to the bar. Two men were standing near the door with a wounded man supported between them. Trent pointed to the back room.

"There is a couch in the back," Trent said, "Put Cole there, and I'll call the doctor." The two men headed for the door to the back. Emily cleared off the couch and then held the door open for them. They laid Cole gently down on the couch and then went back into the bar. Cole had two bullet wounds, one in the shoulder and the other in his side. Emily went into the bathroom and found a first aid kit. After cutting away Cole's shirt she began cleaning and dressing the wounds.

Emily had cleaned up and was sitting on the stairs when the doctor arrived ten minutes later. The doctor looked over the bandages, while Trent stood nearby.

"You must have some medical training," the doctor said.

"I still don't remember," Emily replied.

"Did you take out the bullets?" the doctor asked.

"Both went right through without hitting anything important," Emily answered. The doctor nodded.

"He should fully recover with the proper amount of rest," the doctor said, "He'll be in pain for a while and shouldn't be moved for a couple days. Here are some painkillers he can be given if the pain gets too bad." The doctor set the bottle of painkillers on a small table beside the couch. Emily watched Trent walk the doctor out of the back room. Through the open door she heard the doctor talk to the two men that brought Cole in and then all three left. Several memories came back all at once. A girl of ten declaring she wanted to be a doctor, seeing a man lying on a stretcher dying, and lying in pain with a woman's voice over her saying that everything would be all right.

"Emily?" Trent's voice interrupted her.

"Yeah," she looked up at him.

"You okay?" Trent squatted down to look Emily in the eye.

"I think I'm a doctor."

"You remember?"

"A few things, when I was twelve I used the four thousand dollars to put myself through medical school."

"So, that would be where you disappeared to."

"I guess. All this does is bring up more questions. What was I doing when I was knocked out? Where do I practise medicine? Why would someone want to knock me out? I feel like I found two puzzle pieces that don't fit anything else."

"Doctors must talk to each other, if you ask Doc I'm sure he could ask around to find out where you practise."

"Yeah. Does everyone injured come here?'

"Mostly, I have a phone and know a doctor, so they usually come here if they need help."

"Why not go to the hospital?"

"They come here, the doctor sees them and they don't have to pay an arm and a leg that they can't afford. Why didn't you find a police station after you were knocked out?"

"I don't know, I didn't even think about it."

"I'm sure the rest of the puzzle will come. It may take some time but it will come." Trent brushed a lock of Emily's hair behind her ear.

Grace stepped through the door and walked up to the front desk at the main hospital building.

"Hello, Sandra," Grace said to the receptionist.

"Hello, Grace, what can I do for you today?" Sandra responded.

"I'm looking for a specific person, who is most likely to be injured," Grace answered.

"This is a hospital, we specialize in injuries," Sandra replied.

"Probably came in Tuesday morning or afternoon, female and very likely close to death," Grace said. Sandra looked through the records of the last few days.

"Only three criticals since Tuesday morning," Sandra said, "Two males and one female. The female was a suicide case, found by her boyfriend. Dr. Davidson got a pharmacy out of her stomach."

"Not the person I'm looking for. The person I'm looking for is more likely to be beaten or shot," Grace said.

"Nobody has come in with bullet wounds and so far this week only males have come in beaten, sorry," Sandra said.

"Maybe she is out there, fine and I'm worrying for nothing," Grace said.

"I hope you find her," Sandra said. A man came up to the desk. "Good afternoon, Dr. Richards."

"Good afternoon, Sandra. Nice to see you, Grace," Dr. Richards said.

"Hello, Bruce," Grace replied.

"How is your private practice doing?" Sandra asked Dr. Richards.

"Quite well, two patients in one week and neither one was a lot of work," Dr. Richards answered.

"You've gone into private practice?" Grace asked with raised eyebrows.

"Sort of, I met this great guy, owns a bar in the Dark End as most people call it, anyway people go to him when they need medical attention and he calls me. As a contribution for the community I treat them for free and leave them there," Richards explained,

"Most of it was like today, the guy had a couple bullet wounds. Anyway, what are you doing here? I thought you lived in a cave somewhere and didn't come out except in emergencies."

"I'm looking for a friend that went for a walk on Tuesday and hasn't come back yet," Grace answered.

"That's a long time to be wandering around in this town," Richards said.

"She usually can hold her own in a fight," Grace said.

"Got a picture?" Richards asked.

"No, the only picture there is of her is the one on her ID, which should be on her person," Grace said.

"If you give me a name I'll keep my eyes and ears open," Richards said.

"Her name is Emily Jackson," Grace said, "Thanks Bruce." Then Grace headed for the exit.

"Emily Jackson," Richards muttered as if trying to remember something.

"Dr. Richards, Dr. Evans wants to speak to you," Sandra said.

"Tell him I'm on my way now," Richards told Sandra then started for the elevator, "Emily Jackson."

Travis and Alfred were already sitting in the conference room when Grace arrived.

"Did you find anything?" Alfred asked as Grace took a seat.

"I checked all the clinics and the hospital. Emily hasn't checked into any of them. How did you do, Travis?" Grace asked.

"I had about five volunteers and we started at one end of the city, inquiring at hotels and bars. We only got a quarter of the city done, but nothing so far," Travis answered.

"She has to be out there somewhere, people do not just disappear without a trace," Alfred said.

"Actually quite frequently missing people are never found, alive or dead," Grace said.

"We cannot let it happen to Emily," Alfred stated.

"I agree, but there's still hotels and bars that we haven't checked," Travis said, "And we have all agents out on missions keeping their eyes open."

"I talked to a few doctors who said they would watch for her," Grace said.

"We should find her," Travis said.

"Unless the Black Company has her," Grace said.

Tyler arrived at five, when Trent opened the bar. Tyler was behind the bar and Trent was sitting at a table near the bar when people started to come in. Emily had said something about going to bed early. Rob came in at six.

"Brett decided beer was too much?" Trent asked.

"He decided that drinking was not for him, and so he stayed away," Rob laughed.

"A pity, if you're sober all the time you miss so much," Trent said laughing.

"I think he's too young to be such a stick in the mud," Doug said from where he sat at the bar.

"You guys see the game this afternoon?" John asked coming over.

At two the customers headed for home, with Tyler leaving shortly after. Trent closed the bar down and went into the back room. Cole was asleep on the couch, looking very uncomfortable. Trent went upstairs, opening the bedroom door he saw Emily lying on the bed, sleeping. After gently moving her to one side of the bed Trent laid down on the other side. Trent found himself lying awake wondering who Emily was.

Trent rolled over to find himself in an empty bed, the clock read eleven ante meridian. Getting out of bed Trent wandered downstairs. Emily was sitting on the stairs watching Cole, who overnight had gone white and looked sick. Trent sat down beside her.

"What is wrong with Cole?" Trent asked.

"His shoulder is infected," Emily answered, "I can't really do anything about it, he needs to go to the hospital."

"I'll call Doc," Trent said getting up.

"An infected wound can kill someone, Trent. Doc will say the same thing I have. Cole needs to go to the hospital," Emily said. Trent went to the phone and made the call.

After hanging up Trent went back to sitting beside Emily.

"Doc is coming," Trent said. Emily nodded. "Something else wrong?"

"Some memories have been coming back, my head hurts and nothing makes sense," Emily answered.

"What do you remember?" Trent asked studying Emily's face, she looked exhausted.

"My parents, bits and pieces of my childhood, medical school and then everything just gets weird. Like I deserted a normal life and found myself in a spy novel," Emily said.

"It's good that you remember something," Trent said. Doc knocked on the bar door. Trent got up and went to let him in. Doc came in and examined Cole's shoulder.

"Looks like he'll need surgery to get the infection out, we have to get him to the hospital," Doc said, "I have a car outside."

"Okay, how are we going to move him?" Trent asked.

"You take one end and I take the other, unless you have a stretcher hidden underneath this mess," Doc said. Trent and Doc stood Cole up and supported him.

"Emily, can you please get the door?" Trent asked.

"Sure," Emily said standing up and going to the door. Once Doc and Trent carried Cole through, she followed them and opened the outside door. Using one hand Doc handed Emily his keys and she unlocked and opened the back car door. Doc and Trent carefully put Cole in the back seat. Cole moaned in pain, but didn't wake up. Doc took the keys back from Emily and got into the driver's seat of the car. Doc started the car and pulled away from the sidewalk. Emily and Trent went back into the bar.

Travis was falling asleep with his head resting against his hands on the table, while Alfred paced up and down the conference room. Cynthia opened the door and showed a young gentleman in. Alfred stopped and Travis looked up.

"Alfred, this is Caden Carbrat," Cynthia said, "Mr. Carbrat, this is Alfred and Travis."

"Nice to meet you," Alfred said holding out his hand.

"I only wish it was better circumstances," Caden said shaking Alfred's hand. Cynthia left the conference room.

"Pardon me," Alfred said gesturing for Caden to have a seat.

"We are missing a very valuable and necessary item," Caden said sitting down, "We gave the job of delivering this item to this department. Matt informed me that Emily Jackson picked it up for delivery on Tuesday. The item however has yet to be delivered."

"Emily left Tuesday morning and has not been seen since," Alfred said.

"If the mission is not complete something happened," Travis said.

"According to my sources the Black Company is not in possession of the item," Caden said, "That means my item is out there. It was entrusted to this department."

"And we have been searching for Emily since she went missing," Travis said, "So far there hasn't been a trace of her."

"The Black company is also looking," Caden said.

"We'll find her and your item before Black does," Alfred assured Caden.

"I hope so, I can't afford for this to fall into Black's hands," Caden said as he got up, "Good day." Caden left the conference room.

"We're in deep shit," Travis said.

"Anywhere and everywhere that you can think Emily would go," Alfred said, "Send someone to ask questions, gather information, triple check the route you think she used. Whatever you have to do." Alfred started for the door.

"Where are you going?" Travis asked.

"To get proper help from Warner," Alfred answered before leaving.

Dr. Richards sat in the lounge, after Cole's surgery, sipping coffee. Sitting there relaxing several things connected in Richards's head making him stand up so fast he spilled coffee on himself. Richards quickly wiped the worst up then headed for the front desk at a fast pace.

"Sandra," he said a little out of breath when he got there.

"Something wrong? You look like you ran ten K," Sandra asked.

"Do you have the number for Grace's office?" Richards asked.

"I should have it here somewhere," Sandra said looking through some papers on her desk. "Here it is," Sandra pulled it out and handed it to Richards, "If you don't mind me asking, why do you need it?"

"I think I found Emily," Richards said then headed for his office. Entering his office he sat down and dialed the number Sandra had given him. There were three rings and then a machine told him that no one at the number was available. Frustrated, Richards put the phone back.

"I'll phone her later. Emily isn't going anywhere," Richards said to himself as he tried to relax.

Grace opened the door to the medical lab as the last ring sounded and the machine came on. Oh, well, whoever that was will phone back later, Grace thought as she entered her office. Sitting down at her desk Grace turned on her computer. Absently she took a sip from the coffee mug on her desk as she watched the computer boot up. Instead of swallowing Grace spat the tequila back in to the mug.

"One day I'll figure out why Emily leaves her mug on my desk," Grace muttered to herself, "Or better yet, I'll lock her in a small room until she promises to quit drinking." Grace got up and poured the tequila down the sink. Sitting back down she was going to set the mug back where it was, only to see a folded piece of paper sitting there. Putting the mug down she picked up the piece of paper and unfolded it.

Grace

Be back to help out with Jerry's crew,

Hoping for a better mission,

Sorry about the tequila.

Emily

"That tells me you were planning on coming back that day, but gives me no clue to where you are," Grace said to thin air.

"That sounds like you're talking to Emily," Travis said from where he was leaning on the doorjamb.

"I would be yelling at her, but she isn't here," Grace said.

"I'm sure we'd all have something to say to her, if she were here," Travis said, "Caden Carbrat dropped by for a visit earlier."

"Why?"

"Emily hasn't dropped off what she was supposed to be delivering."

"Think she's been kidnapped by the Black Company?"

"They're looking for her too."

"I know that Emily can disappear if she wants but this is ridiculous."

"We've missed something and I'm not sure what it is, but Alfred is having me triple check everything."

"I haven't heard anything, but I can go back out tomorrow and check."

"Rumour is Jerry's crew is supposed to be coming back tomorrow."

"They are, but I should have time tomorrow evening."

"I really hope we find her soon."

Trent opened the bar at the usual time, with Tyler arriving late. Trent stayed in the bar and talked to the regulars. Emily took some painkillers for her headache and searched through the piles of junk in the back room for something to read. Finding Alice in Wonderland she sat down and started to read. At two Trent closed the bar. Going into the back room he saw Emily sitting on the couch.

"You seem to enjoy reading," Trent commented.

"It's a way to relax," Emily shrugged, "You have some interesting things back here."

"Most of it came with the bar," Trent said sitting on the other end of the couch.

"Why haven't you cleaned it out?"

"Haven't been bothered, besides it's a treasure hunt to go through the piles."

Emily laughed, causing Trent to smile.

"Leave it a few years and an archaeologist might be interested in digging it out of the dust," Emily said.

"If I deal with it, I might make money on the sale of some of this stuff," Trent said.

"And that would be a bad thing?"

"Yeah, Alex will want his loans back."

"How did you get Alex to loan you money?"

"When I first opened he came in with the protection scheme that all the other bars are paying. I had no clue who he was at the time. He started saying something about new bars not lasting long and before he got into the rest I interrupted to tell him that the bar probably wouldn't last a year. I talked his ear off about my plans for the bar and that it was a good bet that the bar wouldn't make money. When I'd run down he offered to give me a loan. I, of course, took him up on it, and then I found out who he was."

"So, other bars are paying Alex, while Alex pays you?"

"Yeah, that's about it. And if I start making money Alex will want his money and interest. I don't have that yet."

"You sound like you're getting there."

"I have a few investments Alex hasn't found out about."

"For how long will he go on being ignorant?"

"It's been five years, and I'm about three months away from being able to pay Alex back in full."

"If you pay him off then the situation will switch, you'll be paying protection."

"That's why I'm not in any hurry to pay of the loans."

"Probably time to go to bed," Emily said getting up. She placed the book open to the page where she last read on the small table next to the couch and then headed up stairs.

"Good night."

"Night." Trent got ready to go to sleep on the couch.

Dr. Richards immediately went to his office when he arrived at work. Barely pausing to take off his coat Richards picked up the phone and dialed Grace's number. Grace picked up on the second ring.

"Hello?"

"Hello, Grace, it's Bruce," Richards said.

"Hello, Bruce. What can I do for you?" Grace asked.

"Your friend that is missing, Emily Jackson, I think I've found her," Richards said.

"Really. Where?" Grace asked.

"The bar owner I told you about took in a lady with a concussion on Tuesday. She had no memory, but she had a piece of ID with the name Emily on it. I treated her concussion, but memory has to come back on its own. On Thursday she bandaged the bullet wounds on the other patient that ended up at the bar," Richards explained.

"Where is this bar?" Grace asked.

"It's on old Oak Street, just passed where Nancy's café used to be, but not as far as old Pine Street," Richards told Grace.

"What is the name of the bar?" Grace asked.

"I don't remember, everyone just calls it Trent's place," Richards said. Richards's watch beeped, he looked down at it, the face read: You are needed in surgery. "Well, I have to go, talk to you another time.

"Bye," Grace said. Richards hung up and headed for surgery.

Grace hung up the phone and turned to Alfred and Travis, who were standing behind her waiting.

"That was a doctor from the hospital and an old friend. I told him about searching for Emily and he thinks he has found her," Grace told them.

"Where?" Travis asked.

"A bar that is on old Oak Street, just passed where Nancy's café used to be, but before old Pine Street. Bruce didn't remember the name but everyone calls it Trent's place," Grace said.

"Where is that?" Alfred asked.

"I have no idea," Grace answered.

"Maybe if we found an older map and overlapped it with a new map in the computer it will show us where," Travis suggested as he sat down at Grace's computer and started to work. Grace and Alfred watched over his shoulder.

Half an hour later Travis was trying to find a map that was old enough to have Oak street, Nancy's Café and Pine street, all of which were on completely different places on each map they tried.

"I don't think we'll find it," Travis said.

"All three have to be in the same area," Grace said, "Bruce called the area the Dark End."

"They don't mark anything that on any of these maps," Travis said.

"He said a bar right?" Alfred said.

"Yes," Grace said.

"Then we just need to finish checking the bars. Travis, you said that the city was half done," Alfred said.

"Yes," Travis said.

"Then eliminate all the bars that you have checked from the map," Alfred said.

"Okay," Travis brought up the new map and got rid of the areas that had been checked, "That's still a lot of space."

"Now using just that area search for the three land marks," Alfred said. Travis did.

"Why didn't Emily contact us?" Travis asked.

"She has a concussion and suffering amnesia," Grace answered.

"I got it," Travis said. The screen was zoomed in on one area; Travis printed the map, "It's still fairly big area to cover and there is supposed to be a lot of bars in that area."

"Then getting started would be a good idea," Alfred said.

"I'll gather my volunteers," Travis said getting up. He left the medical lab. Alfred followed and Grace went back to work.

Trent got up at eleven thirty. He went to the store and got breakfast. When he got back he ate and then started getting ready for opening. At one o'clock Trent went upstairs to check on Emily. He found Emily sitting on the bed staring out the dirty window.

"Emily," Trent said. Emily didn't respond. Trent entered the room and stood by the bed.

"Emily," he repeated a little louder. Emily jerked as if she had just woken up. She looked at him. Her eyes had so many emotions they were hard to look into, but Trent could not look away.

"Are you okay?" Trent asked.

"I will be," Emily said turning back to stare out the window.

"Will be?"

"My memory has returned for the most part. I know who I am, I just can't remember small bits of the incident that took my memory away. But that is normal."

"Then I guess you have to go back."

"Yeah, they'll be looking for me. The briefcase needs to be delivered."

"It must be important."

"It is supposed to be delivered to Caden Carbrat, so I guess it is."

"Caden himself?"

"That was what I was told. Then I have to go back to the department."

"Department H?"

"As in agent for department H."

"Couldn't find a place to practice medicine?"

"I do that there too. I would just practice medicine, but I can't sit still long enough."

"Brett an agent too?"

"Supposed to be. I'm starting to question his alliances."

"Rumour is he is a person to avoid. They say he is taking orders from the wrong person."

"I'll keep that in mind."

"What are you going to tell them?"

“The truth, with the technology today it is easy to verify a medical story. I should head back."

"Why hadn't you?"

"I'm trying to shove all those things that I don't want to deal with back into the corners I had them in before."

"I leave you to deal with that." Trent turned around.

"Thank you for everything." Emily said.

"Around here that's my job," Trent replied before going back downstairs.

Half an hour later Emily came downstairs. Grabbing the briefcase and her stuff Emily left the bar. She walked the distance to the Carbrat Institute. At the front desk Emily identified herself and was quickly escorted to Caden's office. Matt and Caden were sitting around a table in the office.

"Emily?" Matt asked.

"I'm sorry about the delay," Emily said. Placing the briefcase on the table.

"And what caused this delay?" Caden asked.

"A blunt instrument to the back of my head," Emily answered, "I apologize about the handcuffs, but the briefcase has not been opened."

"What happened?" Matt asked.

"I'm not quite sure," Emily answered, "But I need to get back."

"Thank you," Matt said. Emily nodded to both of them and left the office. The person who escorted her to the office was waiting and escorted her back to the door. Emily left the building.

Trent had downed half a glass of bourbon when the door opened and the elderly woman stepped inside.

"The invisible friend has a request," she said.

"What is it?" Trent asked.

"Keep an eye out for Emily Jackson," the woman said.

"Send word back to invisible friend that Emily is headed back home," Trent said.

"She's been here?"

"And gone."

"I will send word back." The woman left the bar. Trent drank the rest of the bourbon and poured another glass.

Emily stopped at Cynthia's desk on her way into the department.

"Emily?" Cynthia asked, "What happened?"

Emily dropped her ID card on Cynthia's desk. Cynthia put it away.

"I got mugged," Emily answered.

"You got mugged?" Cynthia looked bewildered.

"That's was it comes down to," Emily said, "Tell Alfred that I'm back and that I would like to left alone for a couple days."

"I will," Cynthia said.

"Thank you," Emily turned and headed for her room.

Alfred entered the medical lab a week after Emily had returned. Grace was sitting at her computer working.

"Can I help you?" Grace asked Alfred.

"I thought Emily would be here," Alfred said.

"I have neither seen nor heard anything about Emily since Dr. Richards called me," Grace said.

"She apparently came back on her own a week ago," Alfred said, "Cynthia said that she asked to be left alone for a few days, but I figured that she would show up here soon after."

"No, she hasn't shown up here," Grace said.

"Well, I'll try to talk to her another time," Alfred said turning a leaving the medical lab.

Once Grace figured that Alfred would be far enough away she closed up the medical lab and went to Emily's room. The door slid open and the first knock, but the light was off. Grace turned them on. Emily was lying curled up on her bed. Grace checked and made sure she was asleep. Then she noticed the night table. There was a half empty glass of clear liquid, an injection gun and an empty vial with the label thiopental. Grace picked up the glass and took a sniff. It smelled like tequila. Setting the glass down Grace double-checked that Emily was breathing regularly. Grace sighed with relief that she was.

Grace left the room, closing the door behind her and headed back to the medical lab.

Alfred sat at his desk looking over the file that had just come from department C. He carefully read through the entire file.

"It is time," he said standing up to leave his office.

Grace had just come back from breakfast when Emily entered the medical lab. Emily sat down in front of the computer.

"Where have you been?" Grace asked.

"A bar," Emily answered.

"And?" Grace asked.

"Recovering from a concussion."

"Dr. Richards said you had amnesia."

"Yeah, but I'm fine now."

"Now, as in now that you're back here or now as in now that you've come out of your room?"

"I had to straighten my head out."

"And this requires tequila and thiopental?"

"Tequila, yes. Thiopental was to help me get to sleep. It was that or suffer from insomnia caused by nightmares. No, I was not mixing the two."

"That is good, you scared me."

"I'm fine."

"Shall I do a medical check, just to make sure?"

"Not right now."

Alfred stepped into the medical lab.

"Good morning, ladies," Alfred greeted them as the door closed.

"Do you need something?" Emily asked.

"I was wondering how much you know about the twenty-first century," Alfred said extending a mission file to Emily.

CHAPTER 3
CENTURIES

Emily had spent the last hour reading the file. Grace finished the medical check before going over and sitting down in the other chair.

"So, the twenty-first century," Grace said.

"Was a long time ago," Emily said closing the file and started working on the computer.

"How do they plan on sending you to the twenty-first century?" Grace asked.

"A time machine," Emily answered, "According to the file I leave for department C tomorrow and they will ship me to a specific time in the twenty-first century via a time machine."

"Tomorrow?"

"Yeah, the scientist in charge, Jordan, is in a rush to get this done. But once in the twenty-first century I'm supposed to find a guy named Daniel Anderson, who is a scientist of some description. Apparently two guys with time machines are chasing each other through time. I'm supposed to find Daniel and warn him that this guy, Mikael Huston, is trying to kill him."

"And why are they sending an agent?"

"I don't know, but I suspect they are scared that the person they send might come up against Mikael."

"And scientists aren't trained to fight."

"Exactly."

"So, what are you doing?"

"Studying up on everything I can find about the twenty-first century."

"I leave you alone then." Grace got up.

Emily was still working when Grace went to bed for the night.

Grace came in the next morning to find Emily asleep at the desk. Shaking her head Grace got to work. Emily slowly woke up. Once awake she went back to her research.

"When are you supposed to leave?" Grace asked.

"Ten this morning," Emily answered, "Travis said he'll find me about nine-thirty."

"Okay."

No one said anything more, until the breakfast buzzer went.

"You better go for breakfast," Grace said.

"Yeah," Emily said not moving.

"Go," Grace said, "You don't know when you are going to eat again."

"Okay," Emily shut down what she was doing and went for breakfast.

Emily came back into the medical lab about nine o'clock. She looked like she had showered and changed clothes.

"Here for that medical check that I should have done yesterday?" Grace asked. Emily sat down on the examining table.

"Yeah," Emily said. Grace got up and went over to Emily. Emily lay down and Grace did the scan. Emily sat up as Grace studied the results on the computer.

"Anything there that would mean that I can't go on this mission?" Emily asked.

"No," Grace said, "You're fine."

Emily got off the table and sat down at the computer. She started her research again.

"I'm surprised Alfred would give you a mission so soon after the last one," Grace said.

"Especially considering that I got knocked out and disappeared for several days," Emily said, "I asked Travis about it, he said that Alfred was adamant that only I could do this mission. Travis thought it was weird, but didn't feel the need to ask any further questions."

"And if your medical check had come up with something?"

"I don't know."

"I hope nothing happens on this mission. The last two were bad enough."

"According to the file I'm only supposed to be there forty-eight hours. Which means I'm not getting any equipment. I'm also not supposed to have anything on me that could identify me as being from the future."

"Are they giving you clothes from the time period?"

"No, but I'm not exactly sure why."

"So, you are going into this situation with twelve hours of research, nothing but the clothes on your back and a name of the person you're supposed to find?"

"And a description to go with the name."

"What about a description of the guy that is after him?"

"I don't get that because they don't have that."

"This doesn't sound like a well thought out mission."

"The whole thing is set out by department C, no one here has had any input on it."

"Sounds like maybe someone with some common sense should have been consulted."

"Probably."

"You don't seem to have any doubts about this mission."

"I have lots of doubts about this mission, but if I am going to go on this mission I can't let them in. It makes things easier."

"If you say so."

Travis entered the medical lab.

"It is time to go," Travis said. Emily shut down what she was doing on the computer and got up.

"See you when you get back," Grace said.

"Bye," Emily said as she followed Travis out of the medical lab. They left the department building and went to the parking lot. They got into Travis's car and Travis drove to the department C building. Getting out of the car they went into the building. They were in a long white hallway.

"What is with people and white walls?" Emily asked.

"Department H has white walls," Travis said as he led Emily down the hallway to another hallway and along this one.

"Department H has yellow walls," Emily replied. Travis stopped at a door and knocked. There was no answer, so after a minute he knocked again. A white haired man poked his head out.

"What do you want?" he demanded.

"We're from department H," Travis replied. The man looked them over then opened the door enough to let them in. Travis and Emily entered to find themselves in another white hallway. The man closed the door

"Follow me," the man said before turning and walking down the hallway; Travis and Emily followed. The man led them down the hallway, around a corner, up a flight of stairs, through a lab into a large room full of machinery where another white haired man sat behind a desk working on a computer. The man looked up when they stopped in front of the desk.

"The people from department H," the first white haired man announced then left.

"Hello, I'm Jordan," the second man said as he stood up and held out his hand.

"I'm Travis," Travis shook Jordan's hand.

"Emily," Emily shook Jordan's hand. They all sat down.

"Welcome to department C," Jordan said, "Have you both been briefed?"

"Alfred briefed me on the mission," Travis said.

"I read the file," Emily answered.

"Good, so I don't have to go over anything," Jordan said.

"I have some questions though," Emily said.

"Go ahead," Jordan said.

"How do you know where Daniel went?"

"We have a trail through time, you will arrive at the same place he did."

"Do you really think he'll be there?"

"There is no sign that he has left."

"Do you have a picture of Daniel?"

"Yes." Jordan went through the papers on his desk. It took a couple minutes but he finally gave Emily a picture. Daniel looked to be in his early twenties with light brown hair and brown eyes that held a hint of green in them. The picture looked like it was taken from a surveillance camera as he was walking into a building.

"Any description of Mikael Huston?"

"No."

"She'll be only forty-eight hours, right?" Travis asked.

"She'll be in the twenty-first century for forty-eight hours, which will be equal to the same amount of time here. Our time machine is still the one current for this time and there are still some bugs to work out."

"Is there anything that was not mentioned in the file?" Emily asked.

"Asking around for Daniel Anderson might get you into trouble. We did not know that when the file was put together."

"What kind of trouble?" Emily asked.

"There is a man, also called Daniel Anderson, from that time period, who is of questionable reputation and it would be better to avoid meeting him."

"Anything else, not mentioned in the file?"

"No, I think the rest got into it."

"Do I get the watch that the file talked about?"

"Oh yes." Jordan again dug through his desk again. This time after a couple minutes he started going through the drawers. When he got to the bottom one he pulled out a watch and handed it to Emily. Emily put it on.

"That is how we will trace you to bring you back, so don't lose it," Jordan said.

"Let's get this over with," Emily said standing up. Travis and Jordan stood up. Jordan led Emily over to where the machine was. Travis stayed back.

"Stand in that circle," Jordan instructed. Emily stepped into a rubber circle in the middle of the floor. Jordan started pushing buttons.

"Good luck," Travis told Emily. She nodded and then disappeared.

"Are you sure nothing will go wrong?" Travis asked Jordan.

"No, but nothing is likely to. Even if she doesn't find Daniel, there isn't much that can go wrong," Jordan answered, "If you go back to department H, Emily should be back in a couple days."

"I'll see you then," Travis said then left.

Once the darkness faded Emily found herself in an alleyway. Noting no ill effects from the time jump she moved to the entrance of the alley. The first thing she noticed was the number of people. Crowds of people passed the alleyway without a glance in her direction. The people wore all different types of clothing. Some had earphones and were listening to music; others were holding devices to their ears and talking into it. Emily thought they looked similar to telephones, but most were too small. Her clothing was a slightly different style from what others were wearing but there wasn't so much difference that Emily was worried. Vehicles passed at high speeds. Taking a deep breath Emily noticed that the air was cleaner, but smelled off. Looking around Emily wondered how she was going to find one guy among all these people.

Emily guessed it to be about eleven based on the amount of light filtering through the clouds. Emily stepped onto the sidewalk and started walking with the crowd. She tried to pay attention to her surroundings, but the crush of people started to become too much. Emily ended up in the next alleyway, sitting on the ground with her back to the wall of one of the buildings. Taking some deep breaths Emily tried to calm herself down. The people kept going passed, there seemed to be no end to them. Emily had never seen that many people in her life.

She had been sitting there at least fifteen minutes when a commotion at the other end of the alleyway drew her attention. Two men were having a fistfight. Emily just sat still and watched. A third man, this one in uniform, entered the alleyway and broke up the fight, sending each opponent in an opposite direction. The uniformed man did a check of the alley before turning around. He started to leave the alley, when he turned back around. He walked down the alley toward Emily.

"Are you okay?" he asked when he was close enough.

"Just claustrophobia," Emily answered.

"You aren't from around here, are you?"

"No, I arrived today."

"Why brings you to town?"

"Looking for someone to help out a friend."

"You're what?"

"I'm looking for a person because a friend asked me to."

"And why does your friend want you to find this person?"

"Because Jordan thinks someone is trying to kill him."

"Jordan is your friend?"

"Yes."

"Do you know what this person looks like?"

"Yes." Emily took the picture of Daniel Anderson out of her back pocket and showed it to the man. "I just don't know where to look and the crowd of people is too much."

"Perhaps I can help," the man said, "My name is Keith."

"Emily," Emily said, putting the picture away.

"Did you know anything about this guy?" Keith asked helping Emily to her feet.

"No, Jordan didn't give me very much information," Emily answered. Keith led the way to the other end of the alleyway. This street was a lot less crowded.

"Do you know where the guy might be?" Keith asked.

"Somewhere around here," Emily answered.

"Okay, then we'll check with the shop owners in this neighbourhood," Keith said as he started for the first shop. Emily followed him.

They went from business to business asking if anyone had seen Daniel, even occasionally asking a street person that Keith knew hung around this neighbourhood. At six o'clock the businesses started to close up.

"I guess that is all for today," Keith said stopping at a white car with red, white and blue lights on the roof, "I can drop you off wherever you are staying."

"Thanks but I think I will keep looking," Emily said.

"It would probably be better if you went back to where you're staying," Keith said.

"A man's life is hanging in the balance, how could I stop just because the shops are closed?" Emily asked.

"Look, why don't you come back with me to the station and we'll talk to my boss. He should be able to help, without you wandering the streets at night," Keith said.

"Okay," Emily said. They got into the car and Keith drove to the police station. Once the car was parked Emily followed Keith into the building. Keith walked passed the desks that were in even rows across the main room and went straight to an office that was half way down the main room on the left hand wall. The door was closed. Keith knocked.

"Come in," a muffled voice called. Keith opened the door and stepped inside; Emily followed him in. The office was small, cramped with furniture and the man behind the desk appeared to have been working a desk too long.

"Keith, what can I do for you?" the man asked.

"Gregory, this is Emily," Keith said, "She needs help searching a person."

"Have a seat," Gregory told Emily. Emily sat on the edge of the chair he indicated. It looked like it wasn't supposed to be comfortable. Keith left the office closing the door behind him.

"What is the story to this search?" Gregory asked.

"Jordan sent me to town to look for a man. I'm supposed to warn him that someone is trying to kill him," Emily said, "Keith was helpful and we talked to the shop owners along the streets around where I was told the man would be."

"Do you know this man's name?"

"No."

"Do you know where he lives?"

"No."

"Do you know what he does for a living?"

"He's a scientist."

"What kind of scientist?"

"I don't know."

"And you volunteered to find this man, who you know nothing about?"

"It sounded like a good vacation."

"How did you expect to find him?"

"I have a picture of him."

"May I see it?"

Emily dug out the picture and passed it to Gregory.

"Do you mind if I make a copy of it?"

"No."

Gregory placed the photo in a machine that was crammed between his computer monitor and the wall. He pushed some buttons and the machine started to beep and whine. After a minute a piece of paper slid out of the machine and onto a tray. Gregory took the picture out of the machine and handed it back to Emily.

"I will send this out to the rest of the force and ask them to keep their eyes open for the man."

"Thank you."

"I'm sure we'll find him in no time. Now you should go back to where you are staying and rest. If you come back here tomorrow I'll send you out with another officer and you can continue you search," Gregory stood up; Emily followed suit. Gregory opened the door. Emily left the office with Gregory following her.

"Don't worry about it tonight," Gregory said leading her through the desks. Emily could see Keith sitting one of the desks; he appeared to be doing paperwork. Gregory led Emily to the door of the station.

"Alright then, I will see you in the morning," Gregory turned and headed back to his office. Emily left the police station. She paused a moment to get her direction then headed back to the neighbourhood that she had been searching with Keith all afternoon.

Arriving back at the place they left off Emily continued on her search. She asked everyone she met if they had seen Daniel. The sun went down about nine-thirty and it started to get cold, but Emily kept going. One man she asked couldn't tell her much, but willingly gave her half of his supper.

Dawn was breaking when Emily sat down on a bench to rest. The clouds had moved on overnight and sunlight spilled out over the city. Emily watched in wonder at the beauty of it all. Her eyelids lowered and she fell asleep.

Someone shaking her shoulder woke Emily up. She opened her eyes to see Keith standing over her.

"You were supposed to go to where you are staying and rest last night," Keith said.

"Don't have a place to stay," Emily said rubbing her eyes, "Don't have any money. Don't have the time to waste."

"Let's go find you something to eat," Keith said. Emily got up and followed as Keith headed to a nearby restaurant. Entering they were immediately led to a table by a waitress. Emily sat down and Keith sat in the chair across from her.

"Did you find anything?" Keith asked.

"No," Emily answered, "But I covered a lot more territory."

"It is dangerous to be wandering the streets at night."

"Nothing happened."

A waitress appeared and they both ordered breakfast. The waitress moved off.

"Gregory was not much help and I don't have time to wait on other people," Emily said.

"How much time do you have?"

"Until tomorrow, if everything goes right."

"And where do you plan on spending tonight?"

"Wherever I fall asleep."

"And your claustrophobia?"

"Is fine as long as I avoid the busy streets during the day."

"Which means you could be missing a good chunk of the city."

"As long as I get the rest of it."

Keith did not respond to this. The waitress brought their breakfasts a few minutes later.

Once they were finished Keith called Gregory on a device that Keith called his cellphone. Then Keith accompanied Emily as she continued her search.

At lunch they stopped and Keith bought them lunch. Keith checked in with Gregory as Emily ate.

"Well?" Emily asked once he had put his phone away.

"Gregory said that the man had been seen a couple days ago in the area we started with yesterday," Keith said.

"Post meridian and nothing more than we knew before," Emily said.

"Post meridian?" Keith asked.

"Afternoon," Emily said with a shrug.

"Okay."

"Don't you use ante meridian and post meridian?"

"You mean am and pm?"

"I don't know. Let's get back to the search."

They went back to work.

Six o'clock came again and the shops closed. Keith appeared to get tired as Emily continued. It was eight o'clock when Emily stopped at a bench and sat down. Keith sat down beside her.

"No one has seen anything," Keith said, "Can we give it up for the night?"

"We could miss vital information," Emily said.

"Do you ever run out of energy?"

"Yes, but I have a limited amount of time."

"I have a guestroom that you can stay in. We can start first thing tomorrow morning."

"I guess a few hours wouldn't hurt."

"Good." Keith got up and started toward where his car was parked. Emily followed him.

Keith pulled into the driveway of a middle class house. The house looked like it was owned by someone who didn't spend a lot of time working on it, but it was not run down. Keith and Emily got out and went up the steps to the front door. Keith unlocked the door.

"Home sweet home," Keith said as he entered; Emily followed him inside. The inside was neat and organized, but most of it was covered with dust. Keith set his keys in the dustless spot on the table in the hallway. The hallway ran straight with an opening to the living room on one side, what looked like a kitchen at the end, a staircase going up on the left side of the hallway and a door between the stairs and the kitchen.

"You don't spend much time here, do you?" Emily asked.

"I tend to be a workaholic," Keith said taking off his coat, placing it on one of the hooks of the coat rack before going down the hallway. Keith opened the door.

"This is the guestroom," Keith said. Emily followed him inside. The room was painted a light pink with a bed, side table and a closet as the only things in it. The bed had a plastic sheet covering a flowery quilt. Keith pulled the plastic off, rolled it into a ball and put it in the almost empty closet. Emily could see two sundresses inside before Keith closed the door.

"I'll go make supper," Keith said leaving the room. Emily went over and opened the window before sitting down on the bed. Emily lay down.

Keith came in fifteen minute later to call her for supper to find her already asleep. He shut off the light and closed the door without disturbing her. Then he went and ate supper.

When Emily woke up it was still dark out, but the clock said that it was five ante meridian. Emily didn't move, if anything had woken her up it did not repeat itself. Sitting up Emily looked around; everything looked the same as when she went to sleep. Emily got up and closed the window before leaving the bedroom. The rest of the house was quiet as Emily headed for the kitchen.

She was in the middle of eating a sandwich when Keith came down stairs to investigate the noise.

"It is five-thirty in the morning," Keith said when he saw her.

"I know," Emily said, "You said that we would start first thing this morning."

"I'll go shower," Keith said going back upstairs.

Half an hour later he was ready to go and they started the search again

Keith didn't check in with Gregory until nine o'clock.

"Well?" Emily asked.

"A store owner a couple streets from here reported seeing the guy, Gregory suggested we go talk to him," Keith said.

"Then let's go," Emily said. Keith led the way. When they got to the street Keith directed them into a clothing shop. Emily looked around as they entered; the shop mostly sold woman's clothes with only a small section in the back for men's clothes. A man stood behind the counter flipping through a magazine, not appearing to be paying attention to anything. He looked up when Emily and Keith stopped at the counter. The man was a few years before middle-age but looked young enough not to be out of place in this type of shop.

"We were told that you had seen this man," Keith said as Emily showed the man the picture.

"I did," the man said, "The gentleman in the picture stopped by my shop about three days ago."

"Did you speak with him?" Keith asked.

"Briefly," the man said, "He came in to get out of the rain."

"Did he mention anything about where he lived or where he worked?" Keith asked.

"He said that he was a visitor from out of town and he was going to be leaving soon," the man said, "He didn't say where he was staying, just that this is a beautiful city to wander around."

"Did he say anything else?" Emily asked.

"We talked a little bit about the weather and he talked a little about his little girl, but not much else," the man said, "Is he in trouble?"

"No," Keith said, "We just want to talk to him."

"He did leave something with me to give to a friend that he said would drop by," the man said.

"Did he give more instructions on it?" Keith asked.

"He said a friend would stop by and I am to give it to the friend," the man said.

"Did he give an name?" Emily asked.

"Emily Jackson," the man said. Keith looked at Emily with one eyebrow raised. "Do you know who that is?"

"I'm Emily Jackson," Emily said confused. The man looked under the counter he had been leaning on. He pulled out a bag and held it out to Emily. Emily took it. The bag was a dark, heavy plastic that had the top folded and taped so that its contents wouldn't fall out.

"Thank you," Emily said.

"That is all he said," the man told them.

"If you remember anything else, please call," Keith said handing the man his card.

"I will," the man said. Keith and Emily left the shop. Emily pulled the tape off the bag and looked inside.

"Apparently this guy knows you," Keith said.

"As far as I know I've never met the man in my life," Emily said pulling a shirt out of the bag. It was similar type to what she was already wearing. Emily dropped in back in and pulled the second item out. It was a pair of blue jeans. She dropped them back into the bag. "But I now have a few questions for him."

They dropped the clothes off at Keith's car before continuing the search. After lunch Keith had to go back to the station for something, so Emily continued on without him.

About two o'clock Emily stopped to rest on a bench. She checked the watch to see that the time on the watch was exactly the same time as when she had put it on.

"You look tired," a lady said sitting down on the bench next to Emily. The lady had short blonde hair and light blue eyes. Her face was starting to show lines from life full of worry. The clothes she wore seemed slightly out of place, sort of like Emily's were.

"I am tired," Emily replied.

"A common ailment," the lady said.

"It is a symptom of busy lives," Emily replied.

"Perhaps, we should all slow down rather than living twenty-four seven," the lady said.

"You cannot function on that lifestyle for any length of time without suffering burnout."

"That does not seem to stop people."

"It does eventually."

"True."

"Pardon me, I need to get back to what I was doing," Emily said getting up.

"I hope we'll talk again," the lady said.

"Stranger things have happened," Emily said before walking away.

Keith found Emily asleep on a bench about suppertime. He woke her up.

"You're still here," Keith said, "Was there somewhere you needed to be dropped off to get back home?"

"I don't know," Emily said sleepily.

"How about you come back with me for supper, then we'll figure it all out," Keith suggested.

"Sure," Emily said getting up. They got into Keith car that was parked beside the curb.

In fifteen minutes they were back at Keith's place. Going inside Keith started making supper, while Emily sat at the kitchen table. Keith finished making supper and had just served it when his cell phone rang. He answered it and then turned to Emily.

"There has been an emergency," Keith said, "I have to go and I don't know when I'll be back."

"Okay," Emily said. Keith left the house and Emily heard his car drive away. Emily ate supper and put the leftovers in the refrigerator before doing the dishes. When she was finished Emily went out and sat on the front steps. One of the neighbours was out cutting his lawn with a rolling machine that made a lot of noise. Emily ignored it and just sat there enjoying the sunny evening. The neighbour finished cutting the grass and put the machine away. Then he came over to where Emily was sitting.

"Beautiful evening, isn't it?" he asked.

"It is," Emily replied.

"You visiting?"

"Yes."

"How long are you visiting?"

"I've been here two days and I should be going home soon."

"Hardly enough time to see everything."

"Just here looking for someone."

"Oh. My name is Bruce."

"I'm Emily."

"Nice to meet you. What do you do for a living?"

"I'm a doctor."

"Really? So am I. I'm a neurologist."

"Obstetrician paediatrician."

"If you think about staying the hospital is in need of those specialities."

"I don't think I'll be around but if it happens I'll look into that."

"Do you work at a hospital back home?"

"No, I work at a private clinic, but I usually end up doing a lot more general practice than anything else."

"You must get paid quite a bit if you work at a private clinic."

"Not really, most patients don't have money and are usually in need of immediate attention."

"Sounds like a hospital stress level."

"At times."

"I really should get back to yard work."

"It was nice to meet you.

"Nice to meet you too." Bruce went back to his yard work. Emily continued to sit there until the sun went down. Then she went inside and went to bed.

Emily woke up. The sun was shining in the window again. Emily got out of bed and went over to the window. The sun was just rising. Emily had seen those colours in a painting once, but never spread across the sky like that. She watched it until it faded to light blue. She studied the plants that were on people's lawns. The trees were so alive and vibrant, the flowers were the prettiest colours and the grass was almost emerald green.

"What did we do? Why would we do so much harm to the planet we live on?" Emily asked herself, "It was so beautiful." Emily could hear Keith come down stairs and go into the kitchen. From the sounds he was starting breakfast.

"What do I do?" Emily asked herself, "Do I assume that I can't go back? Is the time different? Because Jordan said that it had to be the same. Do I continue searching for Daniel or is he gone by now? What do I do?" Emily checked the watch, according to it only an hour had past since she had left. Sighing Emily finger brushed her hair before putting up in a ponytail. She changed into her new clothes and went out to the kitchen. Keith was putting breakfast on plates.

"Well?" Keith asked as he put the plates on the table.

"I'm waiting for Jordan to contact me," Emily answered sitting down, "He hasn't so far."

"You can stay here until he does," Keith said sitting across from her.

"Thank you," Emily said. They ate without talking.

Once he was finished Keith put his dishes, along with the ones he used to make breakfast, on racks in a cupboard that opened out and down.

"When you finished just put you dishes in the dish washer," Keith said then left the kitchen. Emily heard him leave.

"Dishwasher? Must be something similar to what Trent uses to clean glasses," Emily said getting up and opening the cupboard. She placed her dishes in the rack and studied the machine. "Interesting." She closed the door. Leaving the kitchen Emily wandered the house. The living room had a window with a seat, a couch, a monitor on a table across from it and most of it was covered in dust. Upstairs there was a suite, which looked like where Keith slept. Emily based that on the bed lacking dust, the bathroom looked like it was used regularly and clothes were scattered across the floor. The other door on the second floor led to a storage area that held some boxes, but not much else. Emily went back to the living room.

"Did they not have books in this century?" Emily asked looking around. There was a small pile of magazines at one end of the couch. After picking the top one up and flipping through it Emily put it back. Emily sat down at the window seat and stared out the window.

At five o'clock Emily got up and found a recipe that she could make for supper. She was just finished cooking it when Keith came home. They ate together and then Keith went out for the evening.

The next day was Saturday, Keith left early and Emily was left alone with nothing to do. Sunday Keith slept in and then spent the day in front of the monitor in the living room. Emily borrowed a book from Bruce and spent the day reading.

Emily woke up Monday to dark clouds and rain coming down. This rain was clear and people seemed to be able to go out in it. Emily got up, once again the window attracting her attention. When she realized that Keith was moving around the kitchen Emily went to the kitchen. Keith served breakfast.

"No word from Jordan?" Keith asked.

"None, yet," Emily said. Keith nodded and went back to his breakfast. Once he was finished Keith left for work.

When she was finished Emily sat in the window alternating between watching it rain and reading. At five she made supper and Keith went out after supper.

The rest of the week went about the same as Monday.

Saturday Emily got up and went to the kitchen. Keith was already up and making breakfast.

"It looks like Jordan has forgotten to contact you," Keith said.

"Apparently," Emily replied.

"You can stay here until you find your own place," Keith said.

"Thank you."

"I can loan you some money to buy clothes and other necessities."

"I would appreciate that."

They didn't say anything more as they ate. After breakfast Keith gave Emily the money and dropped her off at the mall. Emily spent the morning shopping before walking back to Keith's house. Keith was out, so Emily made herself at home in the guestroom.

The rest of the weekend was the same as before. Monday Emily cleaned Keith's house after he had gone to work. Keith didn't even seem to notice when he came home long enough to eat supper.

Two weeks Emily did things to keep herself busy, but found herself hoping that she would be pulled back to her own time. The watch seemed to move an hour with the hour or just a minute in a whole day.

Emily sat on the front step feeling homesick. Bruce saw her when he came home from work and went over to her.

"You still here?" Bruce asked.

"Yeah, I haven't been able to go home and it looks like I'm here to stay," Emily answered.

"I'm sorry to hear that you can't go home."

"It wouldn't be so bad, but I have nothing to do."

"The hospital is still in need of doctors."

"The problem there is that the only proof I have that I am a doctor is my say so and I don't think people are willing to take just that."

"That is a problem. Maybe I can talk to a few people and see what I can do."

"You don't even know whether I can do a good job or not."

"I trust my instinct and it says you are good at what you do."

"Thank you, anything is better than sitting around here doing nothing."

"Keith hasn't tried to help you find something?"

"I'm not sure he remembers I'm still here."

"That sounds like what Carol used to say."

"Carol?"

"Keith's ex-wife."

"What happened?"

"He worked too much while she spent his money. Then she met a charming guy with more money and left Keith."

"Doesn't sound like either of them were happy before they split up."

"He seemed to take it pretty hard, he spent two weeks locked in his house."

"How long ago did they separate?"

"Three months."

"That isn't that long. How long were they married?"

"Six years."

A call for supper came from Bruce's house.

"Sounds like my wife wants me to come for supper. I'll talk to people at the hospital and get back to you."

"Okay."

Bruce went home. Emily went inside and started supper.

Keith didn't come home for supper. Emily ate without him and put the leftovers in the refrigerator. She went back to sitting at the window seat.

"Why couldn't everything go as planned? I could be drunk on tequila or something similar," Emily asked out loud, "It is pretty here, but this is not my home. Even getting a lecture from Grace on my drinking would be pleasant right now." Emily rested her forehead on the windowpane and closed her eyes.

When she opened them it was dark out and Keith had just pulled into the driveway. He came into the house and headed straight for the kitchen. Emily heard a cupboard open, but nothing after that. Emily got up and went into the kitchen. Keith was sitting at the table with a bottle of tequila and a full glass.

"Long day?" Emily asked noticing a second bottle on the counter, that one said whiskey.

"Hellish," Keith answered taking a sip from the glass, "Care to join me?"

"Sure," Emily said getting herself a glass.

The white haired man led Travis to Jordan's office. They arrived to find Jordan fiddling with an open panel on the time machine.

"The man is here from department H," the white haired man announced causing Jordan to jump. Jordan turned to them.

"Hello, Travis," Jordan's voice was cheery. The white haired man left.

"Forty-eight hours are up, where's Emily?" Travis asked.

"Yes, well…" Jordan started.

"What happened?"

"A slight malfunction, nothing that isn't fixable."

"You mean an agent is in an unknown situation with nothing to help her and no information."

"I'm sure she'll figure it out."

"And what are you doing about this problem?"

"I'm trying to fix it."

"How long will that take?"

"I don't know… a week maybe."

"A week! And what about Emily?"

"She'll have to deal with things there."

"Are there any more of these machines?"

"This is the only one in this time period."

"Maybe you should have thought this thing out a lot more before sending someone."

"If you go back to department H I will contact you when I have the machine fixed."

"It better be soon." Travis left.

Emily woke to the feeling of pounding in her head. She lay there for a minute hoping it would stop. When it didn't she opened her eyes. Looking around she realized that she was in Keith's room. Sitting up she saw Keith beside her. Quietly Emily got up, put her clothes on, which were scattered all over the floor, and left the room. Once down stairs she took a shower. When she was dressed she went into the kitchen. There were two empty bottles and two glasses on the table. Emily put the glasses in the dishwasher and set the two bottles on the counter. Then she drank a glass of water and started breakfast.

Over the next few days Emily avoided Keith and Keith kept his usual distance.

On Wednesday Keith went off to work and Emily sat down on the step to enjoy the morning. Close to noon she was just about to go in when Bruce's car pulled into Keith's driveway. Bruce got out and went over to her.

"Hello," Emily said.

"Hello," Bruce said, "I talked to the director of the hospital and he said that he would be willing to take you on as a doctor as long as you would be willing to have someone watch you work until he knows you are competent."

"Sounds fine to me," Emily said.

"Good, if you aren't busy the director can meet with you now," Bruce said.

"I'm not doing anything," Emily said standing up. Bruce started toward his car; Emily followed.

"You will be dealing with the problems related to your specialities," Bruce said then got into the car.

"That's fine," Emily said once she was in the car. Bruce drove to the hospital. Once there he took Emily to meet the director. The director talked with Emily a while, then introduced her to the doctor who would be watching her and showed her around. When the director was finished Emily was allowed to start.

Emily went back to Keith's house with Bruce at the end of the workday.

At the end of the second week Emily was allowed to work without having to be supervised.

Emily was sitting in her office doing some paperwork between appointments when there was a knock on her door.

"Come in," Emily called putting her pen down. The door opened and one of the nurses entered.

"Can I talk to you?" the nurse asked.

"Sure," Emily said. The nurse sat down after closing the door. The nurse had brown hair put up, hazel eyes that seemed scared and fingers that twisted around each other in nervousness. The woman's face looked like she had been under a lot of strain.

"I'm scared to talk to anyone here at the hospital, but since you are new I hope this will be easier," the nurse paused. Emily remembered that her name was Kristy.

"Everything said will be kept confidential," Emily replied.

"I've been feeling sick for the last few months, but I didn't think anything of it," Kristy said, "The other day someone made a comment about me gaining weight. I thought that was weird, because I haven't been eating much, but stepping on the scale I found I had. I was trying to figure out what was wrong. I took a home pregnancy test yesterday and it came back positive." Kristy stopped as if she realized she was babbling. She looked like she was ready to start crying. The next sentence came out in a whisper.

"I don't want the baby, I don't want his child."

"When was your last period?" Emily asked.

"I don't remember," Kristy's voice was stronger.

"When did you start to feel sick?"

"Three months maybe."

"I can do another test to make sure that you are pregnant. But I would suggest an ultra sound as well."

"Why?"

"Given that you don't remember exact dates, it will help figure out how far along you are."

"I'm not sexually active. I know the exact date, if I am really pregnant."

"May I ask?"

"He flirted with me before and I've turned him down. I thought that was all. I was getting some sheets to change the beds, when the door opened and closed." Kristy's eyes went to her hands, watching them clench and unclench. "I turned to look and he was standing there. I told him no, but he didn't listen." The tears started to flow. Emily got up and went around the desk. She put an arm around Kristy and let her cry for a few minutes before handing her some tissues.

"How long ago was this?" Emily asked quietly.

"Six months," the replied was muffled.

"Did you report him?"

"You can't report a doctor, not unless you never want to work again. There are plenty of nurses to replace me, but doctors are harder to get. I don't want his child."

"If you are six months along it would not be medically safe for you to have an abortion."

"What else am I supposed to do?"

"A blood test, an ultrasound and no worrying until you come and see me. Because if you are not pregnant than you just wasted a whole week."

Kristy nodded.

"There is water to wash your face," Emily said pointing to the examining room. Kristy got up and went into the examining room. While she was in there Emily wrote up the lab forms. When Kristy came back into the room she looked better. Emily handed her the forms.

"It never looks good when you are seeing the situation fully the first time, but it will work out in the end," Emily said.

"I hope so," Kristy said. Emily saw her out before going back to work for the ten minutes until her appointment.

The next morning Emily knocked on the office door of the other obstetrician.

"Come in," Dr. Hannah Dunton said seeing Emily standing there. Emily entered and sat down in the chair across from her, "You look tired."

"That must be connected to how I feel," Emily said.

"What did you need?" Hannah asked her blue eyes twinkling with laughter.

"Has there ever been a case of a doctor raping a nurse here before?" Emily asked.

"Sure, Dr. Roberts was accused of raping a female nurse about a year ago," Hannah answered, the laughter in her eyes fading, "He hasn't been hitting on you, has he?"

"I've never met the man," Emily said.

"He deals with male problems," Hannah said, "But what brings you here asking about this?"

"What happened to the nurse?"

"The administration suggested that she was trying to get attention and that she should stop trying to ruin Dr. Roberts's reputation. She eventually quit, due to being the centre of the gossip for months."

"Do you think he did rape her?"

"Professionally, I am not sure, there is no evidence either way."

"And personally?"

"He creeps me out and I wouldn't put it passed him."

"Do you think he'd do it again?"

"If he thought he could get away with it."

"What would stop him? He got away with it once."

"People have been keeping an eye on him. The administration may not be, but most of the doctors do. They make sure he is never alone with any female, doctor or nurse."

Emily's beeper went off. She checked it.

"Pregnant ladies will go into labour any time," Emily said.

"Usually," Hannah replied.

"I haven't even had my coffee yet."

"You don't drink anything with caffeine in it."

"Then I better go check on this lady," Emily started to get up.

"Dr. Jackson?" the secretary stuck her nose into Hannah's office, "The results from tests you ordered yesterday are in."

"Thanks, please put them on my desk," Emily said standing up, "I have to go see a woman about a baby." Hannah laughed as Emily left the office.

Emily arrived back at her office after lunch. Sitting at her desk she noticed the file on top. Emily opened it and looked over the results. A knock came at the door. Emily looked up to see Hannah.

"Have a seat," Emily invited. Hannah closed the door behind her and took the chair Emily had indicated. Emily closed the file.

"I talked to Dr. Ellsworth," Hannah said.

"Is he the one you eat lunch with?" Emily asked.

"Yes, he is a surgeon," Hannah replied, "Today I asked about Dr. Roberts."

"And?"

"Dr. Roberts has had three complaints about him that most of the hospital staff never heard."

"Of course not, the administration doesn't want to ruin his reputation."

"Those three have been sexual harassment complaints. One of which claimed that he tried to rape her, but she kicked him in the groin and got away."

"So, he thinks he can get away with anything?"

"Not only that he has figured out that people are watching him and knows when their back is turned, because no one has seen him disappear to do these things. Why did you ask this morning?"

"A patient."

"A nurse here at the hospital?"

"She didn't name the doctor and she won't bring it before administration."

"There isn't much you can do then."

"Yes, there is. I have to figure out what is a good option for someone who doesn't want to keep the child, but is too far into the pregnancy for me to feel safe about abortion."

"You would consider abortion? I thought you would be one of those people who would be morally against it."

"I am, but if the woman is going to do more harm to herself trying to do it without medical assistance then I don't really have a choice."

"True. Adoption is a good choice, especially if the mother can meet the people who want to adopt. I think I have some pamphlets in my office."

"Those would be appreciated. Dr. Roberts may get his in the end, but pressuring this lady to report him is not the way to go."

"Dr. Roberts should be castrated."

"What about the oath about doing no harm?"

"Who says I would do it?"

A knock came at the door.

"Yes?" Emily called. The secretary poked her nose in.

"Dr. Ellsworth is here to talk to you, Dr. Dunton," the secretary said.

"There is another seat in here," Hannah said. The secretary withdrew her head. After a moment a tall man entered the room. He was wearing surgical scrubs under a lab coat.

"Dr. Dunton, Dr. Jackson," He nodded to them before sitting down.

"Emily," Emily corrected him. One brown eyebrow raised itself.

"On a first name basis before we've been introduced?" He asked.

"I prefer to be on a first name basis with everyone," Emily said, "It is a weird quirk of mine."

"Okay," Dr. Ellsworth said.

"What did you need, Galen?" Hannah asked.

"Dr. Roberts went after another nurse this morning," Dr. Ellsworth said, "Since you were asking questions about him this morning."

"Will this one go to the administration?" Hannah asked.

"The director walked in on his attempt to rape her," Dr. Ellsworth said, "If something doesn't happen this time I'd be surprised."

"You don't think they can ignore that?" Emily said.

"The director saw him, that is hard evidence to refute," Dr. Ellsworth said, "Especially since the nurse is going to charge him with attempted rape whether the administration does anything or not."

"Good for her," Hannah said. The secretary poked her nose in.

"Dr. Jackson, your two o'clock appointment is here," the secretary said before withdrawing.

"I see you haven't trained everyone out of calling you by your last name," Dr. Ellsworth commented.

"Every time she says it I want to look around for my grandfather," Emily said, "I guess I have to get to work."

"Then we'll leave you to it," Hannah said getting up. Dr. Ellsworth also stood up.

"Nice to meet you," he said then they both left. Emily pulled out the file she needed as the woman was escorted into the office by the secretary.

A week later Emily sat in her office. It was first thing in the morning, so the secretary wasn't in yet. Kristy entered the doorway and was just about to knock.

"Come in," Emily invited her. Kristy came in and sat down.

"What did the tests say?" Kristy asked.

"That you are pregnant and you're about twenty-four weeks along," Emily answered. Kristy nodded, her eyes dry today.

"Have you thought about the future?" Emily asked.

"You said that abortion was not an option," Kristy said.

"A different doctor might be willing to do it, but I won't," Emily said, "And it would be harmful to your health."

"My sister always wanted a child, but her husband is sterile," Kristy said, "She would never consider using any sperm donors. But I told her I was pregnant and I didn't want the child. She told me that she would take the child and raise it as her own."

"Is that what you want?"

"They live far enough away that I wouldn't see the child much. Maybe someday I can put all this behind me."

"The baby is healthy, but I have nutritional guidelines for you. And I would suggest that you find a counsellor that has no connection to the hospital."

Kristy nodded. Emily dug out the paperwork for her.

"I will need to continue to check your health and the baby's health at least once a month for the next two months, after that we'll have to discuss it."

"My sister said you could tell the gender of the baby already."

"Would you like to know?"

"Yes."

"You are going to have a baby girl."

"Thank you for everything."

"You're welcome."

Kristy took the papers and left the office. A couple minutes later Emily headed to the bathroom and emptied her stomach.

Hannah was waiting her when she got back to the office.

"You don't look good," Hannah said as Emily sat down.

"I'll be fine," Emily said.

"If you have the flu, go home," Hannah said.

"No, based on the symptoms it isn't the flu," Emily said.

"You're pregnant," Hannah said.

"Very likely," Emily said, "Which makes me wonder if I shouldn't give up drinking completely."

"For the next several months you better. When was the last time you had a drink?"

"Two weeks, which coincides with the only time in the past two years I've had sex."

"Two years without sex?"

"He died and the baby was still born."

"Oh."

"What did you want to talk to me about?"

"Dr. Roberts has been cleared of all wrong doing."

"How?"

"He managed to convince the director that it was consensual."

"What about the charges?"

"The director has talked the police into dropping the investigation. The nurse is screaming about how wrong this is and now is out of a job without a reference for five years of hard work."

"Castrating is much too nice."

"Do no harm."

"I'm sure there are people who can be hired to do it."

"You serious?"

"I don't have any money, I haven't been paid yet. My first pay cheque isn't until this Friday."

"If you had the money, would you?"

"Probably not. I'm not that big on doing anyone harm, even if they deserve it."

The secretary came and sat down at her desk. Hannah went into her office and Emily went to hers.

A month passed without too much of interest happening.

Emily was sitting in her office, finishing up some paperwork.

"Good evening, Dr. Walsh," the secretary's voice came in through the open door.

"Good evening, Emily still in?" Bruce's voice asked.

"Yes," the secretary said.

"Thank you."

"Would you like me to tell her that you wish to speak with her?"

"No, I'll announce myself thank you."

A moment later Bruce entered the office and sat down.

"Ready to go?" Bruce asked.

"I'm trying to finish this last thing up," Emily answered without looking up.

"Hannah said that you were pregnant," Bruce said.

"Hannah repeats a lot of things apparently. She seems to need gossip."

"Have you told Keith yet?"

"I see him at breakfast and supper, unless one of us is not there. I'm thinking moving to an apartment closer to the hospital."

"Will you even give him a choice? I know there isn't much of a relationship between you two, but you should at least tell him."

Emily closed the file and put it in to the drawer.

"I'll talk to him tonight, but I doubt it will change anything."

"Maybe he'll turn into the perfect husband when he finds out he is going to be a father."

"Then I'll have to find his ex-wife." Emily got up and grabbed her coat.

"You slept with him, but you don't want to sleep with him again?"

"I was drunk when I slept with him. I have no desire to do either again anytime soon."

Bruce stood up and they left the office.

"At least give him a chance with his kid."

"I'll know by tomorrow whether or not to give him at chance."

They left the hospital.

Emily was sitting at the table with dinner already set out when Keith came in from work. He sat down and started to eat.

"I was thinking of finding a place closer to the hospital now that I have some money," Emily said.

"Okay," Keith said.

"But there is one complication."

"What's that?"

"I'm pregnant, and you are the father."

Keith stared at her.

"What?" Keith asked, "We slept together once a little over a month ago."

"You are the only person I have slept with in two years. I diagnosed myself and have had it confirmed by the other obstetrician and a blood test. I know I am pregnant and you are the father."

Keith didn't say anything as he studied his food momentarily and then ate a couple mouthfuls.

"I can still move."

"No, it would be better if you stayed."

"Okay, but I will continue to stay in the guestroom."

"Fine."

They didn't say anything for the rest of the meal.

Two months went past. Keith spent his time at work and Emily balanced work and pregnancy.

Travis hadn't even bothered to knock or wait for the white haired man; he just went straight to Jordan's office. Jordan was sitting on the floor with pieces of the time machine scattered around him and a circuit with wires coming out of it going in all directions in his hand.

"She has been gone two weeks," Travis said making Jordan jump, "Have you solved the problem yet?"

"No, apparently it is more complex than I first thought," Jordan answered.

"It looks like you have taken it completely apart," Travis said.

"Not quite," Jordan said, "Just enough to fix it."

"I hope you can put it back together so that it works," Travis turned to go, "I'll check back in a week. If you have it done before that contact me." Travis left. Jordan went back to the time machine.

Saturday afternoon found Emily sitting in the window seat watching white stuff falling from the sky and covering the ground. It covered the dead leaves and grass making the world look brand new. Emily could feel the coldness on her forehead where it rested against the window. She didn't look up when she heard Keith enter the room.

"The first snowfall of the season is the most beautiful, isn't it?" Keith asked looking out the window. Emily didn't respond. "You okay?" Keith asked turning his attention to Emily.

"I'm trying to figure out how I ended up here," Emily answered.

"I'm not sure I could give you an answer on that, I'm not even sure how I got where I am," Keith replied as he sat down. Emily nodded.

"I wish I had slippers like the girl in the book who could tap the heels together and be home," Emily said.

"That doesn't work here," Keith said.

"If it did I might be home by now," Emily said.

"What is stopping you from going home?"

"It is impossible to get to my home by walking, running, car, truck, van, plane, train, bus, hot air balloon, or giant moth."

"Then how did you get here?"

"Don't ask me difficult questions. I don't have the energy to answer them today."

Silence settled between them for a few minutes as they watched it snow.

"Giant moth?"

"You need to read more."

Grace was standing in front of Cynthia's desk when Travis came in.

"Any word as when he can get her back?" Grace asked Travis.

"No, currently he is taking the whole machine apart," Travis answered.

"If that's what it takes to get her back I hope it works and I hope he finishes it soon," Grace said then headed down the hallway. Travis shot Cynthia a questioning look. Cynthia shrugged without looking up from her computer screen.

A month and a half went by without much for changes in Keith and Emily's routine. The only changes happening were with Emily's pregnancy.

Emily came home from work, after a stop at the bathroom, went into the kitchen. Keith was already home. Supper was sitting half made on the counter and he was talking on the phone to someone. Emily ignored him and finished making supper. When she was done she set the two plates on the table and started eating. Keith hung up the phone and joined her a few minutes later.

"That was my parents. They were wondering what we were doing for Christmas," Keith said.

"What is Christmas?" Emily asked.

"You don't know what Christmas is?"

"No, I've never heard of it."

"Christmas is a holiday that falls on the twenty-fifth of this month. It is a day where family get together and exchange presents."

"Why?"

"Something to do with Christ being born on that day."

"What does a religious figure have to do with exchanging presents?"

"We celebrate the day the he was born with getting together, exchanging gifts and eating turkey dinner. My parents were wondering if we had anything planned."

"Obviously not, if I didn't know anything about it."

"I already told them we didn't have any plans. They have decided to come and visit. They will show up about a week before and leave after New Years."

"New Years?"

"We celebrate the end of an old year and the beginning of a new one."

"What all is involved with celebrating Christmas?"

"Well, a week before people set up the tree and decorate it. The day before is Christmas Eve and the evening is spent sitting around talking and eating cookies. Christmas morning there are stockings that are filled with gifts to be opened first, then breakfast and then the opening of presents. About mid-afternoon the turkey supper is served, which is usually followed by board games and eating snack food."

"And New Years is celebrated how?"

"Usually by partying on New Years Eve until midnight, having a drink to toast the new year and then sleeping in New Year's day."

"Interesting." Emily cleared her dishes and went to the guestroom.

Emily was just finished her first appointment of the morning and was finishing the paperwork before the next appointment arrived when Hannah came in and sat down.

"Two pieces of good news," Hannah said. Emily looked up from her work.

"You going to tell me both at once or start with the first one?" Emily asked.

"Galen gave me an early Christmas present," Hannah said.

"I thought there was still three weeks until Christmas."

"There is, that is why I call it an early Christmas present."

"What did he give you?"

"This," Hannah held out her left hand. On her ring finger was a gold ring with three large diamonds set side by side.

"Beautiful," Emily commented.

"He wants to wait six months to have the wedding, so that we have time to plan a proper wedding. It will be wonderful."

"He wants? What about you?"

"I'm all for a big, fancy wedding, but I could happily get married tomorrow in blue jeans."

"Plan the wedding, it might be better for the relationship."

"Why is that?"

"If you two can plan a wedding together and survive, you might last longer."

"He claims that his mother will probably try to take over."

"See? What is the other piece of news?"

"Dr. Robert isn't going to be trying to rape anyone again."

"What happened?"

"A prostitute he had hired decided to give him sleeping pills and rob him blind."

"Foolish man."

"Unfortunately for the prostitute he was allergic to something in the sleeping pills. While she was going through his house he went into anaphylactic shock and she came back into the room to find a corpse. The police took her into custody when she called for the ambulance."

"I hope the charge isn't too bad, he doesn't deserve the justice."

"I don't know."

A knock came at the door and the secretary poked her nose in.

"Dr. Dunton, you appointment is here," the secretary said.

"Thank you," Hannah said as she got up. Emily went back to her paperwork as Hannah left the room.

The Saturday before Christmas, Keith spent a few hours digging out the Christmas tree and then set it up. Emily sat on the window seat and watched as he decorated it.

"Why decorate a tree?" Emily asked.

"To put the presents under Christmas Eve," Keith answered. Keith started to hum as he went.

"What day are your parents coming?" Emily asked.

"Wednesday."

"Do they actually know about me?"

"I told them about you when you became pregnant."

"Probably a good thing."

"When they come they will probably treat you as family. I explained the situation to them. They will try to stay on your good side so that if you leave and take the kid they will still get to see their grandchild."

"So far it doesn't look like anything is going to change."

Keith didn't respond as he continued to decorate the tree. Emily stopped watching him and turned her gaze to the snow-covered scene outside.

Keith and Emily continued their routine with only a few changes when Keith's parents arrived.

Saturday Emily spent the morning shopping and went back to Keith's house at noon. After stowing her purchases in the guestroom she went into the kitchen. Karen, Keith's mom, was in the kitchen baking cookies. Emily sat down at the table.

"You look tired," Karen commented.

"I get that comment quite frequently these days," Emily said.

"Sorry, if you hear it too often."

"Not much you can do about that. I probably do look tired."

"The guys took off an hour ago. I doubt they will be back before supper."

Emily nodded.

"I have a request," Karen said, "I spoke to Keith about this earlier, but he felt I was better off talking to you."

"And what is it?"

"I was hoping that the child could be named after my father. He was the last of my family and he died earlier this year. I know this is your child, but I would mean a lot to me."

"Sure, I haven't been able to come up with any names."

"Thank you."

Christmas came and went. New Years came and went. Keith's parents left and Keith and Emily went back to their usual routine.

Emily came in to her office to find Hannah already sitting there.

"You're here early," Emily commented as she hung up her jacket.

"I'm trying to figure out what to do for Galen's birthday," Hannah said, "My sister suggested a candlelit dinner at home followed by snuggling on the couch, but I can't cook and we do the candle light thing every time we go out."

"What does he like to do?" Emily sat down.

"Golf," Hannah said, "He has a weekly poker game depending on his schedule. We both like to dance. He occasionally volunteers at the soup kitchen downtown. But we are both working that day, so I have to do whatever in the evening."

"Take a weekend instead."

"And do what?"

"Find a resort with a golf course and someplace to dance."

"That might be possible, but I don't know which weekends he has off. That and I have like three women that are due soon."

"There is another doctor that can deal with that."

"I know, but you are supposed to be taking it easy."

"I know how much is too much. I'm not going to hit it any time soon. When his birthday comes tell him what you want to do and I'm sure everything can be arranged from there."

"I think I'll do that."

"Beats lighting candles because you don't want him to see how bad supper really is."

Hannah laughed as she got up and left Emily's office.

A week later Emily knocked on Hannah's office. Hannah looked up.

"Heard you weren't available last weekend," Emily said.

"I have a wonderful, but quiet weekend," Hannah said.

"And did Galen enjoy himself?"

"Yes."

"Good," Emily said then went to her own office.

Travis strode purposely into Jordan's office. Jordan stood near the now put back together time machine.

"Well? What is the news this week?" Travis asked.

"I have fixed the problem," Jordan said.

"It's only been three weeks," Travis said.

"I was just about to try it," Jordan said. He started to fiddle with some dials and threw a few switches.

"Here we go," Jordan pressed the last button. Nothing happened.

"What happened this time?" Travis asked.

"I don't know," Jordan said rechecking the machine, "I'll try it again." He pressed the button. Again nothing happened.

"I'll be back in another week," Travis said, "Contact me if there are any changes to the situation." Travis turned and left.

When she was eight months along Emily cut down to part time. Two weeks before her due date she stopped working.

A week later Emily knocked on Hannah's door.

"Come in," Hannah called. Emily opened the door, entered the room and closed the door behind her.

"Emily, a pleasant surprise!" Hannah said as Emily sat down.

"From your perceptive," Emily answered.

"What is wrong?"

"Labour started about two hours ago."

"How did you get down here?"

"Taxi."

"What about the father?"

"I left a message for him. Don't really expect him anyway."

"I'll go find you a room," Hannah said getting up and leaving the office.

Some hours later Emily gave birth to a healthy baby boy. Keith showed up in time to fill out the paperwork.

Three days later Emily was sitting at the kitchen table holding her sleeping son and staring at the birth certificate sitting on the table.

"Daniel Logan Anderson," Emily read to herself. Looking down at the baby in her arms. "Welcome to this insane, screwed up world, Daniel Anderson."

Emily enjoyed two months of being there to comfort and play with her son. Keith worked all day and helped out in the evening.

Travis made his weekly visit to Jordan's office.

"Any changes?" Travis asked.

"I have it fixed this time," Jordan said.

"Okay, then bring Emily back," Travis said. Jordan pressed the button.

Emily paced the living room, holding a screaming Daniel in her arms.

"Please, Daniel, please go to sleep," Emily pleaded, "If I don't get some rest soon I'm going to collapse." Each step didn't seem to help the screaming to stop. "I've tried everything. Keith tried everything, why are you still crying? What is wrong?" The watch on Emily's wrist beeped. Emily looked at it as if she had forgotten it was there. Suddenly the world dissolved into darkness. Emily stopped pacing. The crying stopped. Emily looked down to find Daniel gone. She dropped her arms to her sides. Emily suddenly found herself in Jordan's office.

"Well, I guess you did it," Travis told Jordan.

"Did you find Daniel Anderson?" Jordan asked Emily. Emily shook her head as if to clear it.

"A pity, oh well," Jordan said.

"You okay, Emily?" Travis asked.

"No," Emily answered.

"Well, once back at the department you can go see Dr. Grace," Travis said. Travis led the way outside to the parked car. Emily got into the passenger seat and Travis got into the driver's seat. Travis started the car and pulled out of the parking lot.

"Must be good to be back after a month in the twenty-first century," Travis said. Emily didn’t say anything, she just closed her eyes and rested her forehead against the window. Travis didn't try to talk for the rest of the way back. Once back at the building, Travis pulled into his parking spot. Travis had turned off the engine and had gotten out before Emily moved. She followed him inside then she headed for her room. Inside she locked the door behind her and collapsed on the bed, immediately falling asleep.

The next day Emily entered the medical lab and sat down at the computer.

"Been a while," Grace commented.

"Forever," Emily said.

"So, what is the twenty-first century like?"

"Strange."

"Post mission medical check?"

"Want me to tell you some of what you'll find?"

Grace sat down in the other chair.

"It took a month to get you back here. What happened?"

Keith entered his empty house and sat down in the chair in the living room. Emily and Daniel had disappeared a week ago. Keith had gotten half the police force out looking, had a hotline set up and the media had been informing the public. No one had found a trace of either of them. It was impossible for someone to disappear without a trace; they always left something to follow. Wherever Emily went, the only thing she took was Daniel and left no clues.

Daniel sat down at the computer and started to work. Professor Abbott came into the lab.

"What are you doing, Daniel?" Professor Abbott asked.

"Seeing what I can find about my parents," Daniel answered, "You have been like a father, but after sixteen years I would like to know who my parents are and why they left me here."

"Have you found anything yet?"

"I put both name and picture in the search and I came up with a picture of an older guy that looks like me in a police record in the twenty-first century. The guy was being looked for, with the help of the police, by an Emily Jackson."

"Is that all you can find?"

"Except for some articles that I wrote."

"How about trying the name of the person who was looking for the guy?"

"Emily Jackson," Daniel typed in the name. "Two results. The first is a police record from the twenty-first century. She went missing about a year after she showed up. It doesn't look like she was ever found.

"And the other result?"

"Is classified. It must be in the department though because it wants a password."

"Try 103007891."

"It let me in."

"And?"

Daniel did some more typing.

"Emily Jackson is an agent for department H. She was born and raised in this town and has two medical degrees."

"That doesn't fit with her being in a record from the twenty-first century."

"I think I will try to speak with her. She may have some of the answers I'm looking for."

"Don't be too long."

Daniel got up and left the lab.

Emily had gone back to her room after the medical check. But the next morning she showed up at the medical lab.

"How are you doing today?" Grace asked as Emily sat down.

"Still trying to get used to being home," Emily answered.

"Alfred sent a message that he wanted to talk to me, do you think you could watch the lab?"

"Sure."

Grace left the medical lab. Emily started a research project on the computer. She had been working at it for about half an hour when the door to the medical lab opened. The young man that entered looked like a younger version of the picture Jordan had given Emily.

"Excuse me, I'm looking for Emily Jackson," the young man said, "I was told that I could find her here."

"You've found her," Emily answered. The young man studied her for a couple moments.

"Somehow from the little I've read I thought you would be older," he said.

"I think I should be older too, but time hasn't caught up yet," Emily replied, "Did you need something?"

"I was wondering if I could ask you a few questions," the young man said.

"I can't promise any answers, but you can ask," Emily said.

"I'm Da…"

"Daniel Anderson, I know."

"How did you know?"

"Have a seat, you ask the questions and I'll see if I can answer them."

Emily shut down her project on the computer once Daniel had left. Emily stared at the monitor. Grace came in a few minutes later.

"You seem lost," Grace commented.

"Just thinking about how fast children grow up. I swear only yesterday he was a baby and now he is sixteen," Emily replied.

"To you he was only a baby yesterday."

"These things happen when people are messing with time."

"Abby showed up here about a day after you left."

"And?"

"She has been having trouble with the flu for about a month."

Emily opened up Abby's file on the computer.

"Looks like she is close to three months pregnant."

"I told her that and suggested she see you."

"That gives me something to do."

"I'm sure you'll have a mission soon."

"Yeah, but based on recent history I'm not sure I want one."

"You'll be okay."

CHAPTER 4
RETRAINING

Emily was staring at the computer in the assignment lab pretending she was doing some research when she heard footsteps behind her.

"Busy?" Alfred asked from behind her.

"Depends," Emily answered.

"When you are ready here, is your next mission." Alfred placed a file folder on the table next to the computer and walked away. Fifteen minutes later Nathan came up to her.

"Dr. Grace says she would like to see you in the medical lab," Nathan said.

"Okay," Emily said shutting down what she was doing. Nathan walked away. Emily got up, grabbed the file folder and headed for the medical lab. When she got there, Grace was examining one of the patients that was on a stretcher. There was another patient on a stretcher and four others were sitting with injuries that didn't look as severe. Emily placed the file folder on the desk.

"I was told you wanted to see me," Emily said.

"Start wherever," Grace told Emily. The first lady was holding a bloody cloth to her arm and had a cut on the left side of her forehead. Emily went over to her.

"May I look at your arm?" Emily asked the lady. The lady seemed to be in shock, but she held out her arm to Emily. There was a five-inch cut along her forearm. "I'm going to have to wash the wound and stitch it up," Emily said to the lady. The lady nodded numbly. Emily led her to the office and had the lady sit down on the bed. Emily took out what she needed and started to clean the wound.

"What happened?" Emily asked as she started.

"We were out on a mission. We were close to the objective when we were attacked," the lady said, "And I don't remember much after that."

Emily nodded.

"Not until help came, I woke up and the attackers were gone and the van pulled up. The lady in the van said Leon will never walk again. And Markus was lying there but they didn't pick him up. The lady said he would be brought back here in the other van but I haven't seen him."

Emily finished stitching up the wound and started to bandage it.

"Do you know where he is?"

"No," Emily answered.

"Maybe they took him to the hospital."

When Emily was finished bandaging the lady's arm, she cleaned and bandaged the cut on her forehead.

"I hope he will be okay."

"Anything else hurt?" Emily asked once she was finished. The lady shook her head. "Then I'll get you to lie down and rest."

"But what about everyone else?" the lady asked.

"They will be taken care of," Emily answered. The lady laid down and Emily covered her up. Emily left the office and closed the door behind her. Emily dealt with the next patient in Grace's office. She did the person's after mission medical check before sending them to their room to rest.

Once all the patients had been taken care of, Emily sat down at the desk and started to read the file. Grace came out of the room the two patients were in and closed the door.

"A mystery," Grace said, "Nine went out on that mission, two came back in serious condition, four with less serious injuries, two still missing and one dead."

"Markus wouldn't happen to be the one that is dead, would he?" Emily asked.

"Yes, why?"

"The lady was in shock, she's sleeping in my office. She is really hoping that he is alright."

"That's Bethany. She and Markus were sleeping together. Never could get Markus to admit it."

"Bethany didn't say as much, but she seemed worried."

"Did you do her medical check?"

"No, I thought I would give her time to rest."

"You got another mission." Grace indicted the file.

"Yeah, I start the day after tomorrow."

"Doing what?"

"Helping train the new recruits. I'm supposed to help the two trainers. I think Alfred wants to keep me close to home, but not leave me with nothing to do."

"After all what could go wrong if you are training recruits?"

"I don't want to think about it."

"Will you be able to come back here?"

"Doesn't sound like they want me to, but I probably could if necessary."

"Shouldn't need you to, I was just asking because I know the recruits are in the same building."

"And the farthest corner from everything. I should go and finish reading the file." Emily got up.

"Bethany?"

"Your problem, not mine. She just happens to be sleeping in my office."

"Okay."

Emily left the medical lab.

The next day Emily spent the day with little things. The day after Emily got up and stopped in the medical lab.

Grace did the pre-mission scan.

"Nothing wrong with you," Grace told Emily.

"No surprises," Emily responded. A man opened the doors to the medical lab and held it open for another man pushing a stretcher. The man pushed the stretcher into place. There was a guy lying on the stretcher, who had a very bloody leg. The man, who brought the stretcher in, handed Grace a clipboard.

"This is one of the two missing," the man said as Grace signed the clipboard and handed it back. The two men left and Grace went over to the guy on the stretcher and examined his leg.

"Emily, can you hand me the medical scanner?" Grace asked.

"Sure," Emily pulled the scanner out of its slot and handed it to her. Grace scanned the guy's leg.

"What happened that you weren't with the rest of the group?" Grace asked.

"I chased one of the attackers away from the group, we fought and next thing I know my leg hurts and I can't walk. I saw the van arrive, so I started yelling. The van picked everyone up then left, leaving me in lot of pain until this morning," the guy said while Grace was studying the computer screen.

"Didn't get caught under Delilah's spell?" Emily asked. Recognition was quickly covered up by confusion on the guy's face.

"Who?" he asked.

"Never mind," Emily said. Grace started to clean and bandage the guy's leg.

"I did the medical check on Bethany before she left here yesterday," Grace told Emily.

"And?"

"You should have done it. Technically, she isn't my problem anymore."

Emily sat down at the computer and brought up her file. Grace finished with the guy's leg and rolled the stretcher into the room with the other two. She came back out and closed the door.

"She is less than a month pregnant," Emily said.

"I'm guessing the child is Markus's," Grace said.

"Does she know that Markus is dead?"

"Yes. She asked and I told her the truth."

"How did she take it?"

"Like she knew it, but didn't want to believe it. What is your opinion of Russell?"

"He is a liar. Anyone could see that he wasn't telling the truth. The wounds looked like they were self-inflicted, he had no other bruises or cuts from being in a fight. There was more than one van and he doesn't look like someone who sat out there for two days."

"Which leaves the mystery as who is he working for? Why did they attack that group? And where is Preston?"

"Good luck."

"Who is Delilah?"

"I have to go meet the trainers." Emily headed for the door.

"Emily!"

"Bye." Emily left the medical lab and headed for a different part of the building.

The training area was as far away from everything else as possible without being in a different building. Emily found the door marked “training” at the end of a hallway. It was the only door for at least a hundred metres along the hallway. Emily opened it. On the other side of the door was a landing and then stairs going down. Emily stepped on to the landing, closed the door and then looked down at how many stairs there were. She counted sixteen flights of stairs. Emily climbed over the railing to stand on the outside. Cautiously she reached down to grab the bottom of the railing, then she lowered her feet down and placed them firmly on the next rail. Letting down of the railing she grabbed the one below. Continuing to do that Emily reached the bottom of the stairs in ten minutes. At the bottom of the stairs there was a short hallway that ended at the door. Emily went through the door. The room on the other side was fairly large with five doors going off it, several couches and chairs, a desk and a man sitting at the desk working.

"Most people are out of breath by the time they get here," the man commented, "So either you're in excellent shape or you cheated."

"How do you cheat stairs?" Emily asked.

"That would have been my next question. Anyways, you are?"

"Emily. You are?"

"Jake."

"I was told to report here to help with the training."

"Yeah, we were told that you were coming."

"Is it normal to have an agent help with the training?"

"No, last time they tried this the guy gave up within the first week."

"That doesn't sound good."

"Agents are trained to work alone on missions that get them out of the department."

"There are a few other things to being an agent, but that is what it boils down to. According to the file I was given, I was to do what was asked of me. I have accepted that. The only time I waiver from that is if I'm asked to do something that I consider unethical or amoral."

"What do you remember from basic training?"

"Sufficient."

"I'm going to run through a few things just to make sure."

"Fine with me."

Jake got up and started towards one of the doors. Emily followed him. The door led to a firing range. Jake picked up a gun and held it up.

"Do you recognize it?" Jake asked.

"It is an unmodified glock," Emily answered.

"When was the last time you used one?"

"Basic training."

"Maybe you should practice with it a few time so you can remember how it works."

Emily took the gun from him.

"Pick a place on the target."

"The left shoulder."

Emily shot at the target and the bullet went through the left shoulder.

"I guess you do remember how to use it. The basic handgun is the only gun we will be teaching the recruits. We will be teaching them how to use a combat knife and basic hand to hand. Have you used those since basic training?"

"Yes, though hand to hand more recently than a knife."

"That is good." Jake went to the door on the other side of the range. Emily followed. Jake tested her knowledge on basic training as he gave her a tour. At the end of the tour they ended up back in the room they started out in. Jake sat back down on the desk chair.

"You will be teaching the recruits basic weapons," Jake said, "Clean up and stuff like that is shared."

"Okay," Emily said.

"The recruits will arrive tomorrow and training will start then."

"Okay, I have to take care of something and then I'll be back."

"You didn't do it before coming down here?"

"No, I didn't know how long I had before the recruits arrived and it could have waited." Emily started for the stairs.

"The elevator is that way," Jake pointed at the door behind him. Emily went over to the door, opened it and stepped into the elevator. She closed the door and the elevator started upward. A few minutes later the elevator stopped and the door opened. Emily stepped into the hallway and closed the door behind her. Emily headed back to the medical lab.

When she got there Grace was studying the computer screen and Bethany was lying on the examining table.

"What happened?" Emily asked Grace.

"I thought you were busy." Grace said.

"I was, and will be again soon, but right now I'm not."

"Bethany passed out, so she was sent back here."

Emily looked at the scan on the computer.

"There doesn't seem to be anything wrong," Grace said.

"It may be the stress on her body. My suggestion would be to keep her here in the medical lab for a while so she can rest and someone is here to make sure she eats properly."

"What am I supposed to do if there is a miscarriage?"

"If there is a miscarriage she goes back to being your patient."

"And?"

"Painkillers are a good suggestion, so might be a suicide watch."

"Probably."

"How are the other three doing?"

"I had to send Leon to the hospital. Clark is slowly healing, and Russell is resting or biding his time, it's hard to tell which."

"He's in the same room as Clark?"

"And Leon earlier."

"Put Bethany in my office then."

"Why?"

"Call it a suspicion."

Grace opened her mouth to ask when Bethany groaned.

"Where am I?" Bethany asked.

"The medical lab," Emily answered, "You passed out."

Bethany nodded as she slowly sat up.

"How are you feeling?" Grace asked.

"Tired," Bethany answered.

"That is somewhat expected. Your body is having trouble adjusting to everything that is going on," Emily said.

"What do you mean?" Bethany asked.

"You pregnant and you are currently in a stressful situation," Emily replied.

"I'm pregnant," Bethany's voice seemed small and far away.

"About two weeks. As a precaution on anything more happening I suggest you stay here a while. I also suggest you eat something," Emily said.

Bethany nodded. Grace led Bethany into Emily's office. Emily closed down the files on the computer. A lady came into the medical lab. Emily recognized her as one of the people she had helped to patch up the other day.

"Is Dr. Grace around?" the lady asked.

"Yeah, she just went into the one office," Emily answered, "She'll be out in a minute."

"Are you a doctor?" the lady asked.

"Last time I checked."

"Why aren't you in here all the time, like Dr. Grace?"

"I'm an agent. I have to go on missions and stuff like that. And officially I'm only supposed to be here if Dr. Grace needs me."

"I wondered."

"Hello, Tamara," Grace said coming out of Emily's office, "What do you need?"

"I was wondering how Bethany was doing?" Tamara said.

"She'll be fine, she just needs some rest," Grace said.

"I'm sure it wouldn't hurt her for you to visit her," Emily said, "As long as you don't upset her." Tamara looked at Grace for conformation.

"She is right in there," Grace pointed to Emily's office. Tamara went into the office.

"Probably help for her to talk to someone," Emily said.

"Leaving soon?" Grace asked.

"Right now, why?"

"I would like a few answers, rather than the information block that has developed."

"What information block?"

"What is your suspicion?"

"That the person Russell is working for attacked the group to kill Markus. Russell is here to make sure Markus is dead. If Bethany is pregnant with Markus's child she could be the next target."

"Who would want to kill Markus?"

"I didn't say that I could solve the mystery," Emily headed for the door, "I'll see you after I'm finished this mission."

"See you."

Emily left the medical lab and headed back to the training area.

It wasn't difficult to find the elevator again, but Emily had to wait for it to come back up before she could get in and go down. Opening the door at the bottom Emily entered the main room. Jake was sitting at the desk and a lady was sitting in a chair near the desk. Both turned to look when they heard the door open.

"Back so soon?" Jake asked.

"I wasn't expecting it to take very long," Emily said.

"Emily, this is Sharon. Sharon, this is Emily," Jake introduced.

"Hello," Emily said.

"Are you going to turn out like the last agent that was supposed to be helping us?" Sharon asked.

"I do not know," Emily said.

"He was closer to a pain in the ass than being helpful," Sharon said, "Not that I couldn't see that when he came in."

"I hope you won't hold it against me for being an agent because of one bad experience," Emily said.

"Sorry, but it feels like we aren't trustworthy enough to train the recruits if an agent is sent to help," Sharon said.

"I have no idea why I was assigned here, all I know is that I am," Emily said.

"Jake thinks you are competent enough to teach basic weapons. And unless I see otherwise I will believe him. Did he show you where the first aid kit was?" Sharon asked.

"Yes," Emily answered.

"If the situation calls for a doctor we call Dr. Harvey. He is the doctor for down here, but he doesn't live down here due to claustrophobia or a least that is his excuse," Sharon said.

"It could be true," Emily said.

"I doubt it, he enjoys where he is right now to move anywhere. You do know at least some first aid, right?"

"I went to medical school before I came to work for the department. I know a little more than first aid," Emily answered.

"You have a medical degree?" Sharon asked.

"Two of them," Emily answered.

"I hope we don't need them," Jake commented.

"So far we rarely call Dr. Harvey down, but it is good to have another doctor around," Sharon said, "Anyway. Welcome and be ready for them at six-thirty tomorrow morning."

"I will be," Emily said then she went into the range. After closing the door behind her Emily looked over the collection of handguns. As she went through them, Emily realized most of them were in need of a cleaning. Sitting down with the collection she started with the top one.

Once she was finished and put them away carefully, Emily looked at the combat knives. They were all sheathed but tossed into the container. Emily left them alone and went to find the cafeteria. Jake and Sharon were sitting at a table with a third plate at an empty spot. Emily sat down.

"Until tomorrow lunch, the cafeteria upstairs only sends enough for the people that are down here," Sharon told Emily. Emily started to eat. "What were you doing?"

"Making sure everything was ready," Emily answered.

"How long have you been an agent?" Jake asked.

"I don't remember, feels like forever," Emily answered.

"You don't sound happy," Sharon commented.

"Some days I'm not sure," Emily replied.

"Why don't you quit?" Jake asked.

"Once you are an agent there are only two ways to quit. You can die or you become useless to them," Emily answered, "Neither option is really all that appealing."

"There are times that I'm glad I'm a trainer," Sharon commented.

"You have a retirement plan?" Emily asked.

"Sort of," Sharon answered, "We are only allowed teach for ten years then we are sent on our way."

"Ten years? That isn't very long," Emily said.

"They figure that after ten years the material has changed enough that they need new people teaching it," Jake said.

"According to my son, department C only keeps scientists for about five years unless the scientists come up with new stuff," Emily said, "Seems a little strange to me."

"You have a son?" Jake asked.

"Yeah," Emily answered.

"I thought children were against department policy," Sharon said.

"There are no policies concerning children. The department does not want to admit that agents have children," Emily replied.

"How old is he?" Jake asked.

"Sixteen," Emily answered.

"Sixteen?" Jake asked, "You must have been really young."

"It is a long story," Emily replied.

"You don't sound thrilled about the department policy about children," Sharon said.

"The department doesn't want to admit that agents have children. Like many other faults, they figure if they ignore it, it will go away. It won't. They need to create a policy that will help the mother and the child without making the situation worse. And I doubt things will change," Emily said.

"What happens to a child born to an agent?" Sharon asked.

"The mother gets to keep the child for the first year, but is taken off active duty. After that year is up the child is sent to a foster family and the agent is put back on active duty as if nothing happened," Emily answered.

"Does the mother get to see her child again?" Jake asked.

"Not that I know about," Emily replied as she stood up, "Where do I put the dishes?"

"Just leave them there, they all have to go up at the same time," Sharon said.

"Sorry about the rant. Good night," Emily said before leaving the cafeteria. She went to the room given to her for her stay. Lying down in the bed Emily stared up at the ceiling for a long time before she fell asleep.

Jake stacked the dishes on the cart.

"What do you think of Emily?" Jake asked Sharon.

"Interesting, but why do we need an agent to help us train recruits? We have been doing it without help for eight years now," Sharon answered.

"I talked to Alfred today after her first visit," Jake said.

"What did he say?"

"He said that Emily's temporary placement here has nothing to do with us. Apparently he wants to keep her busy while keeping her close to the department. Sounds like she had some missions go bad or something like that."

"We are supposed to baby-sit an agent?"

"No, he wants her where he can check up on her if necessary. From what I've seen and heard so far, I don't think we'll have the problems we had with Adrian. Adrian's mission was different. He was here to 'improve' our technique; Emily doesn't care. Her mission is just to help us out."

"I still don't like it."

"Like it or not she's here, and she's going to be helping us," Jake said going over to one of the two doors out of the cafeteria, "And you get to take the cart back." Jake left the cafeteria.

"I usually do," Sharon said.

Emily got up at six ante meridian. When she was ready, she went out to the main room. Jake was sitting at the desk and Sharon was leaning against the wall the furniture faced.

"You missed breakfast," Sharon said when she saw Emily.

"I figured that," Emily replied sitting in the other desk chair.

"The recruits should be here soon," Jake said. Emily noticed the door to the stairs was open. Sharon, Jake and Emily didn't say anything as they waited. A few minutes later there was the sound of people coming down the stairs. The sound came closer until eight teenagers entered the room. There were four boys and four girls, all about seventeen or eighteen-years-old. None of them looked thrilled to be there. They all found a place to sit.

"Welcome to basic training," Sharon said once they were seated, "Over the next month you will be taught the basic skills you will need to become agents. I am Sharon, and I will be teaching you survival. This is Jake. He will be teaching the technology end of things. And this is Emily, she will be teaching weapons. Over the month you will learn all this. At the end of the month you will be sent out on a mission. We rarely see anyone go through basic training twice.

"Tell us something we don't know," a guy muttered.

"The sleeping area is through that door," Sharon pointed to the door on the far side of the room, "The cafeteria is through that door," Sharon pointed to the next one, "And the rest leads to classrooms, except that one," Sharon pointed to the elevator, "Which is off limits," Sharon paused for a moment, "Now that you know that, you will start your training. Jake, your turn."

Jake stepped up and started into his class. Sharon went into the first classroom and Emily went into the firing range.

Sitting down in a chair Emily pulled out a book and started to read. An hour before noon Emily could hear the door to the firing range open. She put her book away and stood up as the recruits came into the firing range. The first one to enter was Cass, she was shorter than average with light brown, shoulder length hair and light blue eyes. Next came Sara, she had chin length blonde hair, grey eyes and a hole where her eyebrow had been pierced. Toby was next, he had short, spiky, brown hair and blue eyes that never stopped moving. Nanda had a black braid and dark brown eyes. Logan had short, brown hair, hard brown eyes and two scars, one that went from his hair line to his left eye and the second was a jagged line that went from his right ear down into his shirt. Jen's dark red hair, green eyes and pale skin went with how delicate she looked. Kevin was the tallest of the group and had a black mess of hair with brown eyes. Mike had dirty-blonde hair that wasn't quite chin length and ended up in his face, where the blue eyes seemed to peer out.

"Cool, maybe we get to learn how to use a gun," Toby said looking around.

"More likely we get to learn hand to hand," Sara replied.

"I believe Sharon will be teaching you hand to hand. I am supposed to be teaching you the basic weapons you need to know to move on to the next level of training," Emily said, "First of all, how many of you have used a handgun before?" Five hands went up. "How many of you have used an unmodified glock?" All the hands went down.

"What's the different between an unmodified glock and a modified one?" Kevin asked.

"A basic glock is what they start with when they modify a glock and no two modified glocks are alike," Emily answered.

"Do we get to learn how to use other types of guns?" Toby asked.

"Only if you successfully complete basic training," Emily answered, "Now to the first lesson." Emily handed each recruit a gun.

"Cool," Toby said before pointing the gun down range and pulling the trigger. There was a click, but nothing else.

"Ammo will be handed out as you need it and not before," Emily said.

"Figures," Nanda muttered. Emily ignored it and went on with the lesson. At the end of the time, Emily collected the guns and pointed the recruits in the direction of the cafeteria. Once the guns were put away properly, Emily went to the cafeteria herself. Jake and Sharon were sitting a table away from the two tables of recruits. Emily got a plate of food and joined Jake and Sharon.

"How was the first lesson?" Jake asked.

"Fine," Emily answered.

"Ready for the afternoon?" Jake asked.

"I think so," Emily answered.

"This is one of the better groups we've had," Sharon said.

"I hope it stays that way," Jake said. The recruits talked, but Jake, Sharon and Emily didn't say anything for the rest of the meal.

After lunch the recruits went for another lesson with Jake. Emily went back to the firing range to wait. The recruits came in an hour later.

"Cool, more dealing with guns," Toby said.

"No, for this lesson we will be focusing on a different basic weapon," Emily said, "Specifically combat knives." Emily started the lesson. After two hours went by the recruits went to their next lesson with Sharon. Emily went to supper at five and ate at the table with Sharon and Jake. When she finished eating, Emily went to her room for the night.

At the end of the week Emily joined Sharon in the cafeteria while Jake taught the group.

"What do we teach for the second week?" Emily asked.

"We drill them endlessly on what we just taught them until we go crazy or the month is over," Sharon said.

"Sounds like fun," Emily commented.

"Some days I feel closer to going crazy," Sharon said, "But I think part of that is most recruits aren't normal."

"Most agents or people who become agents are not normal," Emily said, "If the person is normal that automatically disqualifies them as an agent."

"What about you?" Sharon asked.

"They figure I'm insane," Emily answered.

"I'm not sure that you are insane, but I know you aren't what I expected. I was expecting someone similar to Adrian," Sharon said.

"I am much different from Adrian," Emily replied.

"You know him?" Sharon asked.

"I knew him. He died a few years ago. Shot during a mission," Emily answered, "Which was lucky for him."

"How is being dead lucky?" Sharon asked.

"Because when the news of his death reached me, I was in the medical lab dreaming up painful ways for him to die," Emily answered.

"What happened?" Sharon asked.

"We were lovers and I got pregnant," Emily answered, "I was nine months along when I found out he viewed children like the department does. I was a little angry with that. Then he accepted a mission and was elsewhere when I went into labour. The child was stillborn. After that I alternated between shock and rage, with most of the rage directed at Adrian."

"And I thought he was bad when he was supposed to be helping down here," Sharon said.

"He was department through and through, which makes you wonder how this department has survived so long," Emily said, "Of course it helps that enough people don't care about half of what the department says. Some days I wonder if the guy at the top isn't just screwing with people's lives."

"I have no idea, all I know is what I'm told and what I do. Anything else is philosophy that I usually don't have time for," Sharon said.

"I've been spending too much time in places where philosophy is my main source of entertainment," Emily said.

"Is that why you are down here?" Sharon asked.

"Probably," Emily answered.

"Class time," Sharon said as she got up. Emily nodded. Sharon left the cafeteria.

The next week started slow. Reviewing until the recruits knew the information inside out and backwards became the theme. Monday and Tuesday dragged past.

Wednesday morning Emily woke to a knock at the door. Emily got up and opened the door. Jake was standing there.

"Cass won't wake up," Jake said, "We're not sure what is wrong and Sharon couldn't reach Dr. Harvey when she tried."

"How is her breathing?" Emily asked closing her door.

"Shallow," Jake answered. Emily and Jake headed for the recruit's sleeping area. Everybody was standing except Cass, who was lying on her bed. Emily went over to Cass and checked her breathing and pulse. While she was bending over Emily saw an empty pill bottle. Emily picked up the pill bottle and stood up.

"Does anyone know what was in here?" Emily asked.

"Sleeping pills," Jen answered, "She said she had problems with insomnia."

"Sharon, go up and get Dr. Harvey," Emily instructed, "Tell him to bring a stomach pump and adrenaline. Everyone else, go in the cafeteria." Everyone left the sleeping area. Emily sat down next to the cot Cass was sleeping on. Every two minutes she would check Cass's breathing and pulse. Nothing changed in the ten minutes it took for Dr. Harvey to arrive. He had a bag with him.

"How is the patient?" Dr. Harvey asked.

"Still alive so far," Emily answered, "And if you help me, we can keep it that way." Dr. Harvey helped Emily pump out Cass's stomach. Once finished, Dr. Harvey gave Cass a shot of adrenaline.

"Cass," Emily shook Cass's shoulder, "Wake up." Cass didn't respond.

"Her heart rate is starting to go back to normal," Dr. Harvey said, "And her breathing is doing the same."

"I would prefer to see her awake and moving," Emily said getting up and going into the bathroom. She got a cup of cold water and a couple paper towels. Going back into the room she saw Dr. Harvey had packed up his stuff and looked like he was going to leave.

"Do you even care about these kids?" Emily asked.

"My job is to make sure they survive basic training," Dr. Harvey said, "And from the looks of it she will survive."

"And for a second I thought you might actually be a doctor," Emily said.

"What do you know about being a doctor?" Dr. Harvey asked.

"A hell of a lot more than you if you leave a patient in this condition."

"I have a medical degree and forty years of experience! I don't see any reason to put up with this crap!" Dr. Harvey started toward to door.

"Then maybe you should retire," Emily said, "Because after dealing with lots of different doctors and helping to treat agents, I know better than to leave patients just because they aren't currently dying at the moment."

"And you think 'helping to treat agents' qualifies you to make judgements on my skills in medicine?" Dr. Harvey asked turning back.

"Two medical degrees help," Emily replied.

"You're not old enough to have one degree, let alone two," Dr. Harvey said.

"Then yours has worn out," Emily said, "Because they have changed things since you went through, starting with the fact that we are supposed to be helping the patient, not abandoning them!"

"Well, it looks like she is in good hands now," Dr. Harvey said before turning on his heel and marching out of the room. Emily turned back to Cass. She sprinkled some of the water on Cass's face. Cass woke up enough to wipe off her face.

"Cass," Emily said.

"What?" Cass mumbled sleepily.

"It is time to wake up," Emily said.

"But I'm tired," Cass said.

"I know you're tired," Emily said, "But I need you to answer some questions."

"Like what?"

"How many sleeping pills you took?"

"A couple."

"Why?"

"I have insomnia."

"How many sleeping pills did you take last night?"

"Leave me alone."

"I can't. I need you to honestly answer my questions."

"I don't know how many sleeping pills I took, I didn't count them."

"How full was the pill bottle?"

"Half full."

"Why?"

"I don't want to be here."

"So, you were going to kill yourself?"

"That's the only way out."

"There are other ways out. Why do you want out so badly you would kill yourself?"

"They kidnapped me. I never wanted to come here, never wanted to be an agent. All I want is to go back to my parents, my brother, and my boyfriend."

"I know a way to get you out, but you have to finish basic training."

"Why are you willing to help me?"

"Because I'd rather see you out of here than dead."

"Why?"

"I'm a doctor first and an agent second. Will you let me help you?"

"Yes."

"Then I need you to sit up and talk to me."

"About what?" Cass asked as she sat up.

"Tell me a story, tell me about your life, anything that will keep you awake until I know the sleeping pills have worn off," Emily answered. Cass thought for a minute and then started talking.

At lunch Emily had Cass go into the cafeteria to eat. Cass got some food and sat down. The rest of the recruits joined her when they got to the cafeteria. Emily sat down with Jake and Sharon to eat lunch.

"Cass seems to be doing good," Sharon commented.

"As long as she doesn't fall asleep, she can go to lessons," Emily said.

"It is hard enough to stay awake without trying to keep recruits awake," Sharon said.

"I'm sure you'll manage somehow," Emily said.

"I have an idea," Jake said.

'What is it?" Sharon asked.

"I know it isn't part of basic training, but Emily could teach the recruits basic first aid. It would be a change from reviewing and they might need it later," Jake said.

"Sounds like a good idea," Sharon said, "Would you be willing to do it?"

"Sure, it will break the monotony for a while," Emily answered.

"Okay, then we'll review for the rest of this week and next week can be first aid, then the week after we'll go back to reviewing," Sharon said.

"Sounds good," Jake said.

"Fine with me," Emily said. Sharon, Jake and Emily didn't say anything to each other for the rest of the meal. After lunch Emily spent the afternoon in the firing range. She supervised the recruits for two hours and spent the rest of the time reading. At suppertime she ate with Jake and Sharon. Cass seemed to be fine. After supper Emily went to her room.

The rest of the week went by faster with Emily making plans of what exactly she was going to teach. The next week for two hours in the morning and two hours in the afternoon Emily taught the recruits, Jake and Sharon first aid. Once the week was over, the schedule went back to what it had been before. They went back to reviewing.

Emily woke up at six as per usual for the last month. She went to the bathroom and got dressed before going to the main room. Jake and Sharon were sitting there already waiting for the recruits to get up.

"How are you in a wilderness setting?" Sharon asked Emily.

"Wilderness as in?" Emily asked.

"Forest," Sharon answered.

"I do better in the city, but I do okay in the woods. Why?" Emily asked.

"That's where the final test is going to be. Jake will be staying in the van, while we'll be supervising the recruits doing the mission," Sharon answered.

"Fine," Emily said.

"The mission should only take two or three hours, then the recruits go to the next people and you can tell Alfred that you are finished down here," Sharon said.

"Okay, I have a few things I probably should check on when this is done," Emily said. The door to the sleeping area opened and all eight recruits entered the main room. Sharon started once they were seated.

"The mission you are to complete is retrieval. You will have to make your way through the woods to a cabin. In the cabin there will be a computer disk. You are to find it and then head back to the van. This is not a race; you will be doing this as a team. Everyone clear?"

The recruits nodded.

"Then let's head out," Sharon said.

The recruits got up and headed for the stairs. Once the sound of them going upstairs could be heard, Emily, Sharon and Jake used the elevator to get to the main floor. Reaching it, they went to the top of the stairs to wait for the recruits.

"How did they get up here so quickly?" Logan asked once the recruits could see them.

"There's probably an elevator that goes between here and there," Jen said. The recruits reached the top of the stair and Sharon led the way out of the building. A black van was parked just outside the door. Jake got in the back, followed by the recruits and then Emily got in. Sharon closed the van doors and then went around to get into the driver's seat. She started the van and pulled away from the building. Forty-five minutes of the ride was smooth with a few brief stops, then there was thirty minutes of the van going over rough terrain before the van stopped and Sharon turned off the engine. Sharon got out of the driver's seat and went around to the back to open the doors.

"We're here," Sharon announced. Emily got out and the recruits followed. Jake started opening the benches and handing each recruit a bag. Sharon took a bag for herself and then gave one to Emily.

"This bag contains everything you need," Sharon said once everyone had one, "It has a radio you should wear, a gun, a knife, a bottle of water, waterproof matches and a compass. The cabin is northwest from here. Emily and I will be with you to make sure everything goes smoothly." Sharon took out her radio and put it in her ear and attached the bag to the waistband of her pants. The recruits followed suit. Emily took the radio out of the bag and put it in her ear, then tossed the bag back into the van. Sharon gave Emily a funny look before turning back to the recruits.

"You are to wear the radio at all times, it will help you if you get into trouble," Sharon said, "Now let's go." The recruits started to move out with Sharon following on one side and Emily following on the other side.

The recruits sorted themselves into two groups and split up to search for the cabin at once. One person in each group had a compass out. The group slowly picked its way through the trees, being watchful about what was around them. They also kept contact with the other group via the radios. Emily listened and followed but stayed an observer. It was getting close to an hour by the time someone spotted the cabin. They radioed the other group. The cabin was a log structure that was maybe eight by ten and only one storey. The other group took a few minutes to find the cabin. Once they were all together, they went into the cabin to search for the disk. Emily and Sharon stayed outside.

"They are doing pretty good so far," Sharon said.

"Yeah," Emily said.

"Most groups take longer to find the cabin," Sharon said. A yell came from inside the cabin and the recruits came out. Kevin was holding a disk. He tucked it in a pocket. The group was just about to head back to the van when a group came out of the woods surrounding the cabin. They were dressed in dark green and holding guns. The recruits took out the guns they had. Emily and Sharon barely got out of the way as the firefight started. It didn't take Emily long to figure out both sides had stun bullets in their guns and weren't doing any real harm to each other.

"Planned?" Emily asked.

"Of course, they are supposed to use the skills they have learned," Sharon answered. The firefight lasted twenty minutes with most of the recruits still standing and the 'enemy' taken out. The recruits that were standing helped the two that had been hit to stand and they all headed back to the van. Emily and Sharon followed. Once the group got far enough away from the cabin they started to celebrate and talk about the firefight and finding the disk. Emily noticed that even Sharon was relaxing a little bit. They were about thirty minutes away from the van when Emily heard something behind her. She stopped to look back but didn't see anything. Emily turned around and started walking again. She heard another sound behind her. Before she could turn around, a knife went into her lower back.

"Goodbye time for you," Nolan told Emily softly in her ear, and then yanked the knife out. Emily collapsed as the gunfire started. Emily tried to move but she could no longer feel her legs. She reached back and tried to put pressure on the knife wound. Looking up she saw the recruits and Sharon trying to hit a hidden enemy with stun bullets while being shot at with real bullets. Emily saw Nanda fall.

"Jake, we are under attack," Emily said into the radio.

"There is a planned attack on this mission," Jake said.

"I know that, they successfully beat it. If you were listening you would know they have already done that one," Emily said, "This time we are really under attack by people using real bullets. Three people are down and Sharon is at least injured."

"I'm hit on the ankle, that's all," Sharon's voice came over the radio.

"Emily, you're the agent, this is your territory," Jake said, "I have no idea what to do."

"I can't do much, I'm one of the people down," Emily said, "Bring the van in here if you can."

"Then what?" Jake asked.

"We'll figure that out as we go along," Emily said, "A big part of being an agent is taking things as they come." Jake didn't respond, so Emily assumed he was doing what she told him to. The gunfire stopped. Emily looked up. Six recruits were standing. Sharon was kneeling and the people that were shooting seemed to be gone. Two recruits sat down, while the rest checked the ones lying down or started first aid. Cass spotted Emily and went over to her.

"How are the rest?" Emily asked.

"You're injured," Cass said seeing the blood.

"I know. How are the others?" Emily asked.

"Sara and Nanda are dead; Logan, Toby and Sharon are injured. Kevin, Jen and Mike are tending to them," Cass answered, "What happened?"

"We were ambushed. I got caught in the back and can't feel my legs," Emily answered.

"But you're a lot farther back from the rest of us," Cass said.

"This may be a bit of a shock but I'm losing blood fast and talking at the moment is using up energy," Emily said, "But I don't want to be rude, so can you save your questions and comments for later?"

"Yeah," Cass said as she sat down next to Emily. She moved Emily's hand and used her own to apply pressure to the wound. Emily rested her head against her hand. The world seemed to get farther away. The van pulled into the clearing and Jake got out. He started directing people inside the van and directing them to take bodies as well.

"You better go tell him that I can't move and he needs a board to move me," Emily told the person above her. The pressure lifted and a person ran toward the group. After what seemed like forever several people came back with a large, flat object.

"Move her on to the board and we'll take her back to the department," a male voice ordered.

"Wouldn't it be better to take her to the hospital? Isn't the hospital better equipped to handle this kind of injury," a female voice asked. Hands gently rolled her over on to the board.

"The department," the male voice started.

"Hospital," Emily muttered, "Department can't deal." The board was lifted.

"We'll go to the hospital first," a different female voice told them as the board was being carried. Everything stopped for a while. Then everything was moving again. Voices drifted in and out. Lots of motion. Sounds like a helicopter. Blackness.

CHAPTER 5
PROBLEMS

Emily opened her eyes to see Sylvester, wearing a crisp lab coat, sitting backwards on a chair.

"Howdy stranger," Sylvester greeted when he saw that she was awake.

"So you did get a job," Emily replied sleepily.

"I hope so, otherwise you might be in trouble," Sylvester said.

"You're the one who thought you wouldn't get hired. I'm glad you found one," Emily said.

"Are you willing to take orders from a doctor?" Sylvester asked.

"Only while I'm their patient," Emily answered.

"Get some rest and try not to move very far," Sylvester said getting up.

"There isn't anywhere I need to go," Emily said.

"From my basic understanding, not everybody agrees with that statement," Sylvester said.

"They aren't the one who got a knife in the back."

"Go back to sleep." Sylvester smiled as he left the room. Emily closed her eyes and went back to sleep.

The next time Emily woke up there was no one in the room. She could see the sky filled with grey-brown, man-made clouds outside the window. Emily lay there remembering the way the sun shone in the window in the twenty-first century. It was so beautiful. The heart monitor's beeping felt like sledge hammer hits to the side of her head. How do patients stand those things, without ending up on the psych ward, Emily thought, there has been a better way to monitor a person's heart. She let the possibility roll around in her head.

The door opened and Grace came in.

"You are awake," Grace said taking a seat beside the bed.

"I woke up a few minutes ago," Emily said.

"The doctor said you shouldn't move," Grace said.

"I knew that from the time I felt the knife go into my back," Emily replied.

"Jake reported that the people were attacking the group with guns. Why were you stabbed if they had guns?" Grace asked.

"I ended up with the guy who had a knife," Emily answered, "How is Bethany doing?"

"Everything is going well so far. Nothing serious has happened," Grace said, "Russell disappeared about a week after you left. The next morning I noticed that someone had tried to get into your office but failed."

"I figured Russell was gone," Emily said, "It's good to hear that Bethany is all right. Has Abby checked in?"

"Yes, she is healthy, the baby is healthy," Grace said.

"Good," Emily said, "I need your help to fulfill a promise I made."

"If you tell me the promise, I'll think about it," Grace said.

"How about the other way around?"

"Because I want to know what I'm getting into."

"Nothing with the possibility of getting killed."

"Fine, but if I get into trouble, you get full blame."

"And I'll accept full blame. Though if it all works out, I should still be stuck in this bed when you are finished."

"Tell me what you promised."

"I promised to help one of the recruits get away from the department and go home. Her name is Cass and she tried to suicide to get out. All she wants is to go home and live the rest of her life in peace."

"You want me to get her out?"

"I don't know how much time there is to do this and it will be a while before I can do anything."

"I'll see what I can do about the situation."

"Thank you."

"Anything else while I'm here?"

"Not that I can think of at the moment, but something might come to me later. You are coming back to visit, right?"

"Yes, since I'm your regular doctor."

"I wouldn't worry about the doctor too much. Sylvester is a good guy and a good doctor."

"You've gotten that friendly with the doctor?"

"We went to medical school together."

"Ah. You should rest. I'll see you another time."

"See you."

Grace left the room. Emily closed her eyes and went back to sleep.

Alfred stepped outside the doors and went around the side of the building. Brett was standing there.

"Is Emily alright?" Brett asked.

"She is alive and the doctor said that she would recover," Alfred said, "What happened?"

"Nolan was given the job of killing her," Brett said, "Schultz believes that Emily is a danger to him. He thinks she heard something."

"I would be surprised if Emily had not had a run in with Schultz's people before that," Alfred said.

"She may have, but it didn't involve any of Schultz's business," Brett said.

"How much do you think Emily knows about Schultz then?" Alfred asked.

"Whatever she overheard," Brett answered, "And whatever she can find now that he has tried to have her killed."

"You think Emily will go after Schultz?" Alfred asked.

"Not directly," Brett said, "But she'll start gathering information the minute she is out of the hospital."

"Don't tell her anything," Alfred said, "I don't want her too close to this."

"I won't say anything," Brett said, "But she'll do whatever she feels like. If I were you, I would take it and use it to your advantage. Schultz knows she is an agent, but he doesn't believe she can do him serious harm."

"Then why take her out?" Alfred asked.

"Because he does that to everyone that is expendable that knows too much," Brett answered.

"You should head back," Alfred said, "Remember to report back."

"I will," Brett replied before turning and heading away from the department. Alfred went back inside.

Emily spent the next week sleeping and thinking.

Emily woke up to see rain coming down outside her window making it hard to tell what time of day it was. The door opened and Sylvester came in, followed by another man.

"How are you feeling?" Sylvester asked.

"I can feel my feet again," Emily answered.

"That's a good sign. Bored yet?"

"Not as much as I could be."

"I might have something to help deal with the boredom. Emily, this is the hospital director. Director, this is Emily," Sylvester introduced the man.

"Sylvester said that you were a paediatrician," the director said.

"As far as I know I have a degree in that area," Emily replied.

"The hospital has a mystery; a girl that is living here at the hospital has an illness that none of the paediatricians have been able to figure out what it is," the director said.

"Sounds interesting," Emily said.

"It's all in this file," the director placed a file on the table next to the bed and then left the room. Sylvester turned a chair backwards and sat down.

"I accidentally said something to one of the nurses while the director was in earshot," Sylvester said, "Which is a bad thing these days. The director has been looking for a way to get rid of the file and the patient."

"I'm willing to see what I can do," Emily said, "Once I'm up and moving."

"I told him you weren't to be moving very far," Sylvester said, "He wasn't willing to listen."

"I did my second greatest achievement yesterday."

"What was that?"

"I got up and went to the bathroom."

"If that is your second greatest achievement I'm not sure I want to know your first but am compelled to ask: What is your first greatest achievement?"

"Being told that I'm beyond a psychiatrist's help."

"I knew I shouldn't've asked."

"That wouldn't have been fun."

"You don't need a psychiatrist's help. You never have."

"Going back to other things, what do you know about my new patient?" Emily pushed herself up a bit and picked up the file.

"She has been here for two years and no one can figure out what is wrong with her."

"Anything else?"

"That's all I've heard."

"Are you sure I don't need a psychiatrist's help? I have three patients, I'm helping someone out of a bad situation and have someone trying to kill me while I'm lying here unable to move very far."

"I suggest you read the file," Sylvester got up and started to leave as Emily opened the file.

"This girl doesn't even have a name."

"Keep reading," Sylvester closed the door on his way out. Emily read through the file, then laid it down on the table and fell asleep.

A week later Grace came into the room to find Emily sitting up in bed and staring out the window.

"How are you today?" Emily asked without looking at Grace.

"Better than I was yesterday," Grace answered sitting down in the chair next to the bed.

"What happened yesterday?" Emily asked.

"I got Cass out of the department and on her way home," Grace answered.

"How are the rest of the recruits?"

"Still in a little bit of shock and stuck there for an indeterminate amount of time, but other than that not too bad."

"How's Bethany?"

"Doing well. Abby hasn't needed to check in yet since the last time. And no word on Russell or Preston, but Clark is more or less back to normal and Leon is going through therapy so that he will walk again."

"I'm more concerned over Bethany and Abby than the rest."

"You should, they are your patients."

"Two of three, yes."

"Who is the third?"

"A little girl the director of the hospital referred to me."

"That has complications attached to it."

"Probably," Emily looked at Grace, "Want to go for a walk?"

"Can you handle a walk?"

"As long as it isn't far. Besides, this is a hospital, what could go wrong?"

"I refuse to answer that."

Emily got up and then she and Grace left the room. They started to walk down the hall.

"What is the situation with the girl?" Grace asked.

"She was born here, the doctor found that she was sick, but couldn't figure out what it was. Her parents left the minute after they got the news. No one has been able to figure out what the illness is and her parents have disappeared."

"Doesn't sound like a happy story far."

"She is one of the sweetest two-year-olds you will ever meet. Whatever that is wrong with her hasn't affected her in any way, except getting really sick every other month."

"And no one seems to be able to figure it out?"

"She is a charity case. That means that the director has been giving the case to various doctors that give a half-hearted attempt before finding something else to do. Half the tests that should have been done haven't and the tests that were done, have been done several times. I ordered the half of the tests that haven't been done."

"And the staff went with it? Most of the time if they haven't received orders from someone without a person that works at the hospital standing right there, they don't do the tests."

"I told them that if they were too busy that I could do them myself. They jumped at the chance to do them and I'm supposed to get the results tomorrow."

"Well, I know you haven't changed."

"Just two problems."

"What?"

"If it comes out as something I can treat, once she is healthy there is no place for her to go. Her parents abandoned her here and the hospital doesn't care. That, and she is missing something every child should have."

"What should every child have?"

"Their own teddy bear."

"Worry about the treating the illness first and the other after."

"I'm a doctor, once I've finished treating the illness, that is the end of it."

"Emily, when you get involved in things you don't leave it alone until it is over."

Emily sat down on a chair to rest.

"You okay?" Grace asked.

"Fine, just need a little rest."

"You didn't tell me the girl's name."

"She doesn't have one. No one has ever bothered to name her."

"That sucks."

"She's a charity case. The hospital has a number they can refer to her by, why bother with a name?"

"There was an interesting piece of news from the department. Dr. Harvey, who was the doctor for the recruits, was killed."

"How?"

"He was shot several times with one of the training guns. The mystery is that all the guns have been accounted for, none of the recruits or trainers have left the basement, and there isn't any ammo missing."

"How do they know it was a gun used for training?"

"The person who shot him dropped it on their way out."

"Can't they figure who it was by the gun?"

"The gun was clean. They also can't find a motive."

"I can think of a few, but some things are better left unsaid."

"You met him?"

"Cass overdosed and he brought down the stomach pump."

"Wonderful way to meet someone."

"I didn't find anything wonderful about meeting him."

"I never actually met the man."

"I didn't like him." Emily got up and they started back to the room.

"You and someone else."

"Sounds like someone that knew what they were doing. Most people in the department don't know that Dr. Harvey is there, let alone where his office is. The gun was clean and dropped at the scene. Not to mention they could get their hands on an unmodified handgun."

"An unmodified handgun?"

"That is what they use for training. And most people from the department would assume that if it was unmodified that it was a training gun because any agent that uses a gun has modified it."

"Who would want to kill Dr. Harvey?"

"I don't know."

They entered the room and Emily sat back down on the bed.

"I think when I get back, I'm going to be spending a lot more time with Travis," Emily said.

"Don't rush the healing process."

"Sylvester won't let me leave here until he is certain that I can't undo any of his work."

"That is a good system."

Emily shrugged.

"I should be getting back," Grace said.

"See you," Emily said. Grace left the room. Emily lay down. She stared at the ceiling for a long time before her eyes drifted shut.

Grace entered the medical lab and sat down at the computer. Travis came in a few minutes later.

"How's Emily?" Travis asked.

"She seems to be doing well. Physically she's tired and still healing from the stab wound. Mentally, I'm not sure about," Grace answered.

"I don't think anybody has been sure of her mental state," Travis said.

"This is different. She seemed like herself for most of the conversation, then she said something about putting in some time with you and following a doctor's orders," Grace said.

"That is strange," Travis said, "She doesn't like either of those."

"I'm trying to figure out what happened."

"This may sound like a strange thing to wonder about, but how was Emily stabbed if the group was ambushed by people shooting at them."

"I don't know. I asked Emily but she wasn't really into giving me any useful answers."

"I think Emily knows what happened."

"Very likely, but I don't see the connection between that and her current mental state."

"With her it's hard to tell if there is a connection, but you're the only one she talks to. She might tell you more."

"Right now, I'm not sure she'll tell me anything."

"Keep trying, you're her confidant."

"I'm trying and I'm getting frustrated."

"Welcome to how the rest of us feel." Travis left the medical lab.

Grace sat there at the computer a few more minutes before getting up. She locked up the medical lab before heading for one of the back doors of the department. Once outside, she walked quickly. She reached the office building where Edmund's office was. Going inside Grace went directly to his office and knocked on the door before opening it. Grace stepped inside. Edmund sat behind his desk. He looked up at her.

"Grace, what can I do for you?" Edmund asked.

"I need a favour," Grace answered.

"What kind of favour?" Edmund asked.

"Not the usual kinds involving the invisible friends or finding a safe house," Grace said, "I need a teddy bear."

"A teddy bear?"

"I don't have any source of money, or I would go out and buy one myself. Since you have been willing to do me favours in exchange for information from the department, I was hoping you could get one for me."

"And I owe you a good many favours. I understand that, but a child's toy?"

"Yes."

"I can get you a teddy bear. Unfortunately, I can't get it right now, but I will get it for you within the week."

"Thank you."

"I will have it delivered."

Grace turned and left the office building. She headed back to the department.

Two days later Grace entered the medical lab to find a teddy bear sitting on her desk chair. She smiled at it as she picked it up.

"You look perfect for a little girl to hug," Grace commented. Grace heard the door to the medical lab open. She quickly stuffed the bear into the bottom drawer of her desk before going out to see who is was.

Emily got the test results, went over them and then set up the proper treatment for the girl. Sylvester had given Emily a set of exercises for her to do. So, Emily was busy spending time with the girl and dealing with her own recovery.

Emily was released from the hospital the day after the girl was pronounced healthy. Emily took the girl and headed back to department H.

Reaching the building Emily went in the way the recruits had come out, then she headed for the medical lab. The girl rested her head on Emily's shoulder and looked about ready to go to sleep. Grace was sitting at the computer when Emily entered.

Emily set the girl down on the floor. The girl attached herself to Emily's leg.

"So you didn't leave her at the hospital," Grace said.

"You predicted it," Emily said.

"I didn't think you would bring her here," Grace said.

"This is one of two stops I need to make. I don't intend for her to stay here," Emily said.

"I acquired something for you," Grace said pulling something out of a drawer. She came around the desk holding a teddy bear in her hand. Grace offered the teddy bear to the girl, who cautiously took it.

"Should I ask how you acquired it?" Emily asked.

"I don't have any money, so I have to get things other ways," Grace answered, "What's going to happen to her now?"

"Nothing, I hope," Emily answered, "I'm not going out to find her parents or find someone to adopt her. I adopted her."

"Did you give her a name?"

"Adriana."

"Are you sure that is a good idea?"

"I asked if she liked it before I wrote it down on any piece of paper."

"Okay. What are you gonna do now?"

"Find someplace for Adriana to live. I have a few places that I'm gonna try."

"Don't be too long. Alfred will be looking for you."

"I won't be." Emily picked Adriana up and left the medical lab. Emily headed back to the training area. She stopped in front of the elevator, waited for it to come up, stepped inside and went down. Stepping out, Emily saw Jake and Sharon sitting in the main room. They looked up at her when they heard the elevator open.

"Hello," Emily said as she walked into the room.

"You look better," Jake said.

"I'm doing better," Emily answered, "How are things down here?"

"Doing well. Everyone who was hurt is better. Although we're all stuck down here waiting on any word as to what they are going to do with the recruits," Jake said, "They don't want to move them before deciding their fate and we can't get new recruits while they are down here."

"Frustrating," Emily said.

"We're driving each other crazy," Sharon said, "We've had to find stuff for them to do. They know basic training inside out and backwards. And this place has been cleaned from floor to ceiling."

"I was wondering if you could do me a small favour. It might alleviate the boredom," Emily said.

"What is it?" Sharon asked.

"This is Adriana," Emily shifted the sleepy girl on her shoulder, "I'm technically not supposed to have her here, but I need to find her a more suitable home. I was hoping I could get you to baby-sit for a while."

"How long a while?" Sharon asked.

"A few days maximum, a few hours minimum," Emily answered.

"You trust us to look after a kid?" Jake asked.

"Why wouldn't I?" Emily asked, "You have never given me any reason not to."

Sharon stood up and took Adriana from Emily.

"We can look after her," Sharon said.

"Thank you," Emily said.

"Considering that without your help, the ambush could have been a lot worse. It isn't hard to do a small favour for you," Sharon said. Emily smiled and then went back to the elevator. Once on the main floor she left the building and headed for town.

Emily entered the Bar an hour after opening. Most of the regulars were already there. Emily went to sit on one of the barstools. The bartender was new.

"What would you like?" the bartender asked.

"Beer," Trent said placing the bottle in front of Emily. Emily handed Trent the money for the beer. The bartender moved on.

"What happened to Tyler?" Emily asked.

"He was found dead in an alleyway. Police closed the case as random violence," Trent answered.

"Pity, he was a good bartender," Emily said.

"What are you doing back here? I thought non-existence meant not returning to places where they know you," Trent said.

"I needed a drink," Emily said.

"And the ulterior motive is?"

"Hard to explain."

Trent studied her for a moment. He seemed about to reply when Rob came up to the bar for another beer.

"Hey, Trent, Where's your leech?" Rob asked accepting another beer from the bartender.

"Don't know, but if you are looking for her she'll probably be around later," Trent answered looking at Rob.

"I'll pass on that one," Rob said before going back to his table.

"Leech?" Emily asked.

"Hard to explain," Trent answered, "Come into the back." Trent headed for the door to the back. Emily picked up her beer and followed him. He sat down on a wooden workbench and she sat down on the couch.

"I think it's messier in here than last time I was here," Emily commented.

"I haven't exactly had the time to clean anything up," Trent said, "Between problems here and trying to get my house finished. I would take time off here to finish the house but I don't know if I can trust the new bartender. Maybe you can help with one of the problems here."

"The leech," Emily guessed.

"I've tried everything and nothing has worked. With women being more insidious than men maybe you can see a solution that I can't."

"There are a few solutions to your problem," Emily started.

"I would be grateful if you dealt with it, but I don't want to know how," Trent said before she could continue, "You had an ulterior motive for being here?"

"Yes, but I think I'll wait a little while before explaining it to you. To switch subjects, have you seen Alex recently?"

"No, I paid him back all the money he loaned me plus the interest, now he only stops in occasionally to check on things. He hasn't been around for a while so he is due to visit soon. Why?"

"I was hoping to talk to him."

"Considering that according to Alex you stole money from him, you two are on pretty good terms."

"I'm half surprised he hasn't tried to kill me."

"Maybe he is hoping you will be useful later."

"Anything is possible."

"As an agent, aren't you suppose to be on a mission if you're out of the department?"

"Usually. I'm on sick leave, they'll start searching for me in about three days when they figure out that I've been released from the hospital."

"What happens if they find out sooner?"

"I get into trouble when I get back, probably on several counts. That usually results in a long and tedious lecture."

"Sounds like you get off easy."

"When you are as good at your job as I am they can't afford to do anything. Of course, that might change if I get injured on one more mission but I'll worry about that when I get the next mission."

"I never figured out how anyone could do a job like that."

"Insanity, fear, love." Emily shrugged.

"Why do you do it?"

"The popular theory is insanity."

"Why do you do it?"

"Because when I started, I saw it as a good thing, a way to make myself better. Now I have nowhere else to go."

"What about family?"

"My parents are nice people and I love them, but I can't go back there. My son, which is a long story, lives in a lab in a different department. And most of the people I know are either in the department or I can't afford to see them again. And then there are people like Alex, who I wouldn't trust to help me."

"What would happen if you leave?"

"I don't know, I've never heard of anyone who has done it. Most people leave by dying. I'm not sure I am ready to leave yet."

"You don't sound too happy, but you don't want to leave?"

"Everything happens in its own time."

The bartender poked his head in the door.

"It is closing time," he said.

"Okay," Trent said standing up. Trent went into the bar. Emily picked up Alice in Wonderland, which was still sitting right where she left it and stretched out on the couch. Trent came back half an hour latter carrying a bag. He went into the bathroom and came back out a moment later without the bag. Trent stood there as if he wasn't sure what to do.

"What is wrong?" Emily asked as she sat up.

"The bartender has gone home, that's usually about the time the leech shows up if she hasn't already," Trent answered. Emily put the book down and stood up.

"There are ways to make sure she doesn't stay long," Emily said. They heard the door to the bar open and close. Emily stepped up to Trent, wrapped her arms around his neck and kissed him. Trent deepened the kiss as the door opened.

"Trent…" a female voice started. There was a pause, then the door closed, footsteps went back across the bar and the front door closed. Emily broke off the kiss without separating herself from Trent.

"I told you she wouldn't stay long," Emily whispered.

"You did," Trent replied, and then he kissed her.

Professor Abbot entered the lab where Daniel was sitting at the computer.

"Daniel, it is passed time that you should be in bed," Professor Abbott said.

"I'll get there soon," Daniel answered.

"Does this have something to do with Jordan returning the time machine?" Professor Abbott asked, "Because he did apologize for what happened."

"The handheld time machine that I was working on was stolen," Daniel said.

"Are you sure you didn't misplace it?" Professor Abbott asked.

"I have the security footage that shows someone stealing it," Daniel said.

"What?" Professor Abbott asked going to stand behind Daniel. Daniel brought up the video. They were silent as the video ran through.

"How did that man get into our lab?" Professor Abbott asked, "We lock the doors and do security checks regularly."

"I don't know, but I'm trying to figure it out," Daniel replied, "I'm going over the security stuff and running his picture through the database."

"Get some sleep soon," Professor Abbott said.

"I will," Daniel said. Professor Abbott left the lab.

Trent was moving downstairs when Emily woke up. She got up and went downstairs. Trent was in the bar. Emily sat down behind the counter.

"And after last time I thought you were an early riser," Trent said.

"It depends on the situation. I prefer to sleep late but I can get up early," Emily replied. Trent put down the last chair and came over to the bar.

"So, is it lunch or breakfast I'm getting?" he asked.

"Brunch," Emily answered.

"Brunch?" Trent asked.

"Breakfast and lunch in one word," Emily answered, "Used to refer to a meal that happens after breakfast time and before lunch time."

"I'll go pick it up," Trent said starting for the door. He stopped and turned back as he reached the door, "She may show up while I'm gone."

"Don't worry about it," Emily said. Trent left. Emily picked up the newspaper and started to read. A few minutes later a young lady came in. She was about sixteen with dyed blonde hair and the body of an anorexic.

"Most whores don't stay till the next morning," the girl said.

"Most sixteen-year-olds don't look to be sluts," Emily replied.

"Where's Trent?" the girl asked.

"Avoiding you," Emily replied folding up the paper. The girl walked across the bar and opened the door to the back. She looked into the back room before letting the door close and turning to Emily.

"Where is Trent?" the girl asked.

"He went out," Emily answered.

"And he would leave you here?"

"Apparently."

"When is he supposed to be back?"

"You know, being a parasite is not the way to get a guy and going after guys your own age is a really good idea."

"I don't see how that is any of your business."

"I do, but so far you haven't understood."

"Let me guess you show up out of nowhere and have decided that you want Trent for yourself. Well, I don't scare easily, so be prepared for a fight."

"Actually, I'm just visiting. And Trent could have chosen you at any time. What you haven't grasped is that he didn't and he won't. I will be leaving soon enough, but he still won't choose you after I'm gone."

"Are you finished, yet?"

"I suggesting that you find someone that is interested in you, rather than going for what you can't have."

"Whatever. I'll stop by when Trent is here." The girl walked back across the bar and out the door. Emily went to the back and made a telephone call before going back to the bar to wait for Trent.

Five minutes later Trent came back. He set the bag on the counter.

"Here's lunch," Trent said taking two sandwiches and a bottle of pop out of the bag.

"Thank you," Emily said taking one of the sandwiches. Trent took out two glasses and poured pop into them before sitting down and taking the other sandwich.

"Did she come by?" Trent asked.

"Yes, but I don't think she'll be back," Emily answered.

"Okay," Trent replied. They didn't say anything else as they ate. Once they were finished and Trent was cleaning the counter Alex came in with two of his goons.

"Hello, Trent," Alex said sitting down, "How is business?"

"Fine, keeping afloat but don't have enough for anything fancy," Trent answered.

"You're doing better than a few people," Alex said, "Which is making it hard for me to run my business."

Emily came out of the back room.

"You're back?" Alex asked.

"I decided it was a good time for a visit," Emily replied.

"Do you appear and disappear at random or is there a pattern to it?" Alex asked.

"Usually random, I find it easier than trying to stick to a pattern," Emily answered taking a seat at the table with Alex, "And I was hoping to talk to you."

"Talk about what?" Alex asked.

"I'm looking for information on George Schultz," Emily answered.

"You're insane."

"Besides that."

"Mr. Schultz is not someone anyone wants to deal with. Why do you want to know about him?"

"I figure since I'm on his to-die-list, I might as well find out about him."

"You're on his list and you are still alive?"

"Not for lack of trying. The scar from the knife wound is only a bit more than a month old."

"Does he know you are still alive?"

"If he doesn't, he will soon. Now, will you tell me what you know about him?"

"He is the invisible power, if something happens he has okayed it, if it didn't happen he didn't want it to happen. He has people everywhere in every organization. He has a wife and two children."

"Delilah and Nolan."

"Yeah, other than that I don't know much besides people show up dead with no apparent reason."

"Any of his people within your group?"

"There is that possibility."

"Any deaths?"

"Only one recent death. He was shot doing some business that I didn't tell him to do, but Preston is a good replacement."

"There are two MIA's from the organization I work for, Russell and Preston."

"What does Preston look like?"

"I have no idea. I only know he is MIA."

"They could be different people.

"I could find out."

"I'm not sure I want to know," Alex stood up, "I have to get back. See you both another time." Alex left, followed by his goons.

"Alex didn't seem comfortable discussing George Schultz," Trent commented.

"I'm surprised he said that much," Emily said, "Schultz seems to inspire fear in everyone who knows anything about him."

"And you have decided to look for information on him?"

"Why not? He already wants me dead. His son Nolan was the one who put the knife in my back."

"Looking for revenge?"

"I'm not sure what I want, I'm just searching for information. Once I have that, maybe then I'll know what to do."

Trent sat down in the chair that Alex had vacated.

"When Alex mentioned people turning up dead for no reason, Tyler came to mind. He died for no reason and no one looked into it."

"Sounds like George Schultz."

"I wrote his wife a letter to tell her how sorry I was about his death and that she could come and pick up his last paycheque. She still hasn't come to get it."

"She may be dead too. From what I've heard so far, Mr. Schultz doesn't like leaving family alive if he kills a person."

"The cheque is here if she is alive and wants to claim it. How long are you going to stick around?"

"I'm not sure."

"You still haven't told me why you came here, besides you needed a drink."

"I have a predicament. I adopted a two-year-old girl, but I don't live anywhere that she can stay with me. I was trying to see if I could find a place where she could stay and I ended up here."

"She can't stay here."

"I know that."

"But I do have my house that I'm finishing up. Most of what I have to do is a few little things and painting. It is already furnished. And my neighbour is a busy-body, who would love to be asked to baby-sit a small child."

"How do you know that last part?"

"She was asking nosy questions about my personal life."

"You would be willing to take on a two-year-old?"

"The least I can do if you were actually successful at getting rid of the leech."

"And if I wasn't successful?"

"My neighbour will be kept off my back."

"Okay."

"I've only got two questions."

"What?"

"Is she going to left solely in my care? And what happens if you die?"

"I will be visiting her as much as I can. And if I die there is currently nothing set in place."

"Does this girl have a name?"

"Adriana. She is currently under the care of two babysitters within the building the department is in."

"How about a tour of the town? Tyler's place, the department and then my house."

"Fine with me."

"I just need to grab Tyler's paycheque," Trent got up and went into the back room. He came back a minute later.

"Let's go," Trent said. Emily stood up and they left the bar heading for Tyler's house.

Fifteen minutes later they reach Tyler's house. All the curtains were closed and the lawn looked like it hadn't been cut in a month.

"This doesn't look good," Trent commented. They went up the stairs to the door and Trent knocked. There was no sound, no response. A few minutes went past. Trent knocked again. No sound came from the house.

"There doesn't seem to be anyone home," Trent said.

"Are you sure this is the right house?" Emily asked.

"Yes, I happen to own it," Trent answered.

"You own it?"

"Yeah, I own four houses. I rent out two, this one I let Tyler live in and the other one I supposedly live in."

"Okay, so wouldn't Tyler's wife have to tell you if she moved?"

"Yes."

"That leaves two alternatives."

"I know one alternative, but what is the other?"

"She is hiding, which from the movement of the curtain I would say is possible."

The door opened a crack.

"Who are you? What do you want?" a female voice asked.

"I'm Trent, Tyler's former employer and this is a friend of mine, Emily. We were hoping to talk to you," Trent answered. The door closed and after a moment opened again. There was just enough room for Trent and Emily to squeeze in. The house was dark but well kept. Tyler's wife was probably twenty-five but worry lines made her look several years older. She closed the door and locked it before leading them into the kitchen.

"My name is Ruth," she said as they sat down at the table, "What did you want to talk about?"

"Tyler," Emily answered, "Specifically the circumstances of his death."

"The police said someone had put a knife through his neck," Ruth started to play with the mug that was sitting on the table. "They didn't say anything about investigating his death but he knew that would happen. I had hoped otherwise."

"Why did he think the police wouldn't investigate his death?" Emily asked.

"Because there are spies everywhere," Ruth answered.

"Spies for George Schultz?"

"Yes, Tyler could identify the spies but I can't."

"Why would Schultz want him killed?"

"It started three years ago. Tyler helped this guy out. The guy was in trouble and Tyler saved him and brought him home. The guy told Tyler everything he knew and then died. After that Tyler started looking into Schultz. A month after the guy died Tyler received a letter asking for help, then Tyler got sick. After that he seemed to be able tell the difference between spies and people that were not with Schultz." Ruth took a few deep breathes before continuing. "Tyler never seemed that close to anything important as far as I could tell. He wouldn't tell me anything other than which people he trusted. Trent, you were at the top of that list and he mentioned you once too, Emily. I was scared for him but we lived normal lives, now I'm scared to go to sleep at night because I'm sure I wouldn't wake up the next morning."

"Did Tyler keep any record of his findings?" Emily asked.

"Yes, but I have no idea where he hid it," Ruth answered.

"Try to find it," Trent said, "I'm gonna see if I can find a place where you would be safe from Schultz."

"I don't think there is one," Ruth said.

"I'm going try anyway. It is the least I can do for a good friend and a great bartender," Trent said.

"Thank you, but the only way to be safe is if Schultz was dead," Ruth said.

"Perhaps Tyler's findings could be of some help there," Emily said.

"I'll search for it," Ruth said. Trent pulled out an envelope and gave it to Ruth.

"This is the last of Tyler's pay," Trent said.

"Thank you," Ruth said. Trent and Emily stood up; Ruth did as well. They went to the door.

"Tyler said she was looking for help," Ruth said, "And her plans might work if she could get the right person. But he never said who she was, but if you find out it may help."

"We'll try," Emily said. Ruth opened the door and Emily and Trent stepped outside then the door closed behind them. The locked clicked. Emily and Trent went down the steps and continued their walk. When they came in sight of the department Trent stayed where he was and Emily continued on her own. Going around she went in the recruit's door and used the elevator to go down. Sharon was sitting on one of the couches with Adriana asleep beside her. Other than that the room was empty. Sharon looked up when she heard the elevator door.

"You're back," Sharon said quietly, her voice filled with disappointment.

"Yes," Emily answered, just as quiet, "How is everyone here?"

"The recruits are still here and everyone is driving each other nuts, except when it comes to

Adriana. She is just the sweetest little girl," Sharon said.

"I know, but she'll have to come with me now," Emily said.

"I know," Sharon said. Emily gently picked Adriana up.

"Bye," Sharon said.

"Bye," Emily went back to the elevator and stepped inside. She went back through the recruit's entrance and over to where Trent was standing. They didn't say anything to each other as they walked to Trent's house.

The house lacked the finishing touches but looked well kept. They went up the stairs. Trent unlocked the door and they stepped inside.

"The second bedroom down the hall can be hers," Trent said. Emily went down the hallway and found the bedroom. She placed Adriana on the bed and then went back to the hallway where Trent was standing.

"Here's the other key," Trent said handing the key to Emily.

"Okay," Emily said as she put it in her pocket.

"I should get back to the bar and get ready for opening," Trent said, "So, I'll see you later."

"Okay," Emily replied. Trent left. Emily found a book and read until Adriana woke up. Then she took Adriana shopping.

Professor Abbott entered the lab. Daniel was still sitting at the computer working.

"Did you sleep at all?" Professor Abbott asked.

"I figured out how the guy got in," Daniel said, "I also can tell the only thing he was after was the handheld time machine. He even knew approximately where it was."

"Daniel," Professor Abbott started.

"I sent a cleaned up picture to security," Daniel interrupted, "Along with the date, time and how."

"Daniel," Professor Abbott said, "You need to take a break from this. You will not solve this crime overnight, while sitting at the computer. Go get some sleep. If nothing else, it will give security time to look at the information you gave them."

"That was my project. I have nothing to work on until I get it back," Daniel said, "And it hasn't been tested yet. What happens if the guy tries to use it and it blows up in his face?"

"You will get the pieces back and the guy will have made a foolish mistake," Professor Abbott said, "But even if you got it back right now, you would have to sleep before you can go back to working on it. Go to sleep now and when it is recovered you will be rested enough to work on it."

Daniel stopped working.

"I will wake you if anything big comes up," Professor Abbott said.

"Fine," Daniel said as he got up.

"Good," Professor Abbott said. Daniel left the lab.

Emily had fallen asleep on the couch by the time Trent came back. Trent quietly went passed her to get to the kitchen. He poured himself a glass of pop and sat down at the table. Emily came into the kitchen and sat down across from him.

"Sorry, if I woke you," Trent said.

"I'm a light sleeper," Emily replied.

"Are you going to kill Schultz?" Trent asked.

"I don't know what is going to happen," Emily answered, "I'm still looking for information."

"It sounded like you were when we were talking to Ruth."

"I avoided saying that I would kill him because I don't know what will happen. Ruth just wants to not have to be afraid of him. Though I'm pretty sure that Schultz isn't worried about her, she will continue to be afraid of him until he is no longer in a position of power."

"You don't seem like a killer, but agents do what they have to."

"Even though I'm an agent I only kill if there are no other alternatives. There are usually alternatives. Were you serious about your promise to get her some place safe?"

"Yes, I already have a good idea for a place."

"I hope it helps her from being so afraid."

"We'll see. When are you leaving?"

"Tomorrow. I want to introduce you to Adriana so she doesn't wake up and the only person around is a complete stranger."

"Okay."

"I took her shopping and brought her some clothes. She'll probably need some more."

"When will you be here next?"

"I don't know. I hope to try to visit weekly but with my job anything could happen."

"As long as you don't die it, should be fine."

"That wasn't in the plan anywhere in the near future. Sleep maybe, but dying, no." Trent finished his pop. Emily got up from the table and headed for the living room.

"Good night," Trent said. He got up, put his glass on the counter and went to his room.

The next morning Adriana came into the kitchen where Emily and Trent were sitting at the table talking. She climbed onto Emily's lap.

"Hungry," Adriana announced.

"I guess it is time for breakfast," Emily said, "What would you like to have?"

"Cereal," Adriana answered.

"Okay," Emily got up and put Adriana on the chair. She started taking things out of the cupboards. Adriana stared across the table at Trent.

"Who's that?" Adriana asked Emily.

"That is Trent, you will be staying with him," Emily answered as she placed a bowl of cereal in front of Adriana. Adriana smiled at Trent and Trent smiled back. Emily poured milk into the bowl and then put the cereal and milk away.

"You stocked up my cupboards," Trent commented.

"I had to, there wasn't anything in them," Emily said as she sat down. Adriana started to eat.

Once Adriana was finished eating, Emily got her to bring her toys out and play with Trent. Once they were settled Emily headed back to the department.

Emily stopped at the front desk. Cynthia was working at her computer.

"So you are out of the hospital," Cynthia said.

"Yes," Emily replied, "You look like you should be there instead."

"I'm fine, just the flu," Cynthia said.

"I suggest you check with Dr. Grace just to be sure," Emily said.

"I'll try," Cynthia said. Alfred came out of his office.

"Good to see you back," he greeted Emily, "Now that you are I suggest you go back to training with Travis's help. I believe Dr. Grace requires your assistance in the medical lab."

"The medical lab was my next stop," Emily said, "I figured I would check in first."

"That is fine," Alfred said. Emily headed for the medical lab. When she got there she found Grace sitting at the computer.

"Alfred said you were in need of help," Emily said.

"Not at the moment, but you should check up on your patients," Grace said.

"I had thought about doing that," Emily said.

"How's Adriana?" Grace asked.

"Busy doing what any two-year-old does and twisting Trent around her little finger," Emily answered.

"Poor guy."

"He didn't seem to have a problem with it. Any appointments or do I have to find them myself?"

"Abby has an appointment for some time today, but Bethany you will have to find."

"Okay. Anything else happening?"

"Nothing noteworthy."

"Any time Abby is supposed to be here?"

"No, and she hasn't been here yet."

"So, I should probably stay here until she shows up."

"Probably."

Emily sat down on another chair.

"Trent as in the bartender?" Grace asked.

"That's the only one I know," Emily answered.

"Why go to him?"

"Not entirely sure."

"Why do I suddenly feel like I hit an information block?"

"I have no idea, maybe your mind is going. There are times when it might seem like an information block but I don't have the answers myself."

"What about the times you do have the answers?"

Abby entered the medical lab before Emily could answer Grace's question.

"How are you doing?" Emily asked Abby.

"I'm eating enough for two and people are looking at me funny," Abby answered.

"Sounds normal for being six months along," Emily said standing up. Abby got up onto the examining table and Emily used the scanner. Then she put the scanner in its slot in the computer and brought up the results.

"Everything looks fine. The baby looks healthy," Emily said.

"Will it be a boy or a girl?" Abby asked, "Dr. Grace couldn't tell me."

"The baby is a girl," Emily told her.

"Thank you," Abby smiled as she got off the examining table.

"See you in a month unless something comes up or you have any concerns," Emily said. Abby nodded then left the medical lab.

"I have a lot to teach you," Emily told Grace.

"First you would have to find the time for giving lessons," Grace replied.

"I have to find Bethany, then we can discuss a schedule for lessons," Emily said.

"I won't be holding my breath," Grace said. Emily started to leave when Tamara and a male agent Emily sort of recognized came in carrying an unconscious Bethany between them. They carefully placed her on the examining table.

"She just passed out," Tamara said, "She seemed fine."

"It is okay," Grace told Tamara, "She's in good hands now." Tamara nodded and the male agent led her out of the medical lab. Emily pulled out the scanner and did the medical scan. Putting the scanner back in the computer she checked the results.

"Anything serious?" Grace asked.

"I don't see anything," Emily answered, "But it might be best if she goes back to staying in my office for a while."

"Okay," Grace said. Emily and Grace moved Bethany to the bed in Emily's office.

"I'll be back to check on her," Emily said as she started to leave for the second time.

"You better," Grace said. Emily left the medical lab.

After supper Emily went in search of Travis. She found him in the assignment lab talking to Nathan. She waited until he was finished.

"What?" Travis turned to her.

"Alfred said something about training," Emily answered.

"You start tomorrow and work with me every other day after that until I'm satisfied that you are ready for another mission," Travis said.

"Fine," Emily said.

"Was that all?" Travis asked.

"Yeah, pretty much," Emily answered.

"Are you sure you're okay?" Travis asked.

"I'm fine," Emily answered.

"Then I'll see you tomorrow," Travis said. Emily nodded and left, heading for her room.

Daniel entered the lab. Professor Abbott was sitting at the workstation on the opposite side of the room. Daniel sat down at his computer.

"Feeling better?" Professor Abbott asked.

"Somewhat," Daniel answered, "Was there any news while I was asleep?"

"One of the security people recognized the guy," Professor Abbott answered.

"And?" Daniel asked.

"They are looking for him," Professor Abbott answered, "They will bring you all the information they can when they have it. In the meantime, I was hoping you could help me on my project."

"I suppose I could," Daniel said getting up and going over to where Professor Abbott was working.

Emily's schedule started the next day. Every other day was training with Travis, the days in between, Emily either spent the time in the medical lab or at Trent's house. This continued for two months, during which Bethany stayed in the medical lab. Emily slowly got back into shape and Adriana was happy.

Emily got up, dressed and then headed for the cafeteria. When she came back to her room before heading to the gym, she noticed an envelope lying on the bed.

"Where did this come from?" Emily asked. The envelope didn't have anything written on it. Emily picked it up and opened it. There was a folded piece of paper and a key inside. Emily took the piece of paper out and unfolded it. In the middle of the page were the words 'I need your help'. The words were typed and there were no other marks on the page.

"Strange," Emily said. She folded the paper up and put it back in the envelope. The key slipped out and fell onto the bed. Suddenly Emily felt tired and she felt like the room was too hot. Slowly she felt her stomach start to hurt and she started to get light headed. Dropping the envelope on the bed Emily went to the door of her room. Leaving her room she started toward the medical lab using the wall for support.

Emily arrived at the medical lab feeling worse and somewhat unsure of how she got there. Entering, she didn't see Grace, but a young lady. The lady was giving off a bad vibe. Emily wondered if the lady was an illusion.

"Where is Grace?" Emily asked.

"She went to talk to someone," the lady answered, "I can help you."

"No," Emily replied and then went into her office, collapsing on the floor just short of the bed. Emily was glad Bethany had been moved to the other room. Then she blacked out.

Grace was on her way back to the medical lab after talking to Alfred when Travis came up to her.

"Have you seen Emily?" Travis asked.

"No, why?" Grace replied.

"She was supposed to meet me in the gym right after breakfast but she isn't there," Travis said.

"Maybe she slept in. Have you checked her room?" Grace asked.

"I was just on my way to do that," Travis answered. They came to Emily's room. Grace opened the door. Travis entered the room.

"Emily," Travis called. There was no answer. He went over and looked in the bathroom, "She isn't here."

He left the room and the door closed.

"She could be in the medical lab," Grace said. Travis and Grace headed for the medical lab. The intern was sitting on a chair waiting but no one else was there.

"Have you seen Emily?" Grace asked the intern.

"Who is Emily?" the intern asked.

"Sorry, I forgot you haven't met her yet," Grace said.

"There was lady in here looking for you," the intern said.

"Where did she go?" Grace asked.

"In there," the intern pointed to Emily's office.

"That would be Emily," Grace walked over to the door.

"She looked really sick," the intern said. Grace twisted the knob and tried to open the door. It wouldn't budge.

"It won't move," Grace said.

"Is it locked?" Travis asked crossing the room.

"No, you can turn the knob all the way but the door won't move," Grace answered. Travis pushed against the door.

"Don't break it," Grace said. Travis stepped back from the door.

"The hinges are on the other side, aren't they?"

"Yes."

"If it isn't locked, the door must be stuck somehow."

"Is there some way of opening it without breaking the door?"

"Is there another way into this office?"

"No."

"Then I don't think there is a way."

"We'll have to wait for her to come out then."

"Why can't the door be broken?"

"It would set off the security system and we would never get in until the system shut down, which can take up to a month."

"Why put a security system on an office in the medical lab?"

"The security system covers the whole medical lab. It was put in when the department was built.

"I have other things to do while we wait. Tell Emily to come talk to me when she comes out."

"I will."

Travis left the medical lab.

The computer beeped, causing Daniel to put down what he was doing and going over to his computer. He worked on it for a few minutes.

"Finally," Daniel muttered.

"What is it?" Professor Abbott asked.

"Security found the guy," Daniel answered.

"Did he have the time machine on him?" Professor Abbott asked.

"No," Daniel answered, "But they sent me the answers he gave when they questioned him."

"What did he have to say?"

"He was hired to get the time machine. The person that hired him gave him directions to the building, room and where in the room."

"Sounds like an inside job."

"But he didn't recognize anyone when they showed him photos of everyone that works here. In fact, the only thing that is of any use is when they caught him mumbling, but he refuses to tell them what he said. All I have is the name Livia."

"Did you search it?"

"Not yet, but it doesn't sound very promising."

"Search it."

Daniel put the name into the search and then they waited. Fifteen minutes later the search finished without finding anything.

"It must be a nickname or an alias," Professor Abbott said.

"Which means I'm back to where I was before, except that now I don't have a project," Daniel said.

"What are you going to do now?" Professor Abbott asked.

"I don't know," Daniel answered.

Two days after disappearing into her office Emily came out. She looked like she hadn't completely gotten over what she was sick with. She sat down on the computer chair.

"Well, you only look half dead," Grace commented.

"Thanks," Emily replied.

"What happened?"

"I got sick and have spent the last three days in a semi-conscious state hallucinating that I was slowly dying from the inside out."

"What happened besides that?"

"I'm not entirely sure."

"Just because you're not sure doesn't mean you don't have a good guess,"

The young lady, who Emily remembered had been there two days ago, walked into the medical lab. Emily could still feel the bad vibe she was giving off.

"Robin, this is Emily. Emily this is the intern, Robin," Grace introduced them.

"Nice to meet you," Robin went over and held out her hand.

"Hello," Emily replied ignoring the offered hand. After a moment Robin withdrew her hand.

"Robin will be around for a couple weeks," Grace said.

"How's Bethany?" Emily asked.

"Doing fine. Tamara has been visiting, that seems to be helping a lot but I'm not sure she'll ever get used to Markus being dead," Grace answered.

"Some things don't go away," Emily said, "But maybe the child will give her a reason to live."

The buzzer went for lunch. Robin left.

"You don't seem to like the intern," Grace commented.

"This may seem weird, but I feel like she is giving off a sour or bad energy," Emily said.

"I don't trust her but I can't feel anything like that."

"Maybe it is just the flu."

"You didn't give your guess as to what happened."

"I know that when I went back to my room after breakfast I found an envelope on my bed. I opened it and found a note inside and a moment later I started to feel sick."

"There couldn't have been a virus sealed in the envelope."

"No, but there might have been one on the paper."

"Who would send you a virus and why? Or is this someone's attempt to kill you?"

"I don't think it was a murder attempt. There are poisons that kill faster and that make sure I didn't survive."

"But who and why?"

"I'm not sure yet."

"Will you tell me when you know?"

"Yes."

"I want to run some tests. Maybe we can figure out what the virus is."

"Okay." Emily got up and went over to the examining table and laid down on it. Grace used the medical scanner. Emily sat up and looked over Grace's shoulder as Grace studied the results.

"There are no obvious signs of anything. I know this is uncommon, but I'm gonna do a blood test."

Emily laid down again. Grace took a vial of blood from Emily's arm and placed the vial in its slot in the computer. Emily sat up.

"Nothing. According to the results there is nothing wrong with you."

"I would argue that point but computers don't have the programming to admit that they are wrong."

"This doesn't make sense."

"Maybe if you examined the piece of paper."

"Travis and I looked for you and we checked your room. There wasn't any envelope or piece of paper."

"Strange."

"Your door was also unlocked."

"I may not have locked it on my way out. I might not have closed it on my way out."

"Then anyone could have taken it."

"I doubt anyone took it. The person who put it there probably took it."

"That still leaves a lot of people."

"I don't think so, but I'm getting tired so I'll be going back to bed," Emily got up and went back into her office. Grace heard the lock click.

Emily came out two days later, this time looking a lot healthier. She went back to her schedule, with a minor change of not spending time in the medical lab except for five minutes to check on Bethany. She continued this for about three weeks.

After coming back from a day of training Emily showered and got ready for bed. When she was ready Emily laid down. She lay still for a few minutes before rolling over to try and get comfortable. As she lay there Emily slowly became aware of something hard pressing into her back. Emily got out of bed and turned on the light. She looked over the spot and found a key. Emily picked it up and looked it over. It looked like a house key, but there were some markings on the bow of the key. Emily moved the key into the light. The markings said: 583 Elm Avenue, front room back corner. Emily got dressed and left her room. She went to the assignment lab. Sitting down at the computer she typed 583 Elm Avenue into the search. After a moment the computer brought up some newspaper articles. Emily read through the story about the antique store and the fire that happened there. But she couldn't find any information on the owner. Finally giving the search up Emily went back to her room and back to bed.

Emily could hear the pounding on the door and she could see the clock saying three ante meridian but neither registered. She lay there without any thought about the reality that was trying to make itself evident. Slowly the sound filtered into her consciousness. Once she became fully aware of the sound, she became aware of what time it was. Emily got up and went over to the door. The door slid open. An agent, who looked familiar, was standing there.

"You are needed immediately in the medical lab," he said.

"Why?" Emily asked.

"I don't know. Dr. Grace just said that you were needed immediately," the guard answered.

"Give me a minute," Emily said and closed the door. Emily changed clothes, brushed her hair and then headed for the medical lab. When she got there Emily found a young man sitting in a chair and talking coming from her office. Emily entered her office. Abby was lying on the bed in a hospital gown and Grace was trying to calm her down.

"You called," Emily said leaning against the door jam.

"Yes," Grace said. Abby went through another contraction. Emily moved to the side of the bed. Grace left the room.

"How long have you been having contractions?" Emily asked.

"Two hours," Abby answered. Emily checked how far Abby's cervix had dilated.

"Labour is a long process," Emily said sitting in the chair next to the bed, "I would suggest you rest between contractions. Who is the young man sitting out there?"

"Adam."

"Father of the child?"

"No, just a friend."

"Well, I'm going to send him in here to keep you company and Dr. Grace will be out there if you need anything. I will be back in a while to check on you."

Abby nodded. Emily got up and left the office.

"She is in need of company," Emily told Adam. Adam got up and went into the office.

"Call me when her cervix has dilated ten centimetres," Emily told Grace as she headed for the door, "I'll be back later."

"If there are any problems?" Grace asked.

"Call me sooner." Emily left.

Emily went back to bed. At seven she got up, checked on Abby, and then went to the gym and told Travis that she was busy for the day. Then she went back to the medical lab. Abby gave birth to a healthy baby girl at two post meridian.

Abby, Rebecca and Adam were in Emily's office, while Emily and Grace were sitting outside.

"I hope Bethany's goes that smoothly," Grace said.

"We'll see when the time comes," Emily replied.

"Have you checked on Bethany?"

"Yes, I did that this morning. She seems to doing fine."

"When are you going to let her leave?"

"When I feel she is ready."

"What happens if I need that room?"

"Move her to my office. Where's Robin? I haven't seen her all day."

"I'm amazed you noticed with the way you avoid her."

"If you are trying to avoid someone, you take notice if they are around or not."

"She is in class for a week. Does she still give off bad energy?"

"Nothing has changed, except my understanding."

"How has your understanding changed?"

"I'll explain someday when I figure it all out."

"You could tell me everything before. Since you patched up Bethany, Tamara and the rest, you won't answer most of my questions, except with obscure and obtuse answers. What is going on that you can't tell me?"

Emily sighed.

"A lot. Some of it I barely understand."

"If you tell me maybe I can help."

"I appreciate your offer and I would tell you everything but I can't afford to. I know this is frustrating and it is causing problems. I do tell you what I can. I promise that someday I will explain everything."

"You better keep that promise."

"The only reason I don't keep promises is if something like death stops me."

"I know."

The next day Emily was working on a project in the assignment lab when Cynthia sat down next to her.

"Something wrong?" Emily asked glancing at Cynthia.

"I think I have a problem," Cynthia answered.

"What kind of problem?"

"A medical one."

"A little more explanation would be helpful."

"Brett and I slept together before he left. We used protection. Since then I've been busy, but recently I have been noticing a few things."

"Like what?"

"I haven't been having periods, I tire easily, and I'm gaining weight."

"You're scared that you are pregnant."

"Yes."

"The sad truth is protection doesn't always work and what you have described sounds like you're pregnant but go talk to Dr. Grace to make sure."

"If I am I'm in trouble, I'm expected to keep doing my job and there aren't any allowances for this kind of thing," Cynthia said.

"See if you can get in touch with Brett and tell him the situation. And try not to worry about your job right now," Emily said. Cynthia nodded then got up and left the assignment lab. Emily went back to her project.

When the lunch buzzer went Emily shut down the project, got up and headed for the medical lab. Getting there she sat down at the computer and brought up Cynthia's file.

"You have another patient," Grace said coming out of her office.

"Cynthia," Emily said.

"Yes."

"Looks like she is four months along."

"How can anyone miss those signs for four months?"

"Denial and being busy," Emily shut the file down, "Heading for the cafeteria?"

"Yes."

Grace and Emily left the medical lab.

Emily spent the rest of the week and all of the next on her usual schedule.

Before breakfast on Monday morning Alfred stopped in the medical lab. Grace was sitting at the computer.

"Busy?" Alfred asked.

"No," Grace answered.

"I was wondering if you feel that Emily is okay to go on another mission," Alfred said.

"If Travis okays her, then it would probably be a good idea," Grace replied.

"Thank you for your time," Alfred left the medical lab.

Daniel was leaning on the counter looking lost when Professor Abbott came into the lab.

"Something wrong?" Professor Abbott asked.

"I'm trying to figure out what to do next," Daniel answered, "I can't continue my project now that the prototype is gone. My notes were deleted in the last system upgrade and the materials were expensive enough that I was told I could only make one until it was determined that it worked. That leaves me without anything to do, except maybe go after the prototype. And I don't have experience with that type of thing."

"What do you want to do?" Professor Abbott asked.

"Figure out where the prototype is and why someone would want to steal it," Daniel said.

"Why not transfer departments and learn how to become a person that could do that?" Professor Abbott suggested.

"I don't think I could do that," Daniel replied, "Though I think I know someone who can."

"What?" Professor Abbott asked.

"Emily Jackson," Daniel answered, "She is an agent, I can learn from her."

"Daniel," Professor Abbott said, "Agents don't let people hang around while they take missions and they don't just teach things. She may just send you off to get the proper training if you do that."

"She doesn't have to know what I'm doing," Daniel said.

"If you want to go, go. But first think about it for a couple days," Professor Abbott said, "Maybe something else will come up before then."

CHAPTER 6
NEW FRIENDS

Emily had started to count the dots on the second ceiling tile when Travis came into his office.

"You look bored," he commented as he sat down.

"What gives you that idea?" Emily asked.

"There was an emergency I needed to deal with," Travis said.

"Your excuse doesn't interest me. Alfred said something about a mission," Emily said.

"This mission comes with a catch."

"What kind of catch?"

"Warner is worried about you recent record with missions."

"You mean coming back injured and that stuff?"

"Yes, he is pressuring Alfred to take you off being an agent."

"And do what with me?"

"The suggestion that was put up was that you could take Dr. Harvey's place, but Alfred won't do that. So he has given you this mission. Then you succeed without a hitch you can keep being an agent. If you don't get stuck in either Dr. Harvey's position or in limbo until Alfred can find a different position."

"What's the mission?"

"A man important to the department has disappeared. Your mission is to find him and bring him back alive."

"That it?"

"Yes, that is the mission."

"Do I get more information?"

"Yes." Travis slid a file towards her, "His name is Pascal, his address and personal information should be in the file."

Emily picked up the file.

"Everything in here?" Emily asked.

"Everything that is known," Travis answered.

"Then I'm all set."

"Not quite," Travis took a watch out of a drawer and handed it to Emily, "This has a tracking device in it, and you are expected to wear it."

Emily took the watch.

"It tells us exactly where you are at any time," Travis said.

"Tells time too," Emily stood up.

"You will leave in an hour."

"Yeah, okay."

"This may not be as easy as you think."

"It shouldn't be as hard as you pretend or I wouldn't have been given this mission." Emily left

Travis's office and headed for the assignment lab to do research.

An hour later Emily left department H and headed for Pascal's house. The walk took her across town to an upper class neighbourhood. The mansion was huge with a gated courtyard in front. Emily walked up to the gate. She could see a police car parked in front of the door.

"Can I help you?" a guard asked stepping out of the booth by the gate.

"I'm looking for Claire," Emily answered.

"Do you have an appointment?" the guard asked.

"No," Emily answered. The guard stepped back into the booth and picked up a telephone. He spoke into it and then listened for a minute. The guard hung up the telephone and pushed a button. The gate swung open and Emily entered the courtyard. She headed for the mansion; the gate closed behind her. When she reached the door Emily found the butler already waiting.

"This way," the butler said entering the mansion. Emily followed. He led her to a sitting room.

"Claire will be with you in a few minutes." The butler left. The room was twice the size of Emily's bedroom. There was a couch and two chairs. There was a fireplace with a painted portrait of Pascal and Claire over it. Around the portrait were certificates. Emily went over to study them. Most were a show of appreciation for large contributions to charities; two were for heroism.

"May I help you?" a female voice asked from behind Emily. Emily turned around. The lady was slightly over middle age and looked like she was in need of some sleep.

"I'm Emily Jackson. I was sent by one of the organizations your husband helps fund to see if I could help find him."

"Maybe you can help where the police can't," Claire said as she sat down in one of the chairs, "I don't know why they bothered to even send someone if they aren't going to do anything."

"I will do what I can to help," Emily answered as she sat down on the couch.

"What can I do?"

"Start by telling me what happened the day he disappeared."

"It was a usual day. Pascal and I got up, had breakfast and then he went into his study to work. Half an hour later Kent, his secretary arrived. I was busy in the garden all morning. When I went to call Pascal for lunch, he wasn't there. I asked Kent if he had seen him but Kent said he only saw him briefly when he went in there to have him sign some papers. I searched most of the house before calling the police. The police came, questioned me, and then questioned Kent, then left saying to call back if Pascal didn't show up in twenty-four hours. I spent the rest of the day worrying what had happened to him."

"Were you working in the front garden or a back garden?"

"There is only a green house in the back and the cook takes care of that."

"Are there any other ways off the property besides the main gate?"

"No, you have to go passed Marshall every time you enter or leave the property."

"Did you see anyone leave, stranger or not?"

"No."

"Where are the cars parked?"

"Pascal's car is in the garage. Kent parks his beside the garage."

"And the garage is at the back of the house?"

"Yes."

"What do you know of Pascal's business?"

"Everything. He discusses every aspect of it with me; all decisions are made jointly. He doesn't even sign papers unless we both agree on what the paper said."

"What papers did Kent have Pascal signing that day?"

"The finalization of a deal that was made a week ago."

"Was there any business that someone might be offended by or not want done?"

"Not that I know of."

"What exactly does Kent do?"

"He makes sure all the paperwork is in order, he files paperwork, and he runs errands."

"Does he know you and Pascal discuss the business?"

"No."

"Besides Kent, Marshal, the butler and the cook, is there anyone else that works here?"

"There is a maid that comes in twice a week, except she took this week off to attend an out of town funeral."

"What did the police do when you called them after twenty-four hours?"

"An officer came and questioned me. You probably saw his car when you came in."

"Can I see the office?"

"Sure." Claire got up, Emily did the same and Claire led the way out of the room. They went down a hallway, up a flight of stairs, down another hallway, passed a man sitting at a desk working, to a set of doors. Claire opened the doors and Emily followed her into Pascal's office. There was a large desk in the middle with two chairs facing it and one behind it. There was a window behind the desk and the walls were floor to ceiling bookshelves. Emily went over to the desk. It had a telephone on one corner and a blotter with a few pieces of paper on it. Emily felt a bad vibe and the man, who had been sitting at the desk they had passed, stepped into the doorway.

"Can I help you?" he asked.

"Yes," Emily answered, "I was wondering if you could answer a few questions." Emily sat down in the chair behind the desk. Claire sat down in one of the chairs facing the desk. The man stayed standing.

"On what?" the man asked.

"Pascal's disappearance," Emily answered.

"I have told the police all I know," the man said.

"Unless you have a problem with your conscience, I'm sure you would not mind going over it again," Emily said.

"I suppose I could spare a few minutes," the man said.

"You are Kent?"

"Yes."

"Tell me what happened the day Pascal disappeared."

"I came in about quarter after nine. I started working immediately up on arriving. About ten o'clock I came in here and had Pascal sign some papers, and then I went back to work. I was just about to leave for lunch when Claire came to call him for lunch. She found he wasn't there. I didn't remember him leaving, so I helped Claire search the house. When she called the police, I stayed to answer their questions."

"Then you went for lunch?"

"I went back to my desk and finished what I was working on and then went home for the day."

"How do you know what time you came in to get his signature?"

"I happened to glance at my watch just before I knocked."

"Do you know what he was working on that day?"

"No, but he rarely tells me what he is working on until he wants the paper work dealt with."

"Do you know of any reason for someone to want Pascal to disappear?"

"No."

"Any business that might have offended someone?"

"No."

"Did you drive your car on the day Pascal disappeared?"

"I drive to work every day."

"So you did drive your car to work that day?"

"Yes."

"Thank you for sparing a few minutes."

Kent left. Emily got up and went to the window.

"Does this window open?" Emily asked.

"It does open, but Pascal rarely opens it," Claire answered. Emily twisted the handle and pushed. It stuck for a moment before opening.

"What other exits are there besides the front door?" Emily asked as she closed the window.

"The kitchen has a door that goes to the back and a door in the master bedroom that leads to the balcony. The balcony is on the second floor though."

"There does not appear that there was any struggle and nothing looks like it was disturbed."

"You mean he might have just gotten up and left?"

"No, more likely he was drugged so that he could be taken out of here without much fuss."

The butler appeared in the doorway.

"Mrs. Rachel is here to see you," he announced.

"Okay, I'll go down and see her. Perhaps Emily has some questions for you as well," Claire said getting up, "I will be back shortly." Claire left the room. The butler stepped into the room.

"You are investigating Pascal's disappearance?" the butler asked.

"Yes," Emily answered.

"Thank goodness someone is. The police seem completely incompetent," the butler said.

"So I heard. Can you please tell me what happened on the day Pascal disappeared?"

"Certainly. I spent the morning in the kitchen with my wife, who is the cook. I distinctly remember her making cinnamon buns. I stayed after breakfast to help her do the dishes. After that we sat and talked. Then she had to go out and get some vegetables for lunch. A few minutes later the phone rang, so I went into the hallway to get it. It was Marshal; he said there was a salesperson at the gate. I told him to turn the person away. After hanging up I went back into the kitchen. My wife came in a few minutes later and she started lunch. I helped with that. She was ready to serve it when Claire came into the kitchen asking if we had seen Pascal and saying something about not being able to find him. Martha stayed in the kitchen while I helped Claire search. When we couldn't find him Claire called the police. They came, talked to her and Kent and then they left. I spent the rest of the afternoon looking for any sign of him inside and outside. I couldn't find any."

"The search before calling the police must have been quick with you, Claire and Kent all searching."

"Kent was searching? I never saw him."

"What time approximately would you say the phone rang?"

"Ten thirty."

"How long would you say you were out of the kitchen?"

"Three to five minutes."

"Do you and Martha live here?"

"Yes, we have a suite next to the kitchen."

"How long have you been working here?"

"Ten years."

"How long has Kent been working here?"

"Eight months."

"What do you know of the business that Pascal does?"

"He gives a lot of money to charity, but other than that I don't know."

"Do you own a car?"

"No."

"Thank you for taking the time to answer my questions."

"I hope you can help in finding Pascal." The butler left. Emily studied the desk and the office. After a moment, Emily looked at the pieces of paper that were on the desk. Most were how much was being given to each organization this month. Nothing caught Emily's attention. The desk drawers were locked and none looked like they had been tampered with. Emily lifted the blotter a little. Seeing that there was something underneath, she lifted it a little higher. Underneath was a half completed jigsaw puzzle. Emily put the blotter down and made sure it was in the same position. Finished with the desk, Emily turned her attention back to the rest of the room. A cold breeze came through the room, whipped around Emily, and settled in front of the desk. A transparent figure solidified in one of the chairs. The figure was a man. He was white and semi-solid.

"And you are?" Emily asked. The man seemed taken back for a moment.

"Most people are terrified the first time they see me," the man said.

"If you have information it might be helpful, other than that I have no interest in you," Emily replied.

"You are a scary person," the man commented.

"I'm working, I don't have time for nonsense."

"Then why did you bother talking to Kent?"

"Because his lies tell more than not talking to him at all. How do you know he is guilty and what is he guilty of?"

"I saw him."

"What did you see exactly? I would appreciate the full version."

"It started when Kent was hired. Pascal was pressured into hiring him by an unknown caller, who told him that if he didn't, something would happen to Claire. Pascal didn't discuss the decision to hire him with Claire because he didn't want her to know. The next incident was about a month ago, when Pascal gave Kent paperwork to finalize a deal to fund an organization that Kent didn't like. Kent made a comment, but Pascal wouldn't change his mind."

"Do you know the name of the organization?"

"It involved the name Livia, but other than that, I'm not sure."

"Yet you saw everything?"

"They never said the whole name and I can't read. Shall I go on?"

"Please."

"Most of the month went by and I thought Kent had decided to leave it alone. The other day I thought everything was normal when Kent brought the papers to be signed, but after he left Pascal collapsed. I knew Kent drugged him, especially when Kent came in a few minutes later and dragged Pascal away."

"Sorry to interrupt again, but can you go into more details of Kent getting Pascal to sign the papers and Pascal collapsing?"

"Kent entered, waited for Pascal to notice him, handed him the papers and a pen. Pascal signed the papers and then Kent took them leaving the room. Pascal picked up the phone and called someone. When he talks he always faces the window. He talked for about five minutes before collapsing. Kent came in a few minutes later and hung up the phone only to pick it up and call someone to tell them he was ready. Kent then picked up Pascal by the underarms and dragged him out the door. He carefully smoothed out the trail before continuing to take Pascal downstairs. While Martin answered phone, Kent took Pascal out the kitchen door. Kent came back in by the balcony doors in the master bedroom. Kent then went back to work until Claire came to find Pascal. Kent did help in the search. Any evidence he found, he removed."

"Is that all?"

"Everything I saw."

"Did you tell this to Claire?"

"She has been surrounded by people since then and I haven't had a chance."

"Kent must have used the pen to drug Pascal."

"The paper was there too."

"But the paper would be touched by other people. The pen would be easier to get rid of." Emily turned to study the window.

"Good luck," the ghost said. Emily could feel the cold breeze leave the room. Emily turned around when she heard someone come into the room. Claire sat down in one of the chairs.

"Do you have any idea what could have happened to Pascal?" Claire asked.

"A few, but more information would be helpful," Emily answered, "I would like to talk to Martha and Marshall."

"I'll show you to the kitchen. Martha should be there," Claire said as she stood up. Emily stood up and Claire led the way out of the room. They went to a room at the back of the main floor. A woman was busy at the stove.

"Martha," Claire said.

"Yes," Martha turned around.

"This is Emily. She would like to ask you a few questions," Claire said.

"I'm willing to answer any I can," Martha replied

"I have something I have to do. I will be back in a few minutes," Claire excused herself.

"I hope you don't mind if I work while we talk," Martha said.

"Not at all," Emily said. Martha turned back to the stove.

"Martin stopped through a few minutes ago and said that someone was investigating Pascal's disappearance. I assume that is you," Martha said.

"That is correct," Emily replied.

"Then I'm willing to help out any way I can."

"Tell me what happened the day Pascal disappeared."

"My day started at six. I got up and made cinnamon buns for breakfast. Martin joined me for breakfast. After breakfast I washed dishes and Martin dried them. When we were finished, we sat and talked until about ten-thirty when I went out to the greenhouse to get vegetables. I came back twenty minutes later. I made lunch while Martin sat at the table. I was dishing lunch up when Claire came in asking if we had seen Pascal. She said that he wasn't in his office. We told her that we hadn't and Martin volunteered to look for him. I stayed here and kept the food warm. Finally Martin came back. He said that they didn't find Pascal and that Claire had called the police. When the police arrived, they talked to Claire and Kent, then left. Claire was worried. I spent a while with her to try and calm her down but nothing seemed to work. I served what I had made for lunch at supper but only Martin and I ate."

"Do you remember hearing or seeing anything in the last month that was unusual?"

"No, everything was normal."

"Thank you."

"You are welcome." Emily left the kitchen. She was halfway down the hallway when she met up with Claire coming back to the kitchen.

"Finished talking to Martha?" Claire asked.

"Yes. I am going to talk to Marshall next," Emily answered, "You don't have to come with me."

"I'll be in the sitting room if you need to talk to me," Claire said.

"Thank you," Emily said. Emily continued to the front door. Leaving the mansion, she went across the courtyard to the gate.

"Leaving?" Marshall asked.

"Not quite yet. I would like to ask you a few questions," Emily said.

"Why?" Marshall asked.

"I am investigating Pascal's disappearance," Emily answered.

"Sure, I can answer a few questions," Marshall said. He opened the gate and Emily went through and over to the booth.

"Will you tell me what happened the day Pascal disappeared?"

"Not much happened. A salesman stopped by. I phoned the house and Martin told me to get rid of him, which was fine with me. The next thing was Martin calling to say that the police were coming. The police showed up twenty minutes after that. I checked badges and then opened the gate. They left half an hour later. The only thing after that was Kent leaving."

"Why was getting rid of the salesman fine with you?"

"He was creepy. I didn't want him hanging around."

"Anything else about him?"

"He didn't stop at any other houses. He came up the street directly to this place. When I told him to leave, he went back to way he had come instead of on to the next house."

"What do you do when no one is coming or going?"

"I check the security cameras that are around the property."

"Where are the cameras placed?"

"There is one here, three on different sides of the wall and two on the entrances, one on the front door and one on the kitchen door."

"Can you play back what happened at a certain time of day?"

"Yeah." Marshall stepped into the booth; Emily followed him. Marshall typed something into the computer. The front door appeared on one screen and the kitchen door appeared on the other.

"When?" Marshall asked.

"Ten o'clock on the day Pascal disappeared," Emily answered. Marshall typed something in but the picture didn't change. Marshall pushed a button. Nothing happened for a few minutes, then Martha came out and was moving a lot faster than normal speed when she disappeared out of view of the camera.

"Martha going to the greenhouse," Marshall said. A few minutes passed, then Kent, carrying Pascal, stepped out, looked around and headed for his car. Kent opened the trunk and dumped Pascal in the trunk. After closing the lid Kent climbed up to the balcony and out of sight.

"The bastard," Marshall started to rise. Emily put a hand firmly down on his shoulder.

"Beating the crap out of him might make you feel better, but it will not help find Pascal," Emily said.

"Then what do you suggest? Following him in hopes he will lead us to the place where Pascal is," Marshall asked.

"How long have you worked here?" Emily asked.

"A year," Marshall answered.

"What was your first impression of Kent?"

"I didn't like him."

"Do you live here?"

"Yes, I have a room on the other side of the kitchen from Martha and Martin's room."

"Do you enjoy it here?"

"Yes."

"Then you stay here and keep watch, and I'll go deal with Kent," Emily turned to leave.

"You sure you don't need any help?"

"I'll be fine. You need to stay out of trouble so that you can keep your job." Emily left the booth. Marshall pressed the button to open the gates and Emily went back into the courtyard. Going back inside, Emily stopped in the sitting room. Claire was sitting in one of the chairs staring at the picture over the fireplace. Emily entered the room and sat down on the couch. Claire turned her attention to Emily.

"I've figure out how and by whom your husband was kidnapped," Emily said, "But why and where I don't know."

"Pascal never gave anyone any reason to do this," Claire said.

"I think the why might have something to do with the business," Emily said.

"Nothing that the business involves would upset anyone," Claire said.

"You and your husband fund many different organizations. Someone would probably like to control that. That money could go to fund things that would not be good."

"No one can control it except me or Pascal."

"I would have to say someone tried and failed."

"How?"

"Kent. According to the ghost, Pascal was forced into hiring Kent, Recently Kent didn't like one of the organizations you are funding."

"What organization?"

"Something with the name Livia."

"Livia's charity fund. I don't know why anyone would have a problem with that."

"My suggestion, and what I was going to do next, would be asking Kent," Emily stood up.

"I will accompany you, I want to hear his answers," Claire stood up as well. They left the room and started for the office.

"You don't seem surprised that Kent is involved."

"I never liked him and I never understood why Pascal hired him."

When they arrived Kent's desk was empty.

"Where could he have gone?" Claire asked.

"The bathroom?" Emily suggested sitting down in Kent's chair, "What exactly does Livia's charity fund do?"

"I do not know. Pascal was the one who suggested it. We went over some things but that was not anything we discussed."

"I prefer to know where my money is going to."

"He knew and he thought it was a good cause."

A door opened and closed down the hallway and Kent walked towards them. Emily got up and moved to the front of the desk.

"May I help you?" Kent asked.

"We're back to ask you a few more questions," Emily answered.

"I'm working today, I cannot spare any more time to answer questions."

"I am working as well, and unlike you, I cannot do this another time," Emily said.

"I have told you everything," Kent said sitting down.

"I don't think you did because you didn't say anything about drugging Pascal or dumping him into the trunk of your car."

Kent went pale. Emily went around behind him.

"What? I never did any of that. Why would I do that to a man who pays me?"

"Because you are working for Pascal on someone else's orders."

"You are throwing out false accusations!"

"I had to stop Marshall from coming in here and beating your brains out after we saw the security tape of you carrying an unconscious Pascal from the kitchen door to your car and dumping him in your trunk. Who do you really work for?"

Kent didn't answer. Emily took out her knife.

"If you don't answer me, I will skin you alive."

Claire stood in front of the desk, anger on her face and no sign of shock at Emily's suggestion.

"That is illegal," Kent said.

"I was never much on bothering with the law and my job does not require it."

Kent gulped.

"So why don't you just answer my questions?" Emily placed the blade of the knife against Kent's throat. "Who do you work for?"

"George Schultz."

"Why does he have you placed here?"

"To make sure Pascal wasn't funding anything that Mr. Schultz doesn't like."

"What is it about Livia's charity fund that Schultz does not like it?"

"It is set up by the person who is the leader of the group that is trying to get rid of Mr. Schultz."

"Where is Pascal?"

"In a warehouse in town."

"Why kidnap him?"

"I couldn't change his mind, so Mr. Schultz said to take him to a warehouse where they would change his mind."

"Where exactly is this warehouse?"

"In town."

"Where in town? Preferably an exact street address."

"I don't know the exact address, but it was the middle warehouse on Eagle Street."

"That area is full of warehouses. The middle one doesn't tell me much. I need you to be specific."

"I was never told any specifics. I picked up someone who gave me directions."

"Which street did you turn off of on to Eagle Street?"

"Crest."

"Which side was it on?"

"The right.

"Do you have any wire?" Emily asked Claire.

"There should be some in the garage. I'll go check," Claire said then left.

"Get up very slowly and don't make any sudden moves," Emily instructed Kent, moving the knife away enough that Kent could move. Kent slowly stood up. With her other hand Emily pulled both arms behind his back. Putting the knife away, Emily forced him to lie on his stomach on the floor, with Emily still holding his hands behind his back. Claire came back with the wire a few minutes later. She handed it to Emily who started tying Kent's hands.

"I know it will be dangerous, but I want to go with you," Claire said.

"We will be using Kent's car. Can you see if you can find the keys?" Emily asked. Claire started going through the desk. Emily finished tying Kent's hands and stood up. Claire pulled a set of keys out of the drawer.

"I found them," Claire said.

"Good, then we should go," Emily said.

"I will talk to Martin. I'll only be two minutes," Claire handed Emily the keys and went off.

"Why are you doing this?" Kent asked.

"It is my job," Emily answered.

"What kind of job involves this?"

"I'm an agent for one of the organizations Pascal helps fund. I'm also not on friendly terms with Schultz. Something to do with him wanting me dead."

"I amazed he hasn't succeed yet."

"The first two guys were more interested in the information I had than killing me and Nolan was just sloppy."

"Nolan failed?"

"I'm here, aren't I?"

"He never fails."

Claire came back.

"I am ready now," Claire said.

"Then let's go," Emily said pulling Kent to his feet. They went out the kitchen door. Getting to Kent's car Emily opened the trunk and had him climb in. She closed the trunk. Emily handed Claire the keys and then got into the passenger seat. Claire got in and started the car. They drove to the gate. Marshall opened the gate and let them through. Claire drove to the section of town that the warehouses were located. She found Eagle Street and parked.

"Which one do you think it is?" Claire asked.

"I'm not sure, but we can ask Kent," Emily said getting out of the car. Claire followed. They went around to the back of the car. Claire opened the trunk and Emily pulled Kent out.

"Which one?" Emily asked.

"That one," Kent nodded to one in the middle.

"Okay," Emily grabbed a rag that was in the trunk and gagged Kent with it. Claire closed the trunk and all three headed for the warehouse Kent had pointed out. Getting there, Emily directed them around to the side entrance. It was unlocked and opened when the knob turned. Kent was pushed in first, then Emily entered and Claire followed. They entered the main warehouse. There were crates stacked everywhere. It was difficult to see very far and it looked like a maze.

"Stay here and make sure Kent doesn't go anywhere," Emily told Claire.

"Okay," Claire said. Emily climbed the sturdiest looking stack. The maze of crates went from one side of the warehouse to the other. There were steps that went to a walkway that wrapped around the upper half of the warehouse. At one point, the walkway went passed a door that looked like it led to an office. Emily climbed down.

"This way," Emily said pushing Kent in the direction she wanted. Claire followed. It took Emily a few minutes to find the stairs. Emily pushed Kent up the stairs ahead of her and Claire followed behind Emily. They walked along the walkway without seeing anybody. When they arrived at the door, Emily tried the knob. The door was locked. Emily braced herself against the railing and kicked the door. There was a loud crack but the door didn't move. Emily kicked it again. This time the door broke and swung inward. They could see inside the office. There was a desk on one side; the door blocked the view of the other, and Pascal was sitting tied to a chair in the middle. He looked like he had been roughed up but was alive. Claire started to enter the office. Emily grabbed her arm before she moved very far. Claire turned to Emily. Emily shook her head. Claire moved back to where she had been standing and Emily let go of her arm. Emily grabbed Kent and pushed him into the room. Nothing happened for a moment, then Kent moved farther into the room as if instructed to by an unseen signal.

At the first gunshot Emily grabbed Claire and pulled her down so that both were on the ground. Bullets ripped through the wall where they had just been standing. The bullets continued for what seem to Emily and Claire as an eternity. Finally the shooting stopped. Emily waited a moment before raising her head but no more seemed to be coming. A man came into sight, heading toward Kent. Emily stood up. Some debris fell to the floor causing the man to turn towards her. He pulled a handgun out of his pocket and levelled it at Emily. Emily carefully stepped into the office.

"You don't want to shoot me," Emily said as she continued toward him.

"Why not?" the man asked.

"Because if you did, your gun would be loaded," Emily said. The man went to check his gun. Emily grabbed his wrist and then hit him hard with her knee. The gun fell to the floor and the man collapsed. Emily kicked the gun away from him.

Claire came into the office and immediately went over to Pascal. She made sure he was all right and untied him. Once Pascal was untied and moved out of the chair Emily shoved the man into it. She forced Kent to sit behind the chair and using the rope tied them both in place.

"Shall we go?" Emily asked looking around.

"Yes," Claire said. She was supporting Pascal. Emily carefully took the other side and they left the office.

"Was his gun really empty?" Pascal's dry voice asked as they went along the walkway.

"I hope so," Emily answered, "Otherwise I might have been in actual danger of being shot." Pascal's laughter turned to a coughing fit, making them stop so he could rest.

"George Schultz visited briefly to find out what was taking so long," Pascal said as they continued, "When Kent phoned to say that you were on the case, he went red and then purple. I thought he might die but I knew I would be safe soon and here you are."

"Schultz doesn't seem like the type of person to anger easily," Emily commented.

"I don't know what you did, but you have become a pain in his ass," Pascal said with a smile, "You should get in contact with Livia. You two would get along great."

"Let's get out of here and you to a doctor first," Emily said as they went around the crates to the door they came in.

"Going home sounds wonderful. A doctor can be called from there," Pascal said. They reached the door and exited the warehouse. They went over to Kent's car. Pascal gently lay down in the backseat, while Emily drove and Claire sat in the passenger seat. Emily drove back to the mansion. When they arrived, Marshall let them in as soon as he saw who they were. Entering the courtyard, Emily parked next to the curb in front of the door. Martin came to assist as they were getting out. He and Claire helped Pascal up the steps and into the house. Emily followed. They went to the master bedroom where Pascal was placed on the bed. Martin went to phone the doctor.

"Thank you, Emily," Pascal said.

"You're welcome," Emily replied.

"How can you be contacted if we need you again?" Claire asked.

"Leave a message with Warner or Alfred. It will reach me at some point," Emily answered, "If you don't mind, I'll deal with Kent's car."

"Go ahead," Pascal said. Emily left the room. She went down and out the front door. Getting into Kent's car, Emily left the property and headed for her next destination.

Travis and Alfred were talking in Alfred's office when a knock came at the door and Warner entered.

"How is the mission I sent over this morning going?" Warner asked.

"We haven't received word back on any of the agents that are currently out," Travis answered.

"I asked to get updates on that particular mission due to its importance," Warner said.

"We should get word back from Emily anytime on how her search for Pascal is going," Alfred said.

"You sent Emily on this mission?" Warner questioned, "I told you to give her an easy one."

"I didn't have anything else to give her and I didn't have any other agents who were ready to go," Alfred replied.

"If you are expecting to hear back from her, you're wasting your time. Everybody knows how she is at following rules," Warner said.

"Actually, until a little while ago, we were tracking her by the watch she was given," Travis said.

"What happened a little while ago?" Warner asked.

"We lost the signal. We should be able to pick it back up soon," Travis said.

"I hope you do because this mission must be done with no casualties on our side," Warner said before turning around and leaving the room.

"Do you think you will pick up the signal again?" Alfred asked.

"No, but I think the mission might be finished, so there is no need for it," Travis said.

"If it isn't?"

"There could be a problem."

Warner arrived back at his office twenty minutes later. He stopped at his secretary's desk.

"Any messages?" he asked.

"A lady came in wanting to talk to you. She is waiting in your office," the secretary told him.

"Okay," Warner went into his office. He found Emily sitting in his chair.

"Good afternoon," Emily greeted him.

"Aren't you supposed to be on a mission?" Warner asked.

"Done," Emily answered, "Pascal is lying in his own bed with Claire sitting beside him and a doctor is coming to check on him."

"Sounds like it is all wrapped up," Warner said.

"With a nice little bow on top. And I didn't get a scratch. Well, except for the paper cut I got looking through the mission file," Emily said, "But that's healing fast. The lack of serious injuries, despite the bullets and debris, is the reason I stopped here before going back to the department."

"Very thoughtful," Warner said.

"And to give you a warning," Emily said.

"I suspected as much," Warner said.

"If I am not working as an agent for the department, I'm not working for the department at all," Emily said, "I have other things I could be doing."

"Then why are you still with the department?" Warner asked.

"Why should it matter to you? I am still here, are I?" Emily stood up.

"I would like to know if I'm going to have an agent desert," Warner said.

"I'll let you know when I'm leaving for good," Emily said then left the office. As the door closed behind her, Warner sat down in his chair.

"Some days I wonder who is really in control," Warner muttered.

George Schultz sat behind his desk as a king sits on a throne. Kent and Steven stood in front of Mr.

Schultz like peasants waiting to be executed. Mr. Schultz sat, pondering the story that he had just heard. The inevitable seemed to hang in the air waiting to be presented.

"Gentlemen," Mr. Schultz finally addressing the two men, "The situation seems to be ripped from your control. You have failed, but I will not punish you for what you could not control. Leave and wait for further orders."

The men left the office. Nolan started to follow.

"I have other work for you," Schultz told Nolan. Nolan stopped and turned towards Schultz.

"I want you to kill Emily. This time I want you to bring back proof that she is dead."

Nolan nodded and left.

CHAPTER 7
HEAD ON

"How did the mission go?" Grace asked as she put the scanner into the slot in the computer.

"There were no serious problems," Emily answered.

"Then why does Travis want to know the results of this scan?" Grace asked.

"Because Warner was getting on Alfred's case about my record," Emily answered.

"Well, the scan says you're fine, so either you are messing with the results or there is nothing wrong with you," Grace said.

"I'm hoping for the second," Emily said.

"You didn't have time to do the first," Grace said.

"How's Bethany?" Emily asked.

"Since the last time you checked on her?"

"Yeah."

"That baby is hanging on and not letting go. By medical standards I'm surprised there hasn't been a miscarriage yet."

"I wonder."

"You wonder what?"

"Many things, but at this time of night I should be asleep," Emily stood up.

"Good night," Grace said.

"Good night," Emily left the medical lab and headed for her room. When she got there she went to bed.

Emily got up, showered, dressed and was tidying her room when there came a knock at the door. Emily pressed the button and the door opened. Daniel stood there.

"Come in," Emily invited him.

"You aren't busy?" Daniel asked.

"Not right now," Emily answered, "What are you doing here?"

"I'm finished what I was doing. Now I have to decide where I'm going from here. I decided to visit you for a while so I could think," Daniel said, "And we didn't really get to know each other on my last visit."

"Well then, welcome to department H. This slightly organized mess is my living space," Emily said. Daniel looked around.

"You don't spend much time here, do you?" Daniel asked.

"I sleep here and spend time here when I'm not busy with something else, which is maybe once a week."

"You can't be working the rest of the time. They won't even let scientists work that amount of time."

"I spend time on missions, personal projects, and the medical lab. And lately quite a bit of time with Trent."

"Who is Trent?"

"A bar owner that I've made friends with and he takes care of Adriana for me. The thought had occurred to me to visit Trent today."

"What would you do on a normal day?"

"It would depend on the day. Some days I help Dr. Grace in the medical lab, other days I sit and work in the assignment lab. Occasionally I go to Trent's place. Today I thought I would check with Grace and then if she didn't need my help, I would go to Trent's. You can join me but if I get stuck in the medical lab, it might get boring."

"I can handle boredom."

Emily grabbed her wallet and her jacket before she and Daniel stepped into the hallway. After Emily closed and locked her door, they headed for the medical lab.

"Where have you been?" Grace asked when they entered.

"In my room. Why?" Emily answered.

"Cynthia was looking for you," Grace said.

"I'll find her soon. Daniel, this is Dr. Grace. Grace, this is my son Daniel," Emily introduced them.

"Hello," Daniel said.

"Nice to meet you," Grace said.

"What is with Jerry?" Emily asked pointing to the guy on the examining table. Jerry was semi-conscious, muttering to himself and was squirming as if in pain.

"I'm not sure. His whole crew has it," Grace said, "But I've never seen anything like it."

"Need help?" Emily asked.

"They are all being sent to the hospital. I'm just supposed to make sure they survive until transport arrives," Grace said.

"That should be easier with them flat on their backs," Emily said.

"I moved Bethany to your office while they are here," Grace said.

"That's fine. I'm going to Trent's," Emily said, "I will find Cynthia on my way out."

"See you when you get back," Grace said. Emily and Daniel left the medical lab.

"Does that happen all the time?" Daniel asked.

"Which?"

"Unknown illnesses."

"It is a rarity but seems to have become a recent trend."

"That doesn't sound good."

"When you are dealing with human systems there will always be something you don't know out there. Doctors just try to keep pace."

They arrived at Cynthia's desk. Cynthia looked up at them.

"I was told you were looking for me," Emily said.

"I was," Cynthia replied, "I tried to talk to Brett. The department he is working for said that he is currently missing."

"I thought he was working here," Emily said.

"He finished that mission and the other department asked for him back," Cynthia said, "He didn't even stop in and say goodbye. Just went back. Now they can't find him."

"Hopefully he'll turn up soon," Emily said.

"Yeah," Cynthia replied. Daniel and Emily headed for the exit.

"So we are headed for a bar?" Daniel asked once they left the building.

"No, we are headed for Trent's house, and we hope that he is up," Emily said.

"Do you visit him often?"

"I go weekly, or have been. My schedule may change."

"Is he like your boyfriend?"

"He is a good friend. I usually go there to see Adriana. Adriana is a two-year-old I adopted."

"So I have a little sister."

"Yes."

"Strange, for the longest time I thought I didn't have any family."

"At this point, you probably have grandparents out there but I don't know whether they are still alive or not."

"Close family."

"When you become an agent, you are supposed to leave everything behind. You are not supposed to have a personal life. I tried it that way but I found a way out."

"How can you not have a personal life? Even scientists are allowed families."

"There are differences in the departments, but the system is screwed up. The again, some days I'm sure the world is screwed up."

"My world has mostly been department C. I've never really paid much attention to anything else."

"Department H is trying for that but agents need to know what is going on in the world to be able to do their jobs properly."

"One of my choices is to become an agent."

"My advice is to take a different option. Being an agent isn't a good career choice. I made that choice and now I wish I hadn't."

"Why don't you leave?"

"They don't actually give you that option but I'm trying." Emily started up a driveway to a freshly painted house. "This is Trent's house."

Daniel and Emily went to the door. Emily knocked before opening the door and stepping inside. Daniel followed her. A small head poked around the doorway to the kitchen.

"Mom!" Adriana came flying down the hallway. Emily bent down and picked her up.

"Hello, Adriana," Emily hugged her, "This is Daniel." Emily pointed to Daniel.

"Hello," Daniel said smiling. Adriana smiled back.

"Where's Trent?" Emily asked Adriana.

"At this time of the morning I should be in bed," Trent answered stepping into view.

"Sorry to wake you," Emily put Adriana down. Adriana went into the living room.

"You usually don't show up until afternoon," Trent said.

"I started cleaning my room and decided to get out of there," Emily said, "And I wanted to introduce you to my son Daniel."

"Nice to meet you, Daniel," Trent said holding out his hand. Daniel shook his hand.

"Nice to meet you, too," Daniel said. Adriana came out of the living room holding two dolls. She handed one to Daniel.

"Play with me," Adriana said to Daniel and went back into the living room. Daniel followed her.

"She is going to be scary when she grows up," Trent commented, "What are you really here for?"

Emily and Trent went into the kitchen.

"Well, part of it was seeing Adriana. I also would like to talk to Alex," Emily said.

"And you brought him along?"

"He came to visit me and I couldn't just turn him away because I had my own agenda. Besides it gave me a good opportunity to introduce him to Adriana."

"You must have had him when you were pretty young."

"No, just someone messing with a time machine. He was born in the twenty-first century and got lost on the way back."

"If anyone else told me that I wouldn't believe it."

"I don't expect anyone to believe it."

"Alex will probably stop by the bar tomorrow. You can talk to him then."

"Okay. You going back to bed?"

"No, now that I'm up I might as well start my day. Probably won't get any more sleep anyways."

"Sorry."

"You will never sound sincere saying that word."

"Don't you have to start your day? Or are you going to wear the same jeans you slept in?"

"I'm getting there," Trent kissed her and then headed for his bedroom. Emily went into the living room.

Emily spent the day with Adriana and Daniel. That night Emily let Daniel have the guestroom and she went to sleep on the couch.

Emily woke up to the sound of the door opening and closing. She sat up. Trent passed the living room doorway and went into the kitchen. She got up and went to the kitchen.

"Sorry if I woke you," Trent said when he saw her.

"That's okay," Emily said.

"Alex showed up around closing time. I told him you wanted to talk to him. He said he would be at the bar tomorrow afternoon," Trent said.

"Okay."

"Apparently he came in to ask if I had seen you recently because he wanted to talk to you."

"Should I be worried?"

"I doubt it is anything like that."

"Well, I'll see."

"Did you think about what would happen to Adriana if you were killed?"

"A little bit, but I haven't made any decisions. I will soon."

"What about Daniel?"

"He is responsible for himself. If I started making decisions for him now, I would be forfeiting any chance of a friendly relationship with him. But when I make all those decisions, I will include him."

"He seems to enjoy playing with Adriana."

"From what he has said, it sounds like Daniel has never been around small children before. I don't think he would mind looking after her tomorrow."

"You'll have to ask him later. Sleep would be good for tonight."

"Yeah." Trent kissed Emily before going off the bed. Emily turned off the light and went back to lie down on the couch.

When Trent got up, Emily was playing with Adriana in the living room and Daniel was in the kitchen making lunch. Trent sat down at the kitchen table.

"Afternoon," Trent greeted Daniel.

"Good afternoon," Daniel replied.

"I'm surprised you can cook," Trent said, "When I first met Emily she couldn't and she still doesn't cook much."

"I was raised in department C. If you don't learn to cook, you die of food poisoning or something worse. Sometimes I wonder if one of the scientists is in charge of the cafeteria," Daniel said.

"That doesn't sound good."

"That's life. How long have you known Emily?"

"Several months."

"And you willingly took on Adriana in just several months?"

"Several months can seem like a long time when tomorrow can be uncertain."

"Are you and Emily more than just friends?"

"The world has yet to figure that question out yet."

Daniel gave Trent a strange look that reminded Trent of Emily.

"What do you do?" Trent asked.

"I'm a scientist by training but currently I'm at a crossroads. My future could lie in any direction."

"Everyone hits at least one of the those in their life."

"Have you hit one?"

"Yes. I had a choice between marrying the girl next door and working under her father, taking over the family business or moving away and starting a new life."

""And you picked the last one?"

"Yes, it was the only one that I could do without going crazy."

"I can't decide which choice is best or which one I want."

"Do you know all your options?"

"I think so."

"Well, write them out and write out the pros and cons of each. That should narrow down the choices. Or at least tell you what is in your heart."

"Maybe I'll try that." Daniel put the food on the table and then went into the living room to call Emily and Adriana.

After lunch Emily and Trent left Daniel in charge of Adriana and went to the bar. When they got there Emily sat down behind the bar while Trent got ready for opening. Half an hour later Alex came in followed by his usual goons. Alex sat down on one of the barstools.

"Did you check out that Preston missing from where you work?" Alex asked.

"Yes, I even got a picture," Emily pulled a picture out of her pocket and handed it to Alex.

"That's him," Alex said handing the picture back, "He, unfortunately, had a little accident. But, what else would be expected if he was caught skimming profits?"

"I'll inform someone that if they want the body, they should check the city morgue," Emily said.

"And I found out some information about Mr. Schultz but I don't know if it would interest you," Alex said.

"Tell me and I'll decide whether or not I'm interested," Emily replied.

"Nolan and Delilah are Schultz's step-children," Alex said, "There is some question about whether or not he is married to their mother. Schultz is also doing most of his schemes on her money. She is either on drugs or not all there; I'm told she is rarely seen and when she is she seems to be in her own world."

"That's it?" Emily asked.

"Yes," Alex answered

"It is interesting information, though not all of it is news," Emily said.

"Just telling you what I've heard," Alex shrugged.

"And I thank you," Emily said, "It might be helpful."

"Trent said you wanted to talk to me," Alex said.

"Yes, I need a favour," Emily replied.

"What kind of favour?" Alex asked.

"I need blood from someone who is dead," Emily answered, "The morgue keeps samples of blood from people who have died in the last two years. That should be good enough."

"Do you want any dead person's blood or is there someone specific?" Alex asked.

"Tyler," Emily answered, "as in the former bartender for this place."

"Why?" Alex asked.

"Why not?" Emily said.

"Because it is freaky to want blood, especially the blood of a dead person," Alex answered.

"I want to examine it," Emily answered.

"Why not go through official channels?" Alex asked, "You are a doctor."

"Because they ask too many questions and they take too long or they don't give it to me," Emily answered, "Will you get it for me?"

"What do I get out of it?"

"What do you want?"

"Preston skimmed profits; I would like that money back."

"How much?"

"About a thousand dollars."

"That's it?"

"Yes."

"Fine with me. You'll get the money when I get the blood sample. And if it isn't from Tyler I will take the thousand back out of your flesh."

"I do have honour."

"I hope so."

"You will have to give me a few days to get it."

"Fine."

"Anything else?"

"Not that I know of."

"Then I'll be going." Alex got up and left followed by his goons.

"Why do you want a sample of Tyler's blood?" Trent asked.

"I want to examine it to prove or disprove a theory I have," Emily answered.

"How will examining Tyler's blood do that?" Trent asked.

"I'm going to examine several samples of blood," Emily answered.

"Okay," Trent said.

"I'm going back to the house," Emily said. "See you later."

Emily kissed Trent and then left the bar. She started toward Trent's house but before she got very far she turned down a street that went a different direction. Emily walked for about ten minutes before stopping outside a boarded up store. She stared at it for a few minutes. It looked like no one had gone near it in years. She went around back. Using a key she pulled out of her pocket Emily unlocked the door. She put the key away before turning the knob. The knob turned. The door did not move. Pushing on it made it move inward a little bit. Emily shoved the door. The door opened enough for her to enter the store. Holes in the ceiling let enough light in that Emily could see a little bit. She carefully walked through the rooms filled with debris. She uncovered a metal lockbox in the back corner of the front room. .

"Good," Emily said as she placed the debris back on top of it. Wiping her hands off on her pants, Emily went back the way she came. Leaving the store, she pulled the door closed and locked it. Getting back to the street, she headed to Trent's house.

When she got to Trent's, she found Adriana playing in the front yard, while Daniel sat on the steps talking to a girl Emily didn't recognize. Emily walked up the steps and passed them. They were so absorbed in their conversation that they didn't notice her. Emily went into the house. She went to the telephone, picked up the receiver and dialed a phone number. After two rings, it was picked up and the voice was a familiar one.

"Hello?"

"Hello, it's Emily," Emily said.

"What have you been doing that you haven't called?" Lara asked.

"I have been very busy," Emily said, "I called to ask if you wouldn't mind a few visitors."

"Maybe tomorrow. Your father is not feeling well today," Lara said, "How many visitors?"

"Including me, two or three," Emily answered.

"That should be okay. Why don't you come for lunch tomorrow?" Lara suggested.

"That's fine," Emily said, "See you then."

"Good bye."

Emily hung up the telephone. She went back outside. The girl was gone, but Daniel was still sitting on the steps. Emily sat down.

"Your grandparents are still alive," Emily said.

"That is good news," Daniel said.

"We're invited for lunch tomorrow," Emily said.

"Don't you have to go back soon?" Daniel asked.

"Probably, but I'm waiting for something that will take a few days, so I'm not in any hurry."

"What are you waiting for?"

"A blood sample. I have a theory about something and I need blood samples from certain people to confirm it."

"What kind of theory?"

"It is fairly complicated."

"We seem to have time on our hands."

"There is a guy out there who is killing people. It isn't random. He kills whomever gets between him and his evil schemes."

"So there is a guy who is evil and is killing people. How does that require blood samples?"

"He has someone, I'm still trying to figure out who, trying to stop him. That is the simple part. At least two people, who are against this guy, have gotten sick, but the illness is unknown and undetectable after the initial symptoms. One man who was against the evil guy has a girlfriend, who is currently seven months pregnant. The girlfriend has been emotionally unstable since his death. Usually that would have an adverse effect on the pregnancy, like a miscarriage, but hasn't."

"So, you have an unknown illness and a pregnant lady."

"I don't know whether the guy who has the kid ever had the illness but because he was on this evil guy's to die list I think he did have the illness at some point. I think the effects of the illness is the reason the baby has survived."

"You found an 'illness' that changes a person's immune system to help them survive medical situations that would kill them? I'm still confused. What would that have to do with the evil guy? And why do you need the blood samples?"

"I need the blood samples so that I can see not only whether the baby's father had the illness but to see what all it effects. Which means, I need six blood samples. Two from people who had the illness, one from the baby's father and three from people who never had the illness."

"I'm still confused."

"Maybe it is better that way."

"Why?"

"Because I'm on the evil guy's to die list and the less you know, the more likely you won't end up on his radar."

"Why does he want to kill you?"

"I know too much."

"He wants to kill you for knowing too much so you are purposely searching for information?"

"Beats sitting around waiting to die."

"I'm willing to help if you need it."

"So are many people. I've told Grace to back off. Trent I've dragged in too far. And Alex deserves whatever he gets. I'm not sure I want one more person that could get killed helping me. I've already told you more than I should have."

"People make their own choices and you may need the help. You're deciding all this without talking to them. Trent doesn't seem to mind being dragged in, and Grace probably wouldn't mind knowing what is wrong. I'm willing to take the risk to help you."

"It is better for you to decide where you are headed and go that way than help me. With what I'm doing now, I don't need much help."

"I'll provide one of the other blood samples you need, though if the illness is unknown, I don't know whether I had it or not."

"Have you touched something like a piece of paper and within minutes felt like you have the flu and hallucinations?"

"No."

"Then you probably never had it. The blood sample I will accept."

"How do you know so much about the illness if it is unknown?"

"I opened a letter and shortly after got sick, but when Grace did the tests, nothing came up. My blood is one of the samples I will be examining."

"Is the illness from the evil guy?"

"I don't think so, but when I examine the sample, that will be on my mind."

"Why would someone who is not against you make you sick?"

"I'm not sure. Everything I've found out so far has just brought more questions than answers."

"I've decided what I would like to do, as to the direction of my future."

"What direction?"

"One they didn't offer me. I want to stay here, if Trent will let me, and learn about the world that I was shut off from in department C."

"I'm sure Trent wouldn't mind."

"I'll talk to him tomorrow."

Emily was quiet. Daniel glanced at her. Emily was staring straight ahead, focused on something that wasn't present.

"Trent seems like a good guy," Daniel commented.

"I know," Emily replied, still lost in thought.

"I should go start supper," Daniel got up and went into the house. Emily didn't move.

"Mom," Adriana interrupted Emily's thoughts. Emily looked down at her and smiled.

"What?" Emily asked.

"Look," Adriana said holding up a shiny rock.

"That is pretty," Emily said. Adriana smiled before going to playing with the pile of rocks. Emily watched Adriana play until Daniel called them in for supper.

That night Emily laid down on the couch to sleep but found she couldn't. She lay there trying to sleep until Trent came in. Trent was sitting at the table with a bottle of beer in front of him when Emily came into the kitchen. She sat down across the table from him. Trent reached into the bag at his feet, pulled out a beer and handed it to Emily. Emily opened it and took a sip.

"You don't look like you have gotten to sleep yet," Trent said.

"I haven't. For some reason I can't sleep," Emily said.

"It happens to everyone once in a while."

"Yeah."

"How was the rest of your day?"

"I talked to Daniel, and spent time with Adriana."

"Sounds like it was quiet."

"Quiet is nice."

"For now. If it was quiet for too long, you would be out causing trouble."

"I'm in enough trouble for right now, the quiet is nice."

"You'll survive whatever it is. You are a survivor, if you weren't I don't think I would've had a chance to meet you."

"We'll see how survivor does against a well-trained assassin and his evil boss."

"That sounds like a plot for a book."

"Probably is."

"Then we just have to wait for the happily ever after."

"I think it will be a while before we hit that." Emily finished her beer. Trent took the bottles and put them in the cupboard under the sink. Emily stood up and Trent pulled her to him.

"Some days happily ever after just means you lived through another day," Trent said. Emily kissed him.

Emily lay there, still unable to sleep. She could hear Trent snoring softly beside her. After a while Emily got up and dressed. Quietly she left the bedroom. The other two doors were open. Emily paused in each doorway. Daniel looked like he had flopped down on the bed and passed out. Adriana was curled up around her teddy bear. Emily went to the living room. She paced a little and sat down only to get up and pace a little more. The sky was starting to lighten when Emily finally laid down, this time she went to sleep.

Emily found herself on a twenty-first century street that was completely empty of people. She recognized the buildings as one of the main streets.

"Why don't you have a seat? You look tired," A female voice asked from behind her. Emily turned around. She recognized the woman as the one she had talked to while resting on the same bench when she was looking for Daniel. Emily went over and sat down on the bench that had just appeared across from the one the woman was sitting on.

"Sorry to keep you up for most of the night but many people wake up from my dreams if they aren't tired enough," the lady said.

"Unless you are part of my subconscious, which I doubt, how did you get into my head?" Emily asked.

"I've found this is the best way to talk to people without George discovering, so I figured out a way to do it."

"And you're?"

"George's enemy; the one you have been looking for."

"Actually I was looking for a name, not a description but that tells me your name is Livia."

"Pascal said you were intelligent."

"And you want my help dealing with George Schultz."

"Most people don't believe half of what I tell them and you have already figured out some of this stuff for yourself."

"I've figured out a few things and I have a question."

"Ask."

"Why would George Schultz's wife be his enemy and try to get people to help her stop him?"

"You figured that out too."

"A minute ago you referred to him as George instead of George Schultz, Schultz or Mr. Schultz."

"I never thought of that. What else have you figured out?"

"You didn't want me dead, so you requested to Nolan that he not succeed at his assassination attempt."

"I only wish that I could have done more."

"He didn't do as much damage as he hoped to."

"But he did put you out of commission for a month."

"That month gave me time to think."

"I decided that now was a good time to ask if you are willing to help me or whether you will continue alone."

"Maybe you should have asked months ago, like shortly after I was attacked the first time for knowing too much."

"I had other things to do at the time and I didn't think you would be around that long."

"Schultz didn't think I would be around long either. Since you both have underestimated me, I think I will continue on alone."

"Some things cannot be done alone."

"I'm willing to help you to a certain extent, but only on the condition that you tell me the whole story. Other than that, I can find my own help."

"I will tell you the whole story, but not tonight. Tonight was just for asking for your help. I need to go

and you need some sleep." The street and Livia dissolved.

"Mom," Adriana's voiced called in Emily's ear. Emily opened her eyes. Adriana was standing beside the couch in her pyjamas.

"What do you need?" Emily asked sitting up.

"Breakfast," Adriana answered. Emily could hear Daniel in the kitchen. Adriana grabbed Emily's hand. Emily got up and followed Adriana into the kitchen. Adriana let go of Emily's hand and climbed onto a chair.

"Would you like something to eat?" Daniel asked.

"No, I have to go out. I'll be back before lunch," Emily said.

"Okay," Daniel said.

"Mom," Adriana cried when she saw Emily leaving. Emily came back to squat next to the chair Adriana was sitting on.

"I'll be back soon," Emily told Adriana, "In the meantime, Daniel will cook you breakfast. Okay?"

Adriana nodded. Emily smiled at her then got up and left the kitchen.

Trent got up, dressed and then went out into the living room. Daniel was sitting on a chair reading a book.

"Where's Emily?" Trent asked.

"I don't know," Daniel answered, "After Adriana woke her, she said she had somewhere to go and she would be back before noon."

"Okay," Trent said.

"She should be back soon," Daniel said.

"I was just wondering," Trent said.

"I thought over my options and I was wondering if it was okay if I stayed here for a while," Daniel said.

"Fine with me," Trent said. The front door opened and Emily stepped inside.

"Good morning," Emily said when she saw Trent.

"Morning," Trent replied. Emily handed Trent a business card. He looked at it for a moment and then put it in his pocket.

"Where's Adriana?" Emily asked.

"In her room searching for one of her dolls," Daniel answered.

"Should find her," Emily said starting down the hall.

"Going out for lunch?" Trent asked.

"Yes," Emily answered, then entered Adriana's room. Emily came out a moment later carrying Adriana, who was clinging to her teddy bear. Daniel got up and put his shoes on.

"We're going to visit my parents," Emily said, "Want to come?"

"No, thanks," Trent replied, "I'll see you later.

Emily, Daniel and Adriana left the house. Emily held Adriana's hand and led the way.

"Trent said I could stay there," Daniel said.

"That's good. The world holds many different things to discover, but they may not let you back if you leave," Emily said.

"I'm willing to take that chance," Daniel said, "Where did you go this morning?"

"I went to visit a lawyer to complete my will," Emily said, "The card I gave Trent has the information he needs if I die."

"You talk like this guy trying to kill you as if it is nothing, yet completing your will sounds like you are worried that he might succeed."

"Since I started training to become an agent the possibility of getting killed has always been there. I've learned not to let it bug me. When I adopted Adriana, Trent suggested that I complete my will so that Adriana will be taken care of if I die."

"That makes sense. When are you dealing with the blood samples?"

"In a few days. I have to wait until I get one of the samples."

"Why do you have to wait?"

"Because the unusual channel through which I am obtaining it, has to have time to get it. If I went through the usual channels, I would have to wait a couple of weeks anyway. A couple of days isn't going to do any harm, but it means that I'm not waiting back at the department."

"So that's all you are waiting for before going back?"

"The idea of a short vacation from the department sounded good as well." Emily stopped in front of a house in a suburbia neighbourhood. "Here we are."

Daniel followed Emily up the walk. The door opened just as they reached the steps. A woman stood there. She seemed too young for the silver that streaked through her otherwise brown hair.

"Hello," the woman greeted them.

"Hello, Lara," Emily said, "This is my son, Daniel, and my daughter, Adriana."

"Hello," Daniel said.

"Nice to meet you," Lara said. She moved so that they could enter. "Lunch is just about ready."

Lara headed for the kitchen. Emily and Daniel took off their shoes and jackets. Adriana followed their example. Emily led the way into the living room.

"Your mother told me we were having guests, but seems to have a memory problem, because she never told me who," the man sitting in the chair said, looking up from the book he was reading.

"How are you doing?" Emily asked as she sat down. Adriana climbed onto her lap and Daniel sat down in a chair beside the door.

"As good as I ever was," Pasha answered.

"Lara said you weren't feeling well yesterday," Emily said.

"That's nonsense, I'm fine," Pasha said.

"As in no doctor has said that there is something wrong with you, or as in you won't go to a doctor because he might say there is something wrong with you?" Emily asked.

"And you are?" Pasha turned to Daniel.

"Daniel," Daniel answered.

"Must be a relative. You look like splitting image of my grandfather, and I'm pretty sure that he is dead," Pasha said.

"Daniel is your grandson," Emily said.

"Are you sure? Because I know I only had one kid and you are too young to have a sixteen-year-old," Pasha said.

"It is long and complicated story that I'm not sure all the details of," Emily answered.

"Sounds like the first time I met your mother. What do you do with your time?" Pasha asked.

"I'm trained as a scientist," Daniel answered.

"Good profession. Scientists are a much-needed profession. Without them, we would be in the dark ages still," Pasha said.

"I'm not sure it is better now," Emily said.

"So what if it was a scientist that created the nuclear bomb that was used to destroy half the world. The areas are no longer dangerous for human habitation," Pasha said.

"The population went from six billion to eight million," Emily said, "A good portion of those people were just going about their daily lives. Not only that, half the technologies that the scientists created were wiped out."

"World war three did cause some minor set backs," Pasha said.

"Most of those set backs will never be recovered. Most of the advancements are completely new but not necessarily advancements from where the technology level was," Daniel said.

"Maybe it was meant to be that way," Pasha said.

"Lunch is ready," Lara said from the doorway. They all got up and went into the kitchen. Once they were all sitting down, Lara dished lunch up.

"So who are you?" Pasha asked Adriana.

"Adriana," Adriana said.

"That's a nice name. Where did you get it?" Pasha asked.

"Mom gave it to me," Adriana answered.

"I ordered mine from a catalogue," Pasha said, "Do you know what my name is?"

Adriana shook her head.

"Pavel. It was the best name I could find, even if it did cost a little more," Pasha said.

"In copyright or just for the name?" Emily asked.

"I paid by the letter," Pasha said, "So, what do you do?" Pasha turned back to Adriana.

"Play," Adriana answered.

"That must be fun. You should come over and play with me once in a while. Most people who come over want to talk, not play," Pasha said, "After lunch, if you can stay, I'll show you my toys."

Adriana smiled at him.

"What have you been doing?" Lara asked Emily.

"Probably getting to trouble," Pasha said.

"If not on purpose, accidentally," Emily answered.

"That last letter we got was that you were going to go to medical school," Lara said.

"I went through medical school. I am a doctor," Emily replied.

"Good then you know there is nothing wrong because there isn't anything wrong with me," Pasha said.

"My specialty is in pediatrics, not gerontology," Emily replied.

"Ouch," Pasha said.

"Other than that I've been busy," Emily said.

"Are you working in a hospital?" Lara asked.

"No, I'm working for a private organization," Emily answered.

"Your mother works as a nurse at the clinic nearby and I retired so that I could spend my time on my toys," Pasha said.

"You must have filled the basement by now," Emily said.

"I sell a few every now and again or I give them to children at the clinic," Pasha said, "They have a duck I made on display in memory of the little boy I gave it to. They never did figure out what was wrong with him."

"That seems to be a popular trend these days to have something wrong with you that the doctors can't figure out," Emily said.

"I hope it doesn't last long," Lara said.

"I hope so too," Emily said. Lara stacked the dishes.

"Want to see my toys now?" Pasha asked Adriana.

"Yes," Adriana nodded. Pasha got up, followed by Adriana, and Daniel joined them as they headed for the basement. Lara put the dishes on the counter and sat back down at the table.

"The doctor said it might be cardiopulmonarymentia. His memory is worse than ever before, his heart beat is so irregular the doctor is surprised that he hasn't had serious problems associated with it and his lungs are as bad as a life long smoker's. All he seems to have are those toys," Lara said, "I'm scared to leave him alone when I go to work because I'm afraid something might happen. The doctor keeps cutting the amount of time he has left every time Pasha sees him."

"That isn't good," Emily said.

"I'm grateful for those toys, other people have committed suicide because they found they didn't have anything," Lara said.

"He has you as well as those toys," Emily said.

"I know," Lara sighed, "It is good that you could visit."

"The time seemed right," Emily said.

"How can you have two children, on being sixteen, and not wear a wedding ring?"

"Daniel was a combination of a time machine and alcohol. Adriana was a girl that was abandoned at the hospital. I treated and adopted her. There is a guy out there but now is not a good time."

"Don't make him wait too long. Very few people wait forever."

"I don't expect him to wait forever."

"Mom," Adriana came running holding a wooden toy in one hand and her teddy bear in the other, "Look what Pasha gave me."

"Nice," Emily smiled at Adriana. Adriana climbed onto Emily's lap and showed off her new toy.

Daniel came into the kitchen a moment later, looking scared.

"Pasha collapsed into a coughing fit and now he is barely breathing," Daniel said. Emily set Adriana on her feet and headed for the basement. Lara picked up the phone and started to dial. Emily found Pasha lying in the middle of his workshop, gasping for breath. Emily carefully moved him onto his side.

"It was nice to see them before I die," Pasha said.

"You're not dead yet," Emily told him.

"I went to my doctor last week. He said I didn't have much time. I've been dying for years before your mother ever found out," Pasha said.

"Doctors aren't always right," Emily said sitting down next to him. She took his hand and squeezed it.

Five minutes later two paramedics came in. Emily got out of the way so the paramedics could work. They carefully placed Pasha on the stretcher and took him upstairs. Emily followed at a distance. Lara went with the paramedics leaving Emily, Daniel and Adriana behind.

"What a now?" Daniel asked.

"You two go back to Trent's house and I'll go to the hospital," Emily answered. Daniel nodded. Emily made sure the door was locked before they left. They walked in silence back to Trent's house. Once at the house, Adriana and Daniel went inside, Emily headed for the hospital. Half way there Emily sensed someone following her. Checking she spotted Nolan. Emily ignored him and continued.

When she arrived at the hospital, Emily reported in with the reception desk. The receptionist directed

Emily to a room on the second floor. Emily went to the elevator, stepping inside she saw Nolan was waiting near the entrance she had come in. The door closed and Emily pressed the button for the fifth floor. The elevator went up. Reaching the fifth floor, Emily stayed in the elevator. A couple entered. They pressed the button for the main floor. The elevator went back to the main floor. The door opened and the couple left the elevator. Emily looked out and didn't see Nolan. A nurse stepped into the elevator and pressed the button for the second floor. When the elevator stopped Emily and the nurse stepped out. Emily headed for the room the receptionist said. In the room Pasha was lying on the bed hooked up to a machine and Lara was sitting in a chair next to the bed.

"He's asleep," Lara whispered. Emily nodded as she sat down in the chair across the bed from Lara. "The doctor doesn't think he'll survive the week."

They sat in silence. Lara fell asleep in the chair about midnight. Pasha woke up about twelve thirty. He looked around.

"This doesn't look like heaven," he commented.

"You're in the hospital," Emily told him.

"Why are you still here? I thought you had a life elsewhere," Pasha asked.

"I'm waiting for something and Lara needs the support," Emily answered.

"I've been thinking about it a lot lately. I'm not ready to die," Pasha said, "There are still things I have to finish."

"Will any of us leave with everything finished?"

"No, but you always knew that someday you'd die. That is how you have lived your life. That is why people think you're crazy. You aren't scared. I never wanted to die, I'm scared."

Emily reached out and took his hand.

"You aren't dead yet. Doctors have been wrong before, especially when the patient has the will to live."

"I never told you what I did for work. I never told Lara. She never asked, or complained when we didn't have much money. I owe her everything."

"Yeah."

"I worked for a man called Simon Jones. He was a conspiracy theorist. Which means that he collected conspiracies. I helped him figure out what was true and what was not. It was fascinating, but sometimes I felt like I was wasting my talents on a dead end job. I officially retired when he died," Pasha paused. "He didn't pay much and there was no pension, but I got to keep all of his files. When he died, he was looking into a Schultz character. It may sound like a conspiracy theory but I think Schultz killed him." Pasha stopped again. "I have spent the time since his death trying to find the truth. I never told Lara this and she doesn't seem to suspect that I have been doing anything other than making toys. You know the world, you have always been able to tell a lie from the truth. I know you have connections out there. Will you find the truth? Will you finish my search for me?"

Emily didn't respond.

"Please," Pasha said.

"I can look into it," Emily replied.

"Thank you," Pasha said, "Everything I have found is in Jones's files in his office. I don't remember what street it is on, but the name of the business is Jones and Jackson."

"You need to rest," Emily said letting go of his hand, "I'll require your help later."

"I need that answer before I die," Pasha said.

"I'll try," Emily said. Pasha nodded and then drifted off to sleep. Emily sat there until one in the morning then she got up and left. After going down the elevator, Emily went out the front door. Immediately she could sense someone following her. Emily found an address directory and looked up the address for Jones and Jackson. Finding the address Emily headed for the office. The whole way Emily could feel the person still following her. Reaching the office, Emily turned the knob and the door opened. After closing the door, Emily sat down in the chair and turned on the lamp. A moment later, Nolan opened the door and stepped into the office.

"It didn't take much to lure you here," Emily commented, "I would have taken the person out long before they were in a place where it is easy to be taken out."

"I'm only supposed to kill you, not listen to your commentary on how to do my job," Nolan said.

"Then why haven't you killed me yet? You've had a chance. In fact, you've had several," Emily said.

"And you were given a chance to live," Nolan said, "If you have kept to your record, you would be doing Harvey's job right now."

"If I hadn't messed with your plans, I would have a position I don't want. Though Harvey's death probably isn't much of a loss; he was incompetent."

"Schultz can't let you continue being an annoyance," Nolan said.

"If he had a problem with me, he wouldn't send the person who bungled the last time unless he is stupid."

"Everyone makes mistakes; I won't make another one," Nolan took out a gun. Emily didn't move.

"You wouldn't actually kill me. You're programmed not to."

"Yes, it is likely I'd just hit your shoulder but the bullets explode shortly after impact. Even if I don't kill you, I can make you hurt like hell."

"Why try and kill me?"

"Because Schultz told me to."

"If Schultz told you to kill yourself, would you do it?"

"No."

"Why not?"

"That is stupid. He would never tell me that. He needs me."

"What about Devon and Carl? They are assassins too. How many assassins does a man need? How many more mistakes before you are the hunted?"

"He would not kill his own son."

"Is that all you do this for? So that he will love you as a son instead of using you as a minion? You're relying on false hope."

"It is not false hope."

"Is Schultz the one who told you he was your father? Last I heard he might be your stepfather, if your mother is really married to him."

Nolan stared at her.

"You're lying," Nolan said.

"I'm just telling you what I was told."

"What reason would there be for him to lie?"

"Loyalty, obedience, someone he didn't have to pay. The list does go on, but I think you get the point."

"What about my mother?"

"I haven't gotten her story but I doubt she wanted to lie to you. I think she may be closer to a captive than anything else, but that is a theory. I don't have any proof to back it up."

Nolan put his gun away and sat down in the chair in front of the desk.

"Why are you doing all of this? Looking for information, messing up his plans," Nolan asked.

"I figured since he wanted me dead, I might as well give him a reason," Emily answered.

"Have you talked to my mother?"

"Yes, she asked me if I would help her."

"Help her do what?"

"Deal with Schultz."

"What?"

"Your mother's name is Livia, recognize it?"

"What does she need help with?"

"I don't know, she hasn't told me yet."

"You are the only person who has said that Schultz isn't my father. I would like to know if it is true," Nolan stood up, "I will be back in a week. If you have proof, you have another ally. If you don't I will kill you."

"How about eight o'clock rather than one thirty?"

Nolan left the office. Emily turned her attention to the filing cabinet.

When Trent got up he found Emily sitting at the kitchen table. Daniel and Adriana were nowhere to be seen. Trent opened his mouth to ask where they were when Emily cut him off.

"They went to the park with the granddaughter of your neighbour. They will probably back for lunch."

"You look tired," Trent commented.

"I didn't get to sleep until five and I had a busy day yesterday."

"That explains why you weren't here when I came in. Daniel told me what happened with your father."

"That was part of it."

"Alex had a message last night. He'll have the sample today or tomorrow."

"Good, I want to deal with that soon."

"What happened last night?"

"I woke up a few days ago wondering what I should do next, now I think I might be over my head."

"What happened?" Trent asked as he sat down.

"I made a deal with the devil's right hand man. I don't want to drag you under with me."

"I know how to swim."

"It isn't water."

"I'm willing to take that chance."

"It started when I was walking back to the department. I overheard three people talking. I caught a good portion of the conversation. It was meaningless to me. The one guy spotted me and suddenly I had three people trying to kill me. The one guy left. Brett showed up. He stopped them before they succeeded at killing me. He killed one, and I killed the other. That was the start. Now I'm sinking fast or have information overload."

"Write it down."

"I'm not sure I want to because when you have a written record someone else can get their hands on it."

"Any solution has a down point or two."

"I could try it."

"And if you need to discuss anything, I'm here."

"I need proof that Schultz is Nolan's stepfather, and he is only giving me a week to find it before he is going to kill me. If I succeed, he won't kill me."

"How will you find proof?"

"I'll talk to Alex again. Hope I get to talk to Livia again before a week is up and I will see what else comes up."

"That doesn't give you much to go on."

"I hope it is enough. Not because he said he would kill me, but because he could be a useful ally."

"He's tried to kill you and now you're seeing him as an ally?'

"The best way to get rid of an enemy is by making them a friend and it would be a blow to Schultz's power."

"I hope it works."

The door opened and Daniel and Adriana came in.

Emily went with Trent when he went to the bar. She helped him get ready to open. When he opened, she bought a couple of beers and spent the time reading Alice in Wonderland. After the people left, Emily helped Trent close up. They had just finished when Alex showed up.

"The blood sample," Alex held out a box. Emily took the box and checked inside.

"Your part," Alex held his hand palm up. Emily pulled an envelope out of her pocket and held it out to him. Alex took it.

"Where did you get the information about Schultz?" Emily asked.

"I don't reveal my sources," Alex said.

"I do, especially when my life is on the line," Emily said.

"Are you going to tell Schultz?" Alex asked.

"No, Schultz would never personally stoop that low. I would tell Nolan," Emily answered.

"You are going to sink that low? Even your life isn't worth your pride."

"Your source, please."

"No one would sink that low."

"I blackmailed you when I was twelve, I haven't exactly been moving up."

"My source is a drug dealer, who accidentally overheard a conversation. His body was found in an alleyway yesterday morning."

"That was all I needed to know."

"Would you really tell Nolan that I'm your source for information?"

"I might. It depends on whether I'll ever need your help again."

"I'll talk to you another time." Alex left. Trent and Emily went back to Trent's house. When they arrived, they went to bed.

The next morning Emily and Daniel went back to department H, leaving Adriana with Jenna, the neighbour's granddaughter. When they arrived, Emily led them to a different lab than the medical lab.

"Where are we?" Daniel asked as Emily started going through a refrigerator.

"This is the morgue," Emily answered. Emily pulled out a vial. She put it in a box. "This is the sample from the guy who has a pregnant girlfriend."

"Okay."

Emily and Daniel left the morgue and went to the medical lab. Grace was sitting, working on the computer. There was no one else in there. Emily placed the box on the counter.

"What have you been up to?" Grace asked.

"Drowning in information," Emily answered as she got what she needed out, "How are Jerry and Crew?'

"It was food poisoning," Grace answered.

"Food poisoning? That didn't look like food poisoning," Emily said.

"Since they haven't been out of the department in a month, I can only wonder what they were eating that the rest of us weren't," Grace said, "They will be back tomorrow."

Emily took the blood sample from Daniel and placed his sample with the rest after labelling it.

"How could a doctor diagnose that as food poisoning?" Emily asked as she started to examine the samples.

"No idea, but I wouldn't want to deal with that doctor. He would probably mix up small pox with chicken pox," Grace said.

"Anything of interest?" Emily asked.

"Cynthia is trying not to panic. She keeps calling and they keep saying that Brett is missing," Grace said.

"That doesn't sound good," Emily said.

"And Abby came by looking for you. I told her you weren't here and she left a note," Grace held up an envelope.

"I'll pick it up later," Emily said.

"Alfred stopped by looking for you," Grace said.

"What did he want?"

"He said something about a mission for you."

"I'll have to talk to him later."

"What are you doing?"

"Trying to prove a theory."

"Good luck."

No one said anything as Emily worked. Grace went back to what she was doing. Daniel had found a seat to sit on that was out of the way.

It had been quiet for ten minutes when the door to the medical lab opened and three stretchers were wheeled in. Grace jumped up, signed the clipboard that was handed to her and then went over to the first stretcher. Emily put everything down and went over to help Grace. The person on the first stretcher Emily looked at was bleeding from several cuts and looked like their leg was broken. Emily cleaned some of the bad cuts while Grace used the medical scanner. Once Grace was finished Emily gave the person some painkillers and then dealt with the broken limb. Then she finished cleaning the cuts and moved the stretcher into the other room, where Grace had just put the person she had dealt with. Emily came back to find Grace looking at the third person but not touching him.

"What is it?" Emily asked going over. Grace moved enough that Emily could see the person. It was Jeff, he looked like he was just sleeping. His legs and arms lay at funny angles, there were bruises all over his face and neck that continued to his chest.

"It looks like he ended up at the bottom of the pile," Grace said.

"Yeah," Emily breathed out. Suddenly Jeff started to cough, blood coming up with each outward breath. Grace pulled out the scanner again and did a scan of Jeff. Putting it back into the computer she brought up the results.

"Emily?" Jeff's voice was rough.

"I'm here," Emily said.

"Am I gonna live?" Jeff asked. Emily looked over at Grace. Grace looked up from the computer.

"We're gonna have to send him to the hospital," Grace said.

"If you die, it'll be because you gave up," Emily told Jeff.

"It's a lot of pain," Jeff said.

"I know," Emily replied. Emily looked up at Grace, "Anything we can do here?"

"Painkiller, maybe set the bones, that's it," Grace answered.

"Then let's do that. Then when he gets to the hospital, they will deal with the serious stuff," Emily said.

"Okay," Grace said. After they had given him some painkiller, Grace and Emily started setting limbs as they waited for the people who would take him to the hospital. They finished just before the people showed up and Jeff was taken away.

Grace went back to working on the computer. Emily went back to examining the blood sample and Daniel watched Emily.

"Eureka," Emily said half an hour later.

"You found something?" Grace asked.

"The virus does change a person's body chemistry," Emily answered.

"What?"

"Remember when I got sick not that long ago?"

"Yes."

"It is a virus that appears to change a person's body chemistry."

"That's it?"

"It improves the immune system and something else but I can't tell what the other thing does. That and one of the samples I used to compare it to, is very similar to the ones with the changes, so I suspect that person also had the virus."

"Whose blood sample did you use?'

Emily picked up the vial and read the label.

"All it says is Tony. I don't recognize the name."

"Tony? Where did you get the sample?"

"It was with all the rest."

"Tony has been missing for years. He came back from a mission, checked in, went through the medical check and was never heard from again."

"I just picked two at random, and checked to make sure they were clean before I started."

"Strange. How come this didn't show up when I did the scan?"

"Because you were scanning for viruses and the virus had done its work. There was no virus for the scanner to find, so it didn't find any. And it proved my theory."

"What was your theory?"

"That the child survived because it got half its DNA from Markus."

"So the baby should survive until birth?"

"And after. Which will be good for Bethany."

"Getting her out of the department would help too."

"One problem at a time, please."

"I thought you were into multi-tasking."

"I have one deadline in a week, the other could pass anytime, on top of other things."

"You gonna be okay?"

"I'll figure something out." Emily put the equipment she used away, then went over to the desk and picked up the envelope from Abby. She opened it and read the note inside.

Emily and Dr. Grace

Thank you for everything. Rebecca and I are fine and Adam is supposed to join us soon.

Once again thank you for everything you did.

Abby

Emily put the note back in the envelope and put the envelope in her pocket.

"Make sure you talk to Alfred on your way out," Grace said.

"I will," Emily said. Emily and Daniel left the medical lab. When they got to Cynthia's desk, they stopped.

"You go on ahead, I'll catch up," Emily told Daniel.

"Okay," Daniel said then left. Emily turned to Cynthia.

"Alfred in?" Emily asked.

"Yes," Cynthia answered, "He said that if you showed up to just go right in."

"Brett will turn up," Emily said.

"I hope so," Cynthia replied. Emily went to the office door. She knocked before opening the door. Alfred was sitting at his desk. He didn't look up.

"Come in and close the door," Alfred said. Emily stepped into the office and closed the door. She walked over and sat down in the chair.

"I was told that you wanted to talk to me," Emily said. Alfred finally looked up.

"I need you to do a mission," Alfred said. He passed a file to her. Emily opened it and glanced through it.

"Is that it?" Emily asked.

"Bring back the locket," Alfred said.

"No threats about watching me, or getting a watch from Travis?" Emily asked.

"You will give the locket to Travis when you return, but otherwise you just go," Alfred answered, "Travis has three agents out that he is watching. And since Warner is not breathing down our necks this time, I see no reason for threats or anything else."

"Okay," Emily said getting up.

"Make sure you read the file all the way through before heading out," Alfred said.

"I will," Emily said. She left the office and headed for the assignment lab. Getting there, she sat down at a computer and opened the file.

An hour later Emily left the department. She headed for a higher-class hotel. Reaching it, the doorman let her in. Emily went across the lobby to the elevator. She hit the button for the sixth floor. The doors closed and the elevator went upwards. Once on the sixth floor, Emily went along the hallway until she came to the room she wanted. Pulling out a computer card, Emily slid it into the slot in the door. The door clicked. Emily pushed it open. She grabbed the card before letting the door close. Emily looked around the room. There was a sitting area with a bedroom and a bathroom off it. Emily went into the bedroom. There were women's clothing all over the place and a half empty suitcase was sitting on a chair near the bed. Emily went over to the suitcase and rifled through what was in there. Not finding the locket, Emily went to the nightstand and went through it. Not there. Emily left the bedroom and went into the bathroom. She rummaged through the makeup bag that was sitting on the counter. No locket.

"Of course it wouldn't be that easy," Emily commented, "When you have a microchip in your locket, you would keep it on you to make the job harder for people like me."

Emily was just about to leave the bathroom when she heard the door open. Two people entered the hotel room and the door closed. Both were breathing heavy and it sounded like they were shedding clothing. Emily pulled out her dart gun and loaded two darts into it. The couple moved to the bedroom. Emily left the bathroom and moved to the doorway of the bedroom. The couple were too engrossed with each other to notice her. Emily shot one dart at the man and the other at the woman. Both of them passed out.

"I hate to disturb you," Emily said coming into the bedroom," But I am looking for something." Emily rolled the woman over and off the man. Emily took the locket and chain from around the woman's neck.

"Thanks for your time," Emily said before leaving the bedroom. Emily put the locket in her pocket and the dart gun away. She used the computer card on the door and slipped into the hallway. Emily went down the hallway and into the elevator. She pressed the button for the main floor. The doors closed and the elevator started moving. It stopped on the second floor. A man got into the elevator and the doors closed. The man looked with disgust at Emily's clothes.

"Are you a guest at the hotel?" the man asked.

"Delivery person," Emily answered, "Dropped something off."

"I'm amazed they let you into the hotel," the man said. He turned around to face the doors. The elevator stopped and the doors opened. The man walked quickly across the lobby toward the bar. Emily exited the elevator and headed for the lobby door. The doorman held the door for Emily. Just after Emily stepped outside, the fire alarm went off inside the hotel.

"Idiot with his flaming drinks again," the doorman muttered. Emily walked away from the building, but only as far as the alley across the street. People started pouring out of the building. Emily didn't see the man from the elevator come out, but she did see the couple from the hotel room being escorted out by a security person.

Emily left when the fire trunks showed up. She headed back to the department. When she got there, Emily went directly to Travis's office. Travis had three screens on and was standing there trying to give directions over a radio. He nodded to Emily before going back to giving directions. Emily took the locket out and placed it on Travis's desk before leaving the office. She stopped off at her room before leaving the department. It was suppertime when she reached Trent's house.

After Adriana was tucked in, Emily went back to the office of Jones and Jackson. Emily spent the week sitting in the office going over the files and writing all the relevant information into a notebook.

Trent and Daniel got out of the elevator on the second floor.

"How does Emily stand working in a hospital?" Daniel asked, "This place stinks."

"I suppose you get used to it," Trent said. They walked down the hall to the room the receptionist told them.

"Thanks for coming," Daniel said.

"Not a problem," Trent said. They found the room. Pasha was sitting up in bed when they entered the room. Lara wasn't there.

"Daniel," Pasha said, "It is nice to see you. And who is this?"

"This Trent," Daniel said.

"Just Trent?' Pasha asked.

"Trent Murray," Trent said, "Daniel and Adriana are currently living in my house."

"Then where is Emily's living?" Pasha asked.

"Where she works," Trent answered.

"Well, it is nice to meet you," Pasha said, "Come, sit down. Lara has gone off the get herself something to eat. They really should bring meals for the loved ones that sit at patient's bedsides." Daniel sat in one chair. Trent sat down in the other.

"How are you doing?" Daniel asked.

"I'm not as far gone as the doctor thinks I should be," Pasha answered, "Another week and I'll be back to working on my toys. I like to give them out at the clinic where Lara works. It is a nice feeling to watch a child's face light up when you hand them a toy."

"Adriana loves hers," Daniel said.

"What do you do?" Pasha asked Trent.

"I own a bar," Trent answered.

"I used to love going out to bars," Pasha said, "That is how I met Lara."

"At a bar?" Daniel asked.

"No, she was a nurse at the hospital," Pasha answered, "I had gotten into a fight at the bar. I was knocked out and taken to the hospital. I woke up and saw her bending over me and figured I must have died and gone to heaven. Of course, she denied being an angel, but I know better. Emily never believed that story, not until Lara told her that is was true."

"Why not?" Daniel asked. Pasha laughed.

"She would never believe anything after I told her a specific story," Pasha shook his head, "But it was so funny to see her reaction; worth every moment of disbelief. Where is Emily?"

"She hasn't been seen in a week," Trent answered.

"She must be at the office studying the files," Pasha said, "She probably needs help."

"Help with what?" Daniel asked.

"I asked her to do me a favour and go through the files at the office of Jones and Jackson."

Lara came in with the doctor.

"I see you are well enough to entertain guests," the doctor said.

"My grandson visits and you expect me to turn him away?" Pasha asked.

"No," the doctor said, "But I'm letting you go home on the condition that you rest."

"Well, give me my clothes and some privacy," Pasha said, "I have some toys calling."

"You will rest," the doctor said.

"Of course," Pasha said.

"Okay," the doctor said. A nurse brought in Pasha's clothes. Daniel, Trent, Lara and the doctor left the room. The doctor went off down the hallway.

"It will be nice to have Pasha home," Lara said.

"Perhaps Adriana and I can visit later this week," Daniel said.

"That would be good," Lara said, "Just give Pasha a few days to rest first."

"I will," Daniel said.

"I don't believe we have met," Lara said to Trent.

"Trent," Trent said offering his hand. Lara shook it. "Daniel and Adriana are currently living at my house."

"Ah, yes," Lara said, "Emily mentioned you briefly when she visited. Is she not staying with you as well?"

"Emily lives at her work," Trent answered, "Adriana lives with me because Emily isn't allowed to have her stay where she is."

"And you willing took on Emily's children?" Lara asked, "Most people wouldn't do that."

"It isn't a problem," Trent said, "Adriana is sweet. Daniel can take care of himself and he can cook. And Emily is around whenever she can."

"It sounds like all you need is a couple of wedding bands and you would be a perfect family," Lara said. Before Trent could answer, Pasha came out of the room.

"Let's go," Pasha said, "Before they change their mind and decide to keep me."

"They would only keep you if something happened between here and the door," Lara said.

"An even better reason to hurry," Pasha declared. The four of them walked to the elevator.

Once they left the hospital, Daniel and Trent walked Lara and Pasha home before heading back to Trent's house.

Emily woke to find a blanket placed over her and Trent sitting in the chair watching her.

"I'm not sure whether to ask what you are doing here or how you got here," Emily sat up rubbing the sleep out of her eyes.

"I went with Daniel when he went to see your parents. Your father thought you might need help," Trent answered, "Your parents are interesting people."

"How is Pasha?" Emily asked.

"The doctor let him go home today," Trent said.

"That is good."

"Met with Nolan yet?"

"No, that is tonight. I'm ready for it. The rest of the files have some interesting information in them." Emily got up and sat down at the desk. "Anything I've come up with I've been writing down in this notebook."

Emily handed Trent the notebook.

"I started with what I know," Emily said. Trent took the notebook and started to read. Ten minute later he put the notebook down.

"All of this is true?" Trent asked.

"As far as I can tell," Emily answered.

"Wouldn't all this be dangerous to know?"

"Like lying in a bed of scorpions."

"What happened to Jones?"

"As far as I can tell, he disappeared. There is no body, no sign, he just vanished."

"That isn't good."

"I don't think he was kidnapped, I think he left on his own free will."

"Why would he just leave?"

"I don't know. There is no sign and no reason for someone to kidnap him."

"Going to look for him?"

"No, his files give me the information I need."

"Your father seems to think Jones is dead."

"I know, but there is no proof of that."

"Your mother basically asked if there was a chance of marriage in the near future."

"She usually doesn't do that."

"I think she is worried that you have two children and are not married. That, and I had to correct her assumption that you were living with me."

"I don't know where she got that impression."

"I showed up with Daniel. What are you going to do once this meeting with Nolan is over?"

"Keep going through these files, then I have another project I was thinking about."

"Sounds like you're busy."

"Somewhat."

"Have time to go for supper tomorrow?"

"As far as I know."

"Need any help?"

"No, I think I have everything under control."

"I'll get you something to eat, then go get the bar ready to open."

"Thank you." They kissed, then Trent left. Emily went back to going through the files.

Emily was still working when Nolan showed up at eight o'clock. He entered and sat down. Emily pulled a file out of the cabinet and handed it to Nolan before going back to work. Nolan went through the file. When he was finished, he placed the file on the desk.

"So, this Simon Jones is my father," Nolan said.

"That's what it looks like," Emily said.

"What happened to him?" Nolan asked.

"He disappeared. No one has found any trace of him," Emily answered.

"You have proven that Schultz lied," Nolan said, "I'm willing to help you."

"I don't have a grand scheme that I can recruit help for," Emily said, "I don't even have a plan. I have just been going through the information. If I do need help, I will be grateful for your assistance, but right now, the person who might need it is your mother. If she is a captive, then she may have something you can do now."

"I'll see what I can do," Nolan said as he got up. He left the office. Emily went back to work.

CHAPTER 8
INFORMATION

Emily spent two more days going through files. She was starting to run out of notebook pages, but she was running out of files, too.

She had taken the first file out of the last drawer when Trent and Pasha entered the office.

"You had some questions for me?" Pasha asked as he sat down on the couch. Trent sat down in the other chair.

"Yes, do you remember the date of Jones's death?" Emily asked. She flipped through the notebook until she found the page she wanted.

"May something," Pasha answered.

"May seventeenth?"

"Yeah."

"How do you know he is dead?"

"I was supposed to meet him at his house. When I got there, police and an ambulance were in front of the house. I watched them roll a body out of the house on a stretcher. Jones was the only person living in that house. It couldn't have been anybody else."

"Do you know for certain that the body was Jones?"

"No, I talked to the police. They told me someone had already identified the body."

"Did you look for the morgue or police reports?"

"Yes, but I was told that I couldn't get them."

"According to the morgue report, the body taken out of 7352 Maple Avenue on May seventeenth was that of Curtis Mann."

"That doesn't make sense. If that was Curtis Mann's body, what happened to Jones and where did Curtis Mann come from?"

"A family friend by the name of James apparently identified him, but because the police were suspicious of James they used dental records for positive identification. James disappeared immediately after identifying the body. As to where Curtis came from, he was a twenty-one-year-old with heart problems. His mother died about two months before he did. He disappeared a month later. Autopsy results said he died from his heart problems."

"So, where is Jones?"

"I can't find him. There is no record of his death, the house on Maple Avenue is empty and he hasn't contacted anyone. He has successfully disappeared."

"Who is this guy James that identified the body?"

"There is no way of knowing but my guess is Jones. I did find a connection between Jones and Curtis and what Jones was working on."

"Curtis was connected to Schultz?"

"According to Jones's files Curtis was born to Shirley Mann, who claims that the father is George Schultz."

"So, Jones had Schultz's son."

"And Schultz currently has Jones's wife and children."

"How exactly does that work?"

"I'm not sure how it exactly works. I haven't been able the talk to anyone who knows the whole story."

"It all brings more questions."

"And I'm slowly searching for answers."

"I should get back before Lara comes home," Pasha got up. "Please tell me if you come up with more answers or if you have more questions for me."

"I will."

Pasha left.

"How much longer will it take you to finish going through the files?" Trent asked.

"Tonight hopefully. Especially if there are no more interruptions."

"Daniel invited your parents over for lunch yesterday. He warned me before hand and he made lunch, so it wasn't too bad. Your mother is still wondering when the wedding will be."

"That doesn't sound like my mother. She usually doesn't ask once, let alone twice."

"Maybe she figures that you should get married while your father is still alive."

"What was your response to her wonderings?"

"I didn't get to say anything before your father told her to mind her own business and changed the subject."

"I'm guessing they have had that discussion before."

"We've never discussed our relationship."

"What would you like to discuss about it?"

"Nothing at the moment."

"At the moment? There is another time when you want to discuss it?"

"I have a few things to do before opening. I'll see you tomorrow," Trent answered as he got up.

"See you tomorrow," Emily said. Trent left the office and Emily went back to the files.

Half an hour later the door opened, this time Livia entered the office.

"I thought you didn't get out much," Emily commented.

"We made a deal and this was the only way to visit," Livia said.

"How can you physically visit now when the last time you had to visit me in a dream?" Emily asked.

"Last time I didn't have much time and George would have noticed my absence if I had used the machine."

"As in you are using something other than a vehicle."

"I use a machine kindly invented by Daniel Anderson."

"You are using a time machine to travel, which explains how you could show up in the twenty-first century."

"You heard of it."

"Yes."

"Most people haven't."

"Most people don't have the connections I do. You are here to tell me the whole story?"

"That was our agreement."

"Start with Simon Jones, please."

"You figured that connection too, have you?"

"I'll tell you that story once you are done yours."

"I met Simon at school. It was crush at first sight. He didn't notice me until after school was finished. We married at seventeen. I had Delilah shortly after. Simon worked while I was a mother. A year later Nolan came. Less than a month after that, Simon started working a lot more. I thought he was doing it on purpose so that he didn't have to spend time at home. One day I watched him playing with the children. He was enjoying playing with them, so I figured the reason he worked so much was because I did something wrong. I was foolish. I never talked to him, otherwise I would have known that work was the reason."

"What was his job?"

"I'm not exactly sure what all his job encompassed but it is similar to what job George is doing now. But without the power hungry, kill everyone who gets in his way part. After a while of those thoughts going through my head, I met George, who worked under Simon at the time. George could see my fear and he used it. I'm still not sure what all happened or how it all happened but I became George's prisoner, my children became his loyal followers and Simon disappeared without a trace. I heard rumours about all sorts of things, from he joined department H to George had him killed and buried. After a while I figured I had to do something about George, especially once I found out he was killing people. I got my hands on a time machine and a virus and started using people to try and stop him. I learned quickly that I didn't have the information I needed, so I got the people to help me by finding the information and putting blocks in George's way. So far, the only thing that is changing is the height of the pile of bodies. I never wanted anybody to die, but George doesn't care."

"Fits the information I have found."

"Now, you had a story."

"Jones disappeared after you joined Schultz. I can't find any trace of him for several years. Then he opened this office and hired my father. He gathered information about everything and anything. A few years ago he found Schultz's son, Curtis. But Curtis died and Jones disappeared again. My father asked me to see what I could find. Shortly after Nolan found me and we had an interesting discussion. Once he left, I started going through Jones's files. That is how I found out about the connection between you and Jones. A week later Nolan came back for a second discussion. He has decided that Schultz isn't that great after all."

"How did you convince him of that?"

"I told him that Schultz wasn't his father and showed him his birth certificate."

"Thank you. George won't let me close to him or Delilah."

"I haven't met Delilah. I've only heard about what she is doing."

"Maybe I should have asked for your help earlier."

"What else does the virus do besides improve the immune system?"

"It makes you more susceptible to telepathic messages."

"Like you entering my dream?"

"Yes. I was told it also helped people identify George's minions but I'm not sure how that works."

"If the virus makes it easier for you to get into my dreams, how are you able to do it?"

"I'm not sure. I've always been able to do it to some extent. It is harder without the person having had the virus."

"Even with the virus, it seems you have trouble."

"Some."

"How did you know where to find me in the twenty-first century?"

"The same way the people who sent you did. The watch was a tracker. I should get back. I don't know when I'll be able to talk to you again."

"I'm sure you'll find me when you can."

Livia got up and left the office.

No one else disturbed Emily as she went through the last of the files. It was morning by the time she finished with the files. Having finished, Emily locked up and headed for Trent's house.

When she got there, Trent wasn't up and Daniel and Adriana weren't home. Emily went into the kitchen and made herself a sandwich. When she was finished eating, she picked up Wuthering Heights and started to read.

About noon Trent came into the kitchen.

"Finished?" Trent asked.

"With the files, yes. The information, no," Emily answered not looking up from her book.

"Well, I knew you wouldn't be done with the information," Trent said, "What are you going to do now?"

"I have to go back to the department soon," Emily replied.

"Why didn't you go back after you finished with the files?"

"I haven't slept in close to twenty-four hours. I need to let the adrenaline go through my system so that I can sleep."

"Going to sleep through supper or will you be available to go out?"

"I should be available to go out."

Trent made himself lunch. Emily had fallen asleep in the book by the time Trent sat down to eat.

About one-thirty Daniel came in carrying Adriana. Trent was sitting on the couch in the living room. Daniel went down the hall to Adriana's room.

He came out a few minutes later without her. He sat down in the living room.

"Emily here yet?" Daniel asked.

"Yes, she is going to sleep before heading back to the department," Trent said.

"Pasha is back in the hospital. The doctors are sure he won't survive this time," Daniel said.

"We'll see," Trent said.

"He was worse today and then he passed out again," Daniel said, "The doctors couldn't wake him up once he was at the hospital. They said he wouldn't wake up."

"Sometimes that happens. People don't live forever, it is the memories of the people that keep them alive for us."

Daniel didn't respond for a while as he thought that over.

"Thanks," he said finally before getting up and going down the hall to his room. Trent got up and went to check on Emily. She was still sleeping.

"Not always a light sleeper, are you?" Trent asked softly as he brushed some hair from her face. Emily didn't move. Trent went back to what he was doing in the living room.

Quarter to five post meridian Daniel came into the kitchen to start supper. He tried not to disturb Emily. A few minutes later Emily lifted her head and rubbed the sleep out of her eyes.

"Sorry if I woke you," Daniel said.

"That's okay," Emily replied. She got up and headed for the bathroom. Emily came back a few minutes later.

"Do you know where Trent is?" Emily asked.

"He should be headed for work," Daniel answered, "But I haven't seen him since earlier this afternoon."

"Okay," Emily nodded. She left the kitchen and went down the hall to Trent's room. Daniel heard the door open and close. Emily didn't come back.

A few minutes later the door opened again, this time he heard both Emily and Trent's voices. They headed for the front door. Then Daniel heard the front door open and close.

Trent and Emily went down the front steps and started down the street.

"Don't you have to go to work?" Emily asked.

"I asked someone I trust if they would look after the bar tonight," Trent answered.

"I was wondering about something earlier."

"What?"

"Did you find a safe place for Ruth?"

"Yes, she moved two days after we visited her and last I checked she was still alive."

"That is good."

"Tyler's journal is still missing. Ruth searched but couldn't find it. I have to go through and clean the house out. Ruth didn't have time, so I said I would do it. I just have been a little busy lately."

"I'm sure she understands."

"So, what now? Just going back to the department?"

"I have to go back. That is where I work. I have a project at the back of my head that wants to come out and I have two patients there."

"And you left two patients for this length of time?"

"They are pregnant; one is eight months along and the other is five months. Aside from their monthly check ups, there isn't a whole lot to do, unless something goes wrong."

"From my impression, not only from you but also from rumours I've heard, agents don't get paid. Yet you seem to have as much money as you want."

"Ever heard of Emily's restaurant?"

"Yes, it is one of the higher end establishments."

"I own it."

"Wow."

"I bought it off the last owner, who didn't want his children to wreck the place through mismanagement. It was named for his mother."

"In here," Trent directed Emily into a restaurant. They entered. A waitress led them to a table and took their drink order leaving them with menus. They decided what they wanted and gave their order when the waitress came back with their drinks. A while later their supper was brought out. They ate. When they were finished Trent paid the bill and they left the restaurant. They walked a little while without talking.

"You seemed to have something on your mind when you asked me out for supper." Emily said breaking the silence.

"I was thinking about our agreement," Trent said.

"With Adriana?"

"Yes, I'd like to make it permanent instead of temporary."

"And how would you like to do that?"

"By doing what Lara keeps suggesting; marry you."

"What if I say no?"

"Then nothing changes."

"And if I say yes?"

"I'll give you a ring and we'll get married at some point."

"You sure you know all the risks that tie in with marrying me?"

"There may be some I don't know about, but I'm sure I can handle them."

"I don't know."

"Let me put it this way." Trent stopped. Emily stopped. Trent went down on one knee in the middle of the sidewalk. He pulled a ring box out of his pocket and opened it so that Emily could see the diamond ring inside.

"Emily, will you marry me?"

Emily looked at him as a smile slowly spread over her face.

"Yes, Trent, I will," Emily answered. Trent took the ring out of its box and put it on Emily's finger before getting up. Once he was standing, Emily kissed him, which Trent deepened. When they separated Trent and Emily headed back to Trent's house.

Simon walked down the hospital hallway checking over his shoulder every few feet. He would look at the door number on each side of the hallway, then behind him. He jumped at every large sound and tried to avoid people. He slowly progressed until he came to Pasha's room. Pasha was the only one in there. He was lying on the bed, hooked up to various machines. Simon went to the side of the bed.

"Pasha," Simon whispered. Pasha opened his eyes half way.

"Simon," Pasha gasped.

"Yes," Simon said.

"Find Emily," Pasha gasped.

"Emily who?" Simon asked.

"Jackson." Pasha closed his eyes and the machine stopped beeping. Simon hurried out of the room before anyone came to check on Pasha. He left the hospital, keeping more alert of his surroundings than when he entered.

Daniel had gotten up, gotten dressed and was headed for the kitchen to make breakfast when the telephone rang. Entering the kitchen he saw that Emily had picked it up. She was dressed and there was a cup of tea sitting on the table.

"Hello? Yes…I see…okay…bye." Emily put the receiver back. She stood there a moment with her head bowed before she shook it and sat down. She took a sip of the tea. Daniel started breakfast.

"Anything you would like?" Daniel asked Emily.

"No, I'm not hungry," Emily answered absently.

"Something wrong?" Daniel asked.

"That was the hospital," Emily replied in an expressionless tone, "Pasha died last night."

Daniel stopped what he was doing and looked at Emily. She drank the rest of her tea and stood up. She placed the cup next to the sink and started for the door.

"Where are you going?" Daniel asked.

"Back to the department," Emily replied. Then she left.

Emily stopped at Cynthia's desk when she arrived.

"How are you doing?" Emily asked.

"Aside from the fact that Brett seems to have disappeared off the face of the earth, I'm doing okay," Cynthia answered.

"Dr. Grace done a scan recently?" Emily asked.

"Last one was when she checked to see if I was pregnant," Cynthia said.

"Stop by the medical lab today," Emily said, "I need to do another one to make sure everything is going smoothly, especially with the stress you are under."

"I will try," Cynthia said.

"You will or I'll be talking to Alfred about your work load," Emily said.

"I'll get there," Cynthia said. Emily nodded and then headed for her room. Getting there she dropped her jacket on the bed. Emily turned to head for the medical lab and found Stephanie standing in the doorway.

"I was wondering if you could do me a favour off my medical record," Stephanie said.

"Probably," Emily answered, "What is wrong?"

"I'm not sure, but I don't want to be taken off missions just because of some minor thing," Stephanie said.

"Okay," Emily said, "What are the symptoms? I can't help you if you don't tell me those."

"Stomach pain, nausea," Stephanie said.

"It could be food poisoning," Emily said, "That would pass in a day or two. But come to the medical lab and I'll run a scan. It won't go into your medical files, but it will tell me what it is. Okay?"

"Okay," Stephanie said. They headed for the medical lab.

Grace was nowhere to be seen when they arrived. They went into Emily's office. Stephanie let Emily do the scan. Emily put the scanner into the computer and brought the results up on the screen.

"What is it?" Stephanie asked after Emily had been studying the results for five minutes. Emily looked at Stephanie.

"Your problem does not have a quick fix," Emily said, "And for you to get treatment I have to report it."

"What is it?" Stephanie asked.

"Peritoneal mesothelioma," Emily answered.

"What is that in English?" Stephanie asked.

"Cancer," Emily answered, "A rare form and very deadly unless treated quickly."

"People can recover from cancer," Stephanie said.

"Yes, they do," Emily said, "But I need your permission to pass this information along to the cancer clinic at the hospital."

"Pass it along," Stephanie said, "I'll talk to Alfred. Then I'll have to find my parents and see if they will pay for the treatments."

Emily typed a few things into the computer.

"There they have the information," Emily said, "They will be waiting for you."

"Thank you," Stephanie said, "I wish it had been food poisoning, but hopefully, I'll be back soon."

"Good luck," Emily said. Stephanie left Emily's office. Emily left her office a lot slower. Grace was sitting at the desk. She looked up from what she was doing.

"What is wrong with Stephanie?" Grace asked.

"Advanced peritoneal mesothelioma," Emily answered.

"Damn," Grace said, "Does she know that?"

"Part of it," Emily answered, "I couldn't take all hope away."

"As long as it doesn't backfire," Grace said.

"Anything new happening around here?" Emily asked.

"Three things," Grace answered, "Jeff is going to be fine, but will probably never go back to being an agent. And Jerry and crew came back. They looked fine. Then I did medical scans. Now they are in quarantine with a virus that has yet to be identified."

"Why in quarantine if it hasn't been identified?"

"Because it gave all the signs of being contagious."

"Doesn't that mean you have to check everyone for it?"

"The doctor and nurses from the hospital have the virus as well. Somehow it seems like the person needs to be exposed for long periods of time. Other people are working on what it is and how to cure it."

"How did Jerry and crew get it?"

"They are working on that too. The other thing that happened was the recruits that were stuck here have, been checked over to see if there was anything physically wrong with them and then sent elsewhere so that the next batch of recruits could come in."

"Where were they sent?"

"Department F."

"Heard the name but I've never heard about what they do there."

"When something serious goes wrong in training or a person goes off the deep end to the point that they can't do their job, they are sent to department F. There they are evaluated and given a job based on that evaluation."

"Interesting."

"Apparently there is a search for a doctor to replace Dr. Harvey. Someone realized that you were a doctor and suggested to Alfred that you would be a good replacement."

"What did Alfred say?"

"He told the guy that you were an agent and that you were going to stay an agent."

"Glad he cleared that up."

"Wouldn't you want the job?"

"No."

"I guess the recruits aren't young enough."

"How is Bethany been doing?"

"Learning a lot of first aid. Other than that, she has been wondering as to the gender of the baby, which I take as a good sign. She is in my office."

Emily went into Grace's office. Bethany was sitting on the bed reading a magazine. She looked up at Emily.

"How do you feel?" Emily asked.

"Fine," Bethany answered, "Dr. Grace said to ask you what my baby's gender is." Emily went to the computer and brought up the results from the last scan.

"You are carrying a healthy baby boy," Emily told her.

"Thank you," Bethany said.

"You're welcome," Emily replied as she shut down the computer. Bethany put down her magazine.

"Do you know someone named Schultz?" Bethany asked.

"I've heard of him but I have not met him."

"I think he wants to kill me."

"Why do you think that?" Emily asked as she sat down in the chair beside the bed.

"He killed Markus and he sent Robin to watch me."

"Markus was killed during a mission and Robin is an intern."

"I know what is going on, Markus was killed because of Schultz and it was made to look like an accident. And Robin is here as a spy for Schultz, I can feel it."

"And what do you want me to do about all this?"

"Right now, all I want to do is raise my son in safety. I was hoping you could find someplace safe to stay."

"I can see what can be done," Emily stood up.

"Thank you."

Emily left the office closing the door behind her.

"What was that about?" Grace asked.

"She is looking for safety for her son," Emily replied as she sat down.

"From you?"

"I know why she wants the help, but why she is asking me? I don't know."

"Maybe she can tell you are getting the same bad vibe off Robin that she is."

"It is possible or she is taking a gamble on the basis that we stopped Russell's attempt to kill her."

"Why if there was one attempt why hasn't there been another?"

"Schultz may have backed off until she had the kid."

"So she has the child, then what?"

"Probably kill the child."

"Who is this Schultz and why would he do this? And how do you know so much about all this?'

"Would you like me to start at the beginning, answer those questions or tell you what I know?"

"Yes."

"It started with Simon Jones, who after breezing through school, got a job making important decisions for a company. The company happens to have been run by a former friend of the guy in charge of the government, David, and was funded by a friend of mine, Pascal. It also happens to be what is referred around here as department A. When the paperwork got too much, Mr. Jones hired a recently released con artist, George Schultz. Schultz saw this as a government job that would get the law off his back while he made money for his next scam. He spent a while just mindlessly dealing with papers. Then one day he read one and realized what kind of decisions Jones was making. His interest was piqued. Using his finely tuned skills as a con artist, Schultz set to work. His plan was to kill Jones, take over the position and corrupt it from there. His plan changed when he met Livia, Jones's wife and learned that she had money that Jones was not connected to in any way except through marriage. Schultz carefully got Livia on his side and practically adopted her and Jones's children, Nolan and Delilah. When Jones realized what was going on he disappeared, leaving his post open for Schultz to step into."

"So department A is run by a power hungry con artist?"

"No, Schultz corrupted everything he touched. David, the former friend of the guy in charge of the government, gave the department to a retired government official to run and cut it off from the rest of the company. Pascal's money went with the departments and away from Schultz's corruption. The rest of the company was sold to Black for about a quarter of its worth. Schultz realized after the final paper was signed that David had just screwed him over. Instead of Jones being his first kill, David was, or so most of the information I have found claims. In his bid to move up in the world, Schultz took control of everything he could and removed anyone who got in his way. Now he seems to feel that he has control of everything."

"What about the departments?"

"The retiree is still in control because the red tape prohibits Schultz from trying. Schultz has spies around here and pretends to control it but between the retiree's orders and Schultz's orders, the departments jump at the retiree's orders."

"So, we are not Schultz controlled."

"The departments, the Carbrat Institute, and Pascal along with businesses Schultz considers insignificant."

"Is that the end?"

"No. Livia, Jones's wife, realized her big mistake a little too late. This realization came with her being a prisoner and her children being told that Schultz was their father. So Livia decided to correct her mistake. She stole the time machine from department C and a virus from Black. With these and her telepathic ability, she began to recruit people to help her. She would find someone, send them the virus, talk them into helping her and then most of them would do something to piss Schultz off and he would have them killed. While all this was going on, Jones reappears and sets up shop as a conspiracy theorist. He started searching for information and hired the late Pavel Jackson to help him."

"Schultz killed Pavel?"

"No, he died last night of cardiopulmonarymentia. Anyway, Jones found Schultz's son and hoped to use him against Schultz. Unfortunately, the plan didn't work. Curtis died of heart problems, which had been there all his life. Realizing his plan just crashed in, Jones once again disappeared. Somewhere in that time period, Schultz realized that the people he was killing off, because they were annoying him, had this particular virus. So, he stole the second virus from Black and gave it to his minions. This was supposed to give them the ability to tell them when they came across one of Livia's help. What no one told him, probably for fear of dying, is that all the virus does is tell Livia's help who Schultz's minions are. The virus that Livia is giving her help, is the one that I tested a while ago.

"Markus got one of Livia's damsel-in-distress letters, thus receiving the virus and Preston found out. The ambush on the mission was to kill Markus. A realization Schultz made at some point was that a person passes on the traits that the virus provides onto their offspring. Russell was sent back to make sure everything had gone as planned and nothing was missed. Like Leon being killed instead of Markus. We accidentally told him what was missed. Now Schultz wants Markus's child dead because it carries the virus. My guess is that the child transferred the wonderful traits of the virus to Bethany by the umbilical cord and placenta. Which means, Bethany is getting the same bad vibes off Robin that I am. And having read Markus's journal had figured out her situation.

"How I got mixed up in this is simple: I overheard a conversation that caused the near death experience I had and Schultz putting me on his to die list. So I went in search of information, which bothered Schultz, so he sent Nolan, his assassin trained foster son, to kill me. It was Nolan who put the knife in my back during the recruit's training mission. The ambush was to cover my assassination."

"Is that everything?"

"How much more do you want to know?"

"Keep going."

"On Nolan's most recent attempt, I gave him some of the information I had found, like his birth certificate, and his parents' marriage certificate; which I found when my father told me about the office of Jones and Jackson. As well as most of the rest of the information I've just told you. The other interesting piece of information I found was that Livia and Pascal used to be neighbours so they know each other. Which gives a good reason for Pascal to give money to Livia's charity fund. The fund goes to help people who have had a loved one taken from them by Schultz or his minions. And that is about where my information ends."

"Was this what you couldn't tell me about before?"

"Yes."

"One question."

"What is it?"

"Who is the retiree that runs the departments?"

"His name is Alfred."

"As in the one who took over from Benjamin?"

"Yes."

"Then why does he pay attention to Warner?"

"That you would have to ask him."

"Does he know that you know all this?"

"I don't know."

"How do you plan to keep Bethany and her child from Schultz's evil plan?"

"I don't know. I could kill Robin before she can report back to Schultz about the birth."

"Self-defense is questionable but acceptable. Murder I will not tolerate."

"I know that."

"What are you going to do now?"

"Sit here working on the project going through my head until Cynthia stops by."

"She is supposed to stop by?"

"I asked her to."

"Have fun." Grace went back to what she had been doing. Emily went into her office, but left the door open.

Cynthia stopped in after lunch and Emily made certain that she and the baby were healthy. Alfred came looking for Emily in the afternoon to give her a mission. Emily took the mission and spent the next week guarding a government official with three other agents.

Grace completed Emily's after mission medical check. Emily was now visiting Bethany. When Grace left the medical lab. She headed for Alfred's office. Cynthia was sitting at her desk.

"Is Alfred busy?" Grace asked.

"I think he is dealing with paperwork," Cynthia answered.

"I need to speak with him for a couple minutes," Grace said.

"Knock and then go in," Cynthia said. Grace went over to the office door. She knocked before opening the door. Alfred looked up at her.

"Dr. Grace, what can I do for you?" Alfred asked. Grace stepped into the room and closed the door.

"I need you to not give Emily any more missions until Bethany has had her baby," Grace answered.

"And how long will that be?" Alfred asked.

"Bethany is eight months along, so maybe a month," Grace answered, "Probably less."

"And why is it important for Emily to be here?" Alfred asked.

"She is the obstetrician," Grace answered, "If anything goes wrong, I need Emily here."

"Fine," Alfred said, "But she goes back to having missions after."

"That is fine," Grace said. Grace left Alfred's office and headed back to the medical lab.

Over the month Emily worked on her project, gave Grace basic lessons in obstetrics, and checked on Bethany regularly. She even visited Trent, Daniel and Adriana a couple times.

On the last day of the month Bethany went into labour. Early in the morning she gave birth to a healthy baby boy.

Bethany smiled at the bundle of joy in her arms.

"I think I'll name him Zachary, Zack for short," Bethany said. Emily smiled then left the doorway and collapsed into a chair in front of the computer.

"The problem with being an obstetrician is the unpredictable times when the baby arrives," Emily said yawning.

"It wasn't that long ago you wouldn't mind," Grace said from where she was sitting.

"Then I must be getting old."

"What about Bethany now that the baby is born?"

"She and Zack will have to wait until later. Even if I had someplace for her to go, she shouldn't move right now"

"Are you okay?"

"Besides being tired, I'm fine. Why?"

"I'm not sure. You just look pale."

"Best thing then might be for me to go to bed." Emily got up, "See you later."

"Okay."

Emily left the medical lab and headed for her room.

Later. Emily got up, dressed and then headed for the medical lab. Noticing that Grace, Bethany and Zack were gone Emily placed her latest project on the counter and sat down at the computer. She had been working for ten minutes when Grace came back. Grace saw Emily's project and picked it up. It was a piece of rubber the size and shape of an ID card. One side was sticky and the other side had a monitor in it.

"What is it?" Grace asked.

"A heart monitor," Emily answered.

"They already invented that. What is so great about this one?" Grace asked.

"It doesn't beep to indicate your heart rate. And it hooks into the scanner programs that I created. That means the computer beeps if the patient's heart stops, but doesn't drive the patient nuts," Emily said, "You place it on the patient's wrist and the heart rate appears in the bottom right hand corner of your screen. You place it on the patient's neck and the heart rate, breathing rate and temperature all appear."

"Useful," Grace placed the heart monitor on her wrist, "It says my heart rate is normal."

"I already sent it off to the Carbrat Institute with instructions," Emily said.

"What happens to the money that is earned off the patents?"

"I don't know. I have never bothered to ask."

"You could have money sitting there and not know about it."

"I doubt it. More likely it is used to fund something." The meal buzzer went. Emily got up. She and Grace headed for the cafeteria.

Emily was sitting in the medical lab working on the computer when a young man flanked by two guards entered, followed by Travis. Travis came over to where Emily was sitting.

"Cool," the kid commented, "This looks like the sickbay on the Enterprise."

Neither guard responded.

“Where's Dr. Grace?" Travis asked Emily.

"Elsewhere," Emily answered.

"This kid was found wandering the halls. No one seems to know where he came from. Alfred wants to know if the kid has anything contagious," Travis said.

"He probably wants to know where the kid came from too," Emily said.

"If you can find out, that would be good," Travis said. Travis left but the guards stayed right where they were. The kid sat down on the examining table.

"I've got a good guess," Emily said quietly to herself as she got up. She walked over to the examining table and pulled the medical scanner out of the computer.

"This is a medical lab, not a sickbay and you are still on Earth, not a spaceship," Emily told the kid.

"So, where is this place? A government lab?" the kid asked.

"This place isn't government run. Please lie down," Emily answered.

"Why?" the kid asked, his eyes on the scanner.

"I have been asked to make sure you do not have any contagious diseases or anything like that," Emily answered.

"How are you going to do that?" the kid asked.

"Lie down," Emily said. The kid did what he was told. Emily used the scanner and then put it back in its slot in the computer.

"I'm done," Emily told him. The kid sat up. Emily brought up the results on the computer.

"So you scan me and everything shows up on that computer?" he asked.

"That is the idea," Emily answered.

"Did you find anything?" the kid asked.

"Asthma and a tracer substance," Emily answered.

"What is a tracer substance?" the kid asked.

"A drug or something that is put in the bloodstream so that the person can be traced or use only certain technology," Emily answered.

"How did it get into my bloodstream?" the kid asked.

"No idea," Emily shut down the file. She sat back down at the computer.

"What day and time is it?" Emily asked.

"I don't know what time it is. They took my watch," the kid said.

"From when you last looked, time and date," Emily said.

"Four pm, March fifteenth," the kid answered.

"Year?"

"2003. Why do you want to know?"

"How did you get here?"

"I don't know. I was just looking at my watch, I looked up and I was here."

"People don't usually do that without something happening."

"School was over, I went to a second hand shop and brought the watch. I was walking home, fiddling with the watch, trying to set it. Next thing I know I'm here."

"May I see the watch?" Emily asked the guard. The guard took it out of his pocket and tossed it to Emily. Emily caught it and examined it.

"How can a watch transport me from one place to another?" the kid asked.

"You've watched television," Emily said.

"Yeah, so?" the kid asked.

"Truth is always stranger than fiction," Emily said.

"So what exactly did the watch do?" the kid asked.

"I'm a medical doctor. I would need to consult a chronologist to know what happened," Emily said.

"What does a chronologist do?" the kid asked.

"Deals with time," Emily answered. Grace entered the medical lab.

"Travis wants to talk to you," Grace told Emily.

"Okay," Emily stood up. She left the medical lab and headed for Alfred's office. Alfred and Travis were standing outside Alfred's office talking. They stopped when Emily arrived.

"Did you find anything out about the kid?" Travis asked.

"He thinks it is March fifteenth 2003. And by what he has said," Emily held up the watch, "This is how he got here."

"A time traveler?" Alfred asked.

"Without knowing it," Emily replied.

"So, what now?" Travis asked.

"We keep him isolated and see if there is some way of sending him back before any more damage is done," Alfred answered.

"Okay," Travis said.

"Emily, can you go get Daniel? He will be of some help on this case. I have to talk to Warner," Alfred said.

"Okay," Emily headed for her room, grabbed her jacket and then headed out of building to Trent's house.

Daniel was sitting on the steps.

"Back for a visit?" Daniel asked.

"This is work related," Emily said. She pulled the watch from her pocket and tossed it to Daniel. Daniel caught it and looked it over.

"It is a watch," Daniel said.

"One that, from all appearances, brought a kid from the twenty-first century here," Emily said, "Alfred would like to hear your thoughts on all of it."

"I would need to examine the watch more carefully," Daniel said.

"Whatever you need," Emily replied.

"Let me get my coat," Daniel got up and went inside. When he came back out they headed for department H.

When they arrived Daniel was directed to a conference room, while Emily headed back to the medical lab. Grace was working on the computer. Emily went over to her.

"Anything decided?" Grace asked.

"They're getting a committee together," Emily answered.

"My fate is being left to a committee?" the kid asked, "Oh no."

"Your fate isn't being decided yet, "Emily said, "They are still trying to figure out how you got here and how to send you home."

"Probably be late for supper," the kid said, "If I get home today at all."

"We'll see what happens," Emily said.

"Shouldn't you be at the committee meeting," Grace asked,

"Not yet. They aren't ready to discuss what to do with the kid," Emily said, "They are still examining the watch."

"When the meeting starts, you should be there to tell them about the tracer substance," Grace said.

"I will, but knowing that it is there is not helpful if we don't know what it does," Emily said.

"What caused it?"

"The watch unless he has messed with something else."

"Why would the watch leave a tracer substance in his system?"

"So only he could use it or so that he can't use it again or just to determine the number of times he has used it."

"How do you determine which one?"

"By guessing."

"So how long until the committee meets?"

"Not sure."

"So, the watch I bought is a teleportation device?" the kid asked.

"Not quite, but close to it," Emily answered.

"Then why did it send me here?" the kid asked.

"I don't know," Emily answered.

"Where's the bathroom?" the kid asked.

"The closed door over there," Emily pointed the direction of the bathroom. The kid got off the examining table and went into the bathroom.

"I'm going to check on the progress of the committee," Emily told Grace.

"Okay," Grace said. Emily left the medical lab.

Cynthia directed Emily to a conference room. Warner was standing at the head of the table, Alfred and Travis were sitting on either side of him. Daniel sat further down the table. Emily sat down near the other end of the table.

"So what do we know?" Warner asked.

"He was found wandering the halls. There are no signs of him entering by any of the doors," Travis said.

"He claims that time and date are four pm, March fifteenth, 2003. His clothes and reference to Star trek support that belief," Emily said.

"What about the medical check?" Warner asked.

"All that came up was asthma and a tracer substance," Emily answered.

"What is asthma?" Warner asked.

"Respiratory disease, usually chronic. It is not anything contagious," Emily answered.

"What about the watch?" Warner asked.

"The only way to send him back is by the watch," Daniel replied.

"So, what is the problem?" Warner asked.

"It apparently is a broken two use time machine," Daniel answered, "You use it one way and then you use it to get back. There was a tracer substance on it. The substance is there to make sure that you only go there and back again and only use that machine."

"Meaning?" Warner asked.

"The only way to send him back is by the watch," Daniel replied.

"So, what is the problem?" Warner asked.

"The watch was designed to be used only twice. The guy's use that got him here was the second and last time for the watch," Daniel answered.

"Is there any way to fix it?" Warner asked.

"It is broken, an important component needs replacing, which is impossible," Daniel said.

"How is it impossible?"

"Even if we made the parts today, the last ones melted leaving bits on the parts that didn't. The watch was intended only to be used twice."

"So what do we do with him now?" Warner asked.

"We could send him to department F. He'll probably be re-educated and given a job," Travis suggested.

"Sounds good," Warner said.

"I'll tell him," Emily said.

"Okay, then I guess we are done," Warner said. Everyone got up and left the conference room. Emily headed back to the medical lab. The kid was sitting on the examining table again. Emily went over to him.

"I'm Emily," Emily said.

"James," the kid responded.

"Well, James, the committee made its decision and as much as we would like to we can't sent you home," Emily said.

"What do you mean?" James asked.

"The watch was a time machine that broke after you used it. You went from the twenty-first century to the twenty-seventh," Emily answered.

"This is the twenty-seventh century?"

"Yes."

"Where's all the advanced technology?"

"World war three set back the advancement of technology."

"What will happen to me now?"

"The decision that came out of the meeting was to send you to department F. There you should learn what you missed with the jump in time and they should provide you with a job based on your skills."

"That's it?"

"That is it."

"No one is going to kill me or anything?"

"No."

"Then why are the guards still here?"

"They are to escort you to the vehicle that will take you to department F."

James stood up.

"Then I might as well go."

The guards and James left the medical lab.

"Do you think he'll try to run?" Grace asked.

"No, his eyes said that he couldn't wait for the next adventure," Emily answered.

"He'll get over it. Most people do," Grace said.

"I'm not sure he wanted to go home. It looked like he was hoping that he would get to stay."

"Maybe he didn't have much to go back to."

"Anything is possible." Emily started for the door. "I'm going to spend the afternoon reading. Call if something comes up."

"I will," Grace replied. Emily left the medical lab.

The next morning, Emily headed for the medical lab after breakfast. Grace was sitting in front of the computer looking through one of the stacks of files that were on the desk.

"Oh good, you're here," Grace greeted Emily, "Take the bottom half and start going through them."

"What are the files on?" Emily asked.

"The virus Jerry and crew have," Grace answered.

"What are you looking for?"

"A cure."

Emily picked up the bottom half of the files. Sitting down, Emily started with the to one.

Halfway through the pile Emily stopped.

"Something wrong?" Grace asked.

"No, just the words are blurring on the page," Emily said.

"This from the person who can read a book all day," Grace said.

"Most books aren't this repetitive," Emily said, "These reports say the same thing: it is an unknown virus. They don't even bother using different words to say it."

"In all your searching through the information did you find anything like this?"

"No, how did Jerry and crew get it in the first place?"

"I don't know. The only place they went was the hospital."

"During that month did any one of them leave?"

"I was told no."

"They couldn't have gotten it before that month because the doctor and nurses got sick after a few days. Can I use the computer for a minute?"

"Sure." Grace got up and Emily sat down. Emily went into the security system and checked what Jerry and crew were doing for the month they didn't leave.

"Looks like nothing unusual happened," Grace said.

"Except for Dorian, who came and went from the department at regular weekly intervals. He is usually gone for an hour," Emily said.

"So he brought it in."

"Looks like it. Though the report showed something in their blood." Emily got up and picked a file. She opened it. "Here it is. According to this report, they had a chemical in their blood."

"It is in another report. I looked up the chemical, it is used when people donate DNA to be cryogenically frozen."

"I thought cryogenics was illegal."

"It is, but if you have enough money, people will do it for you anyway."

Emily sat down at the computer. She shut down the surveillance system and opened Dorian's file. Emily skimmed through it.

"Dorian's father is dying, so that would be a good reason for his weekly excursions. His father lives at a home for the sick and dying."

"So what is your theory?"

"I wonder if Dorian didn't catch something when he visited his father. It hit the chemical and mutated into what the group has now."

"Which would explain why no one else showed up with it before and the numbing sensation they have been experiencing."

"Send the idea out and see what the response is." Emily got up and Grace sat down. While Grace worked, Emily stacked the files neatly on the side of the desk.

"Now we wait," Grace said when she was finished. Emily sat down in the other chair.

Three hours later Grace got an answer. She read it.

"Apparently it is not only possible but tests show that it is what we have here," Grace said, "They are currently looking for a cure."

"So Jerry and crew should be back to normal soon," Emily said.

"I was working on this for the doctor and nurses at the hospital," Grace said, "Not Jerry and crew."

"They should be back to normal too." Emily got up.

"Leaving?"

"Unless there is something else you need me for."

"No."

Emily left the medical lab.

A few days later the cure and a sample of the virus arrived.

Emily entered the quarantine area. Jerry and crew were sitting around the quarantine chamber looking bored. Jerry was the only one who looked up when Emily entered.

"What do you want?" he asked. His voice sounded metallic through the vent.

"They figured out what is wrong with you," Emily said.

"So you're here to taunt us," Jerry said.

"We are looking for a test subject for the cure that was created," Emily said.

"Are you serious?" one of the other guys asked. Everyone had perked up.

"Yes," Emily answered.

"I'll do it," Dorian said before anyone else could say anything.

"You sure?" Jerry asked.

"Yeah, I probably brought it in. I should be the test subject," Dorian said. Grace came in with a tray and wearing a face mask. Emily donned a face mask and then pressed a button that sealed the door out of the quarantine area. She pressed a second button and the quarantine chamber unsealed. Dorian came out.

Emily pressed the button to reseal the chamber. Grace had him sit down.

"Actually, you didn't bring it in. You just brought one of the contributing factors," Emily said. Grace injected the cure into Dorian's neck.

"I don't feel any different," Dorian said.

"It will take some time before it takes effect," Grace said.

"So now what?" Dorian asked.

"We put you in a different chamber and check on you tomorrow," Grace answered.

"Okay," Dorian said. Emily pushed a different button and a different chamber opened. Dorian went inside and Emily pressed the button to seal it again. Emily pressed the first button again and the door to the quarantine area opened. Emily and Grace left.

Emily came into the medical lab the next morning. Grace was off checking on Dorian and was not there. Emily went to where Grace was keeping the virus and its cure. Taking out the virus using all precautions, Emily transferred some into another container. Finishing that, Emily put the virus back and the container into her pocket. Sitting down, Emily started to work on the computer. Grace came in ten minutes later.

"Did it work?" Emily asked.

"Yes," Grace answered, "And the rest of them have been given the cure."

"That's done," Emily said.

"You sound like you had plans," Grace said.

"I was thinking of visiting Trent."

"Go. I'll take care of any major emergencies that come along."

"I wasn't asking permission."

"Go. You seem to have run out of things to do, so it will be good for you."

"I'm leaving." Emily got up and left the medical lab. She stopped briefly at her room to grab her jacket and drop off the container before leaving the department. She headed for Trent's house.

When she got there she entered without knocking. In the front hallway were three boxes stacked against the wall. The top one had Emily's name on it. Emily glanced at them before going into the kitchen. Daniel was sitting at the table. Emily sat down in the chair across from him.

"Back again?" Daniel asked.

"For a short visit," Emily answered.

"Lara held Pasha's funeral," Daniel said, "And dealt with the will."

"That was fast," Emily said, "It usually takes longer for the morgue to finish with a body."

"They didn't have the body at the funeral," Daniel said.

"Funerals aren't held until the body has been released. And the body is usually burned just before the funeral, so that the ashes can be there," Emily said, "Sometimes if it takes too long the ashes don't get there on time."

"What do they do with the ashes?" Daniel asked.

"Sometimes the family keeps them. Sometimes the urn is buried in old cemeteries," Emily answered,

"If the family doesn't know what to do with the ashes or the body was unclaimed, the ashes get sent to the government's growers."

"What do they do with the ashes?" Daniel asked.

"Use it as fertilizer for the plants," Emily answered.

"So, the vegetables you can buy are grown using ashes from people as fertilizer?" Daniel asked.

"Yes," Emily answered.

"That is gross," Daniel said.

"Where is Trent?" Emily asked.

"He has been busy the last couple days. I'm not sure with what. He has been keeping the same hours."

"That just makes it easier to go back to his regular schedule."

"Adriana is over at Jenna's for the morning."

"What have you been doing?"

"I got a job. Usually I work mornings but I got this morning off."

"Enjoying it?"

"Yes."

"That's good."

"You talked about leaving the department. What will you do when you leave?"

"Use my medical training at a hospital or clinic."

"I took a job in construction. It isn't a booming industry but there is enough work."

"The experience should be good for you."

"Yeah. I actually enjoy it. I wasn't sure I would when I started." Daniel got up and began lunch.

"Do you cook?" Daniel asked Emily.

"A little bit."

"Trent doesn't seem to."

"Cooking is a new skill for me and I'm sure Trent could learn to cook if he had to."

"Cooking is an essential skill. How can people not learn it?"

"Easily. There are stores that will sell you already prepared food."

"What about the proper nutritional requirements?"

"Welcome to the world outside department C."

Trent came into the kitchen.

"Back already?" Trent asked Emily.

"There wasn't anything going on," Emily replied.

"I found something that might interest you," Trent said.

"What is it?" Emily asked.

"I'll go get it." Trent left the kitchen and came back a minute later. He set a journal down on the table.

"I've been dealing with Ruth and Tyler's stuff for the last few days. I found that. It looks like Tyler's journal," Trent said.

"Thank you," Emily said.

"You're welcome," Trent said. Emily picked it up and started to read. She took a break for lunch and then went back to the journal. Daniel went out for the afternoon and Trent went to work. When Daniel came back he brought Adriana with him. Emily took a break from reading to spend time with Adriana. When Adriana went to bed for the night Emily went back to the journal. She finished it as Trent came back from work.

"So, what did you learn from it?" Trent asked as they sat down at the table.

"Tyler had uncovered a lot of information. I'm surprised he wasn't killed sooner," Emily replied.

"Anything you can use?"

"Locations that Schultz uses, maybe a few allies, who knows what else. Information can be useful even if it doesn't seem like it at first."

"So, have you decided what you are going to do?"

"No, right now I'm just looking for more information. I have a lot of history to the situation but except for Tyler's journal and what happened to me, I don't know what is currently going on."

"Did you find Jones?"

"No, I don't think I will find him. He seems to have a talent for disappearing without a trace."

"I'm sure you'll figure it all out."

"Yeah."

CHAPTER 9
CONCLUSION?

Emily headed back to the department the next morning after breakfast. She stopped by Travis's office. He told her that he didn't have anything for her to do at the moment. Emily left and headed for the medical lab. Grace was sitting working on the computer.

"Nothing to do there either?" Grace asked.

"There are things I could do. I just don't want to deal with it yet," Emily answered.

"Like Schultz."

"Like three boxes of stuff my father left me."

"Why not Schultz?"

"I am waiting to see what direction Livia wants to go next."

"Are you going to kill him?"

"I don't know. Probably not, but depending on the situation, I might have to."

"You know as an agent you are trained to kill people."

"Yes, but I prefer to leave that option for him or me situations."

"Speaking of training, because they haven't found a replacement for Dr. Harvey yet, I'm responsible for checking over the latest group of recruits to make sure they are healthy enough to train."

"Need any help?"

"For eight kids? I doubt it but you can stick around if you want to."

"There doesn't appear to be anything else to do."

"Maybe you need a hobby."

"Like what?"

"I don't know."

"Neither do I, but since these occasional breaks don't last long, I don't think I will bother."

Grace got up and went over to the examining table. She set up the computer. Emily sat down in the spot Grace just vacated. The door opened and the recruits were escorted in. James was one of them, also there were three of the ones from the group before; Mike, Jen, Kevin and four Emily didn't recognize. Emily turned her attention to a project she had on the computer.

The door opened, shedding light across the floor of the bedroom. The room was small and bare, except for a bed in the middle of the room. A man was trying to make himself as small as possible in one corner. He had greying brown hair and clothes that looked like they hadn't been changed in a month. A second man entered, slowly and with deliberate steps, walked across the room to stand before the first man. The second man squatted down.

"Simon," Alfred's voice echoed off the walls.

"He's dead. We can't do it without him," Simon's words sounded panicky.

"I know he is dead, but we cannot let that stop us. We need to get David out. Brett has told me that David is still alive. The rumours are false," Alfred said, "Jackson would want us to finish this."

"Third person. Need third person."

"I know. Jackson did try to get a third person."

"Said to find Emily, Emily Jackson."

"She is an agent in department H. I can talk to her. We will get a third person. But we need to act soon."

"Need some time."

"You said that when we came up with this plan. You said that last time we had a chance. We have to do it now."

"Two days."

"Okay, but only two days."

"I'll be ready."

Alfred stood up and left the room closing the door behind him. The light disappeared when the door closed.

Emily woke up just as the buzzer for breakfast went off. She got up and got ready to face the day. When she was ready Emily took out the vial with the virus in it. She looked at it for a moment before putting it in her pocket. Getting up, Emily left her room and headed for the medical lab. Robin was sitting at the desk. Grace was nowhere to be seen when Emily arrived. She ignored Robin and went over to the counter.

"What did you do to Nolan?" Robin asked in a cold voice.

"I have no idea what you are talking about," Emily replied, taking a few things out of the cupboard.

"He has been acting strange since he was sent to kill you. What did you do to him?"

"I'm still confused as to what you are talking about and how I'm to blame," Emily said placing the stuff on the counter and turning to face Robin.

"You're lying. You're going to reverse what you did to him!" Robin said.

"Really? How am I going to do that? I don't even know what you're talking about," Emily turned back to the counter.

"You'll figure that out because you won't see Dr. Grace until Nolan is back to normal. Mr. Schultz has her right now," Robin said.

"Is that right?" Emily said, "And why should I believe you? Dr. Grace could merely be late getting back from breakfast."

"You'll just have to wait. While you do, I suggest you think about how you are going to get Nolan back to normal," Robin said. Emily didn't respond. "If you don't hurry, it is possible that Dr. Grace could be in danger."

Emily turned to face Robin again. This time she had a hypodermic needle in her hand.

"What is that?" Robin asked getting up and backing away from Emily. Emily picked up a dart gun from a different counter. She emptied the syringe into the back of the dart gun then put the syringe on the counter.

"Insurance that you will stay out of my way while I retrieve Dr. Grace," Emily answered Robin's question. Robin inched toward the door and away from Emily.

"That is cheating! You have to change Nolan back to normal!" Robin said.

"I did nothing to Nolan so I can't change him back to normal and I don't like to fight fair," Emily fired the dart gun. Robin tried to run, only to get hit in the back with the dart and pass out. Emily put the dart gun away, then threw out the syringe. Going over to Robin's prone body, Emily pulled out the dart and threw it into the garbage can. Then she moved Robin to a post in one corner of the medical lab.

"You really shouldn't provoke me, but I decided to be nice and just give you a sedative," Emily told the unconscious Robin as she tied Robin's wrists behind her back with the post in between. When Emily was finished she gagged Robin.

"That should keep you for a few hours, depending on if anyone comes in before that," Emily said. Emily went to the counter and pulled out a box with another syringe in it. Putting that in her pocket, Emily left the medical lab. She stopped briefly at her room to grab her jacket before continuing to Cynthia's desk.

"Where are you going?" Cynthia asked looking up.

"To visit some friends. I shouldn't be gone more than a day, maybe two, depending," Emily answered.

"When you get back, can you help me find Brett?" Cynthia asked.

"Sure," Emily replied.

"Thanks," Cynthia said. Emily left the building.

"Should I send the note yet?" the man asked.

"No, we aren't quite ready yet. Send it tomorrow. Emily will come right after receiving the note and I want to make sure the trap is ready," Schultz said, "Make sure that idiot doesn't kill the bait."

"Yes, sir."

"Not yet, anyway."

Alfred watched Emily walk away from the building before entering himself. He stopped at Cynthia's desk.

"How are you doing?" Alfred asked Cynthia.

"I'm fine," Cynthia answered.

"Any messages?"

"No."

"Where is Emily headed?"

"To visit some friends."

Alfred nodded and then went into his office.

Emily walked to the boarded up store. When she got there, Emily went around and entered by the back door. The inside looked exactly as she had left it. Scorched walls holding up the roof with pieces of debris scattered across the floor. Emily went to one corner and started digging through the burnt rubble. After a minute she pulled out a lockbox. Taking out the key, she unlocked it and opened the lid. It held a map, a taser and a small box wrapped in brown paper. Emily pulled out the map and laid it out on a semi clear space of floor. Taking little bits of charcoal, Emily placed them on locations Tyler had mentioned in his journal.

"Where could he be hiding?" Emily asked herself.

Brett entered department H and went to Cynthia's desk.

"Is Emily here?" Brett asked.

"No, she left earlier this morning," Cynthia answered.

"Damn," Brett muttered as he turned and headed for the door.

"Brett," Cynthia called, but Brett didn't hear her. He had left the building.

Eleven forty-five post meridian Travis and Alfred had a meeting in Alfred's office. Fifteen minutes later they left Alfred's office and headed for the medical lab.

"Do you have any idea where Emily went?" Travis asked.

"No, but we'll talk to Dr. Grace," Alfred answered. Travis opened the door to the medical lab and they stepped inside.

"Where is she?" Travis asked looking around.

"Apparently not here, but Robin is," Alfred said seeing Robin tied to the post. Travis went over to Robin.

"I didn't think she was supposed to be here today," Travis said.

"As far as I know, she is not supposed to be here at all. She is supposed to be in class," Alfred said as Travis kneeled down. Travis removed the gag and tried to wake Robin up.

"What happened?" Travis demanded when he got Robin to a semi-conscious state.

"Emily…" Robin started.

"Emily what?"

"Shot…me…tried to…get away."

"Why would Emily shoot you? And if she did where is the bullet hole?" Travis asked.

"My guess would be that Emily shot her in the back with a dart gun," Alfred said.

"How do you figure that?" Travis asked.

"The dart in the garbage and she tried to escape," Alfred answered.

"Why would Emily do this? And where is Dr. Grace?" Travis asked.

"Emily after…doctor," Robin said.

"Where is Dr. Grace?" Travis asked.

"Schultz," Robin answered sinking back into unconsciousness.

"Who?" Travis asked.

"I know who," Alfred said, "Get a van and five agents and meet me in the parking lot!" Alfred sprinted toward the door.

"What is going on?" Travis asked standing up.

"I will explain it later," Alfred told Travis as he left the medical lab. Leaving Robin where she was, Travis left to do what Alfred told had him.

Emily dusted off the map prior to folding it up and putting it away. She grabbed the taser before closing and locking the box. Putting everything back Emily left the store and headed for the location she picked. It was a lab not far from the warehouse where Pascal had been held. When she was close Emily went into a nearby building. She went through the building and up to the roof. Emily sat up there, watching the traffic at the back door.

"So, what are we doing?" Travis asked Alfred as they got into the van.

"We are searching several locations," Alfred answered.

"For who?"

"Emily, Dr. Grace and anyone else we might find."

Travis started the van and left the parking lot. Alfred gave him directions to the first location.

Brett tried the door of the bar. Finding it unlocked, he entered. Trent was getting ready to open.

"Can I help you?" Trent asked.

"I hope so. My name is Brett. I'm a friend of Emily's. I was wondering if you had seen her today," Brett said.

"Sorry, I can't help you. I haven't seen her today," Trent said.

"Damn," Brett said and started to turn to leave.

"Why are you looking for her?" Trent asked.

"Know anything about Schultz?" Brett asked.

"Yes," Trent answered.

"Well, Schultz has set a trap to capture and kill her. Emily is guaranteed to take the bait. I am hoping I can stop her or make sure she thinks it through before rushing into it," Brett said.

"Oh."

"You act like you aren't worried."

"I am worried. There is just nothing I can do. I don't know where Emily is and I have made an agreement to remain neutral in all conflicts."

"Then how can you be so close to Emily?"

"There aren't any rules against it. I am not personally involved in any of the conflict."

Brett shook his head and left the bar.

The van arrived at the first location. They all got out. On Alfred's order they entered the building. Alfred stayed by the door while Travis and the five agents went through the building room by room. Half an hour later, they were back in the van and headed to the next location. They continued this pattern all afternoon. They went through ten locations before the sun went down.

"How many more of these are there?" Travis asked as they got back into the van after the tenth one.

"Two more to go," Alfred answered.

"If they aren't there?" Travis asked.

"Then there is a problem," Alfred said. They continued to the next location.

After the sun went down, the traffic at the back door of the lab stopped. Emily sat there for ten minutes before using a cable to get to the roof of the lab. Once across, Emily used a rope to get down to a window. Emily slid it open then climbed inside. The room was bare except for a bed and a desk with a chair. The bed was occupied. Emily pulled out a lighter. The small flame was enough to show that the occupant of the bed was a man. It was the older version of a picture Emily had seen of Schultz while going through Jones's files. Emily put the light out.

"If I were you, I would be in a more secure room," Emily whispered. Emily took the box with the syringe and the vial out of her pocket. She removed them from the box before she filled the syringe with the virus and injected it into his arm that was hanging off the bed. Schultz moved his arm a little but didn't wake up. Emily put the syringe back into the box and slid it under the bed. Getting up she opened the door a crack. There wasn't anyone in the hallway outside the room. Emily stepped and softly closed the door behind her. Emily headed down the hallway. There were doors at regular intervals on each side of the hallway. The route turned left and came to a dead end. There weren't any doors after the corner. Emily turned around and went back down the hallway in the other direction.

She made a right hand turn at the end. This hallway was without doors. When Emily came to the end there was another right corner. This hallway had doors on both sides at regular intervals. At the end of this corridor the right turn took Emily to a set of stairs.

At the bottom of the stairs was a hallway that ran to the right with doors along it. Emily continued along it. The left turn at the end led to a hallway without doors.

"No wonder he wasn't concerned about security, this place is a maze," Emily muttered to herself. Three more lefts brought Emily to another set of stairs.

The hallway at the bottom had doors but this time only on the outside wall. With the same pattern there were four rights and then a staircase. This floor had much shorter hallways. Emily took four lefts and reached the next staircase. This staircase led to an open area that had a door on each side of the room. One door had an exit sign over it.

Emily walked across the open space to the door without the exit sign. She opened it. Upon entry there was a metal staircase that went down. Emily could see a guard at the bottom of the stairs. She quietly stepped out onto the landing, got a good view and shot the guard with the taser. The guard jerked a couple times, then fell to the floor. Emily waited several minutes to see if anyone would check what made the noise. When no one appeared, Emily slowly went down the stairs. At the bottom was a hallway with a door at the end. Emily stepped over the guard and went to the door.

Trying the handle, Emily quickly found it locked. She went back to where the guard lay. After a quick check of his pockets, Emily found the key. Access through the door led to a bigger room. Emily stood on a metal walkway that was a storey above the floor of the room. There were prison cells along the wall on Emily's left. The cells were empty, except for the one at the end. To Emily's right was a staircase that went down to the rest of the room. Emily could see that below the walkway were more cells, with two guards pacing back and forth in front of them. The rest of the room was dedicated to the extraction of information.

"Hey," one of the guards had noticed Emily. He moved out from under the walkway aiming at her. Emily shot him with the taser, while being careful not to get hit. The second guard punched an alarm before moving out from under the walkway. Emily hit the second guard. Both guards now lay on the floor.

A man was standing next to the bars on the upper level. Emily didn't recognize him but he seemed familiar. Emily turned to go down the stairs.

"Hey," the man called. Emily turned to look at him. "Could you unlock the door? The keys are in your hand."

Emily studied the man for a moment. He was tall, white haired, full beard and skinny as if he was unfed. Emily's instinct told her to trust him to help her. She went over and unlocked the cell, leaving it closed.

"Thanks," the man said.

"You're welcome," Emily said. The man sat down on the cot in his cell. Emily went down the stairs. There were three people in the cells on the lower level. Grace was lying on the cot in the middle one, while a man was in another cell and a woman in the third. Emily recognized the man as Kent, but she didn't recognize the woman. Going to Grace's cell, Emily unlocked it. Opening the door, Emily entered the cell and knelt beside the cot.

"Grace," Emily said. Grace opened her eyes. He eyes looked glazed and she seemed to be trying to focus.

"Need antidote," Grace muttered.

"What is the poison?" Emily asked.

"Don't know," Grace muttered.

"Can you move?" Emily asked.

"Sort of," Grace answered. She sat up with Emily's assistance. Slowly Emily helped her stand. Most of Grace's weight was being supported by Emily. She half dragged Grace out of the cell. The door at the top of the stairs opened. Several armed guards entered followed by Nolan, a female Emily assumed was Delilah, and Schultz.

"Hurry," Grace whispered as Emily lowered her to the floor. The guards came down and surrounded Emily and Grace. Nolan followed them, while Schultz and Delilah stayed on the walkway. The man in the cell on the upper level stood up. He leaned against the bars, but made no attempt to open the cell door. Emily counted twelve guards.

"Perhaps I should have had the trap ready when the bait arrived," Schultz said.

"Maybe you should watch your organization for loose mouths," Emily retorted, "Unless Robin's blackmail scheme was part of your plan."

"She will be rewarded as she deserves," Schultz said.

"If you can find her," Emily said.

"I always locate them, you should know that," Schultz said.

"That's why you had to set a trap for me?" Emily said.

"I have two reasons for that: one being that you yourself are bait for another trap and two I want to successfully get rid of you."

"Who would possibly walk into a trap with me as bait?"

"You act like you don't know."

"Any reason I should?"

"You were the one who searched out the information."

"Searching for information and finding it are not the same thing."

"You didn't have trouble finding this place. I'm pretty sure Robin didn't tell you."

"Of course not, but you leave enough breadcrumbs that she didn't need to."

"Capture her alive," Schultz ordered his men. The guards started toward Emily. Emily moved away from Grace and shot the guards. She disabled six of the guards before the taser was knocked out of her hand from behind. Emily started to engage the guards in hand to hand. Nolan stood watching. Schultz stood waiting. The cell door opened and the man stepped out. Emily knocked out three guards. She slowly edged closer to the taser. Schultz started to look worried. The man grabbed Delilah from behind. He wrapped one arm tightly around her throat. Schultz turned to look at Delilah. A shot rang out. Schultz turned to look at Nolan, who was pointing a gun in his direction. Then Schultz collapsed. The guards' attention was distracted by the gunshot. Emily used it to grab the taser and shoot the guards. The man let go of Delilah. Delilah scrambled over to Schultz.

"Dad," Delilah sobbed. Schultz quit breathing. Emily went over and checked on Grace. She was still alive but no longer conscious. Emily carefully wrapped Grace's arm around her neck. Nolan came over and did the same. They carried Grace over to and up the stairs. The man stayed where he was. Nolan opened the door and they went through it sideways. They went along the hallway to the stairs.

"You go first, I'll follow," Nolan told Emily. Emily nodded and released Grace's arm. Nolan picked Grace up. Emily headed up the stairs, Nolan followed. At the top, Emily opened the door. Alfred was standing near the door on the other side of the room. Emily entered, and then Nolan. Nolan lowered Grace down. Emily wrapped Grace's arm around her neck. Nolan and her carried Grace across the room.

"There is a van outside," Alfred said, "Tell the driver to take you to the hospital." Nolan and Emily went outside. There were three vans. They headed for the closest one. They got into the back, lying Grace across one of the seats. The driver closed the door and got back into the driver's seat. The van started for the hospital. Emily used the radio in the back of the van to contact the hospital and relay Grace's condition. When they arrived, attendants came out with a stretcher. Grace was transferred to the stretcher and taken into the hospital. Emily followed. While Grace was taken behind closed doors, Emily stopped at the reception area. There she sat down. Fifteen minute later a doctor came out, checked with the reception desk, then went to where Emily was sitting.

"She is going to be okay. She just needs to rest. She has also been asking for you," the doctor informed her. Emily nodded and stood up. The doctor led Emily to the room. Emily went in and sat down in the chair by the bed. Grace was sleeping. Emily sat there, silently waiting.

Grace's eyes flickered opened. She turned to look at Emily.

"I'm usually the one sitting there," Grace's voice was rough.

"I would switch places with you but I think you need the rest," Emily said.

"I'll be fine," Grace said.

"One of my professors told me that the worst patients were doctors," Emily said.

"Point taken," Grace said as she closed her eyes. Ten minutes later Grace was asleep. Emily left the room. On the right, Alfred was standing a little ways down the hallway. There was a man crouched in a chair across from Alfred. The man had unkempt hair a beard, and clothes that looked like he had been wearing them for months. His face was drawn but Emily recognized him as Jones. Emily turned to her left. She stopped. Nolan was standing outside a doorway. Emily could see Livia lying inside the room on a bed. She touched Nolan's arm. He turned to her.

"There's someone you need to meet," Emily told Nolan. Emily turned towards the other two; Nolan followed. Emily stopped in front of Jones and knelt at eye level with him.

"Simon Jones, I'm Emily Jackson. I would like you to meet your son, Nolan. Nolan, this is your father, Simon Jones," Emily said, then stood up and stepped back.

"Mom is in the room down the hall," Nolan said.

"Livia?" Jones's face lit up.

"Yes," Nolan said.

"Show me," Jones stood up. Nolan led him down the hall to Livia's room. Emily sat down in the chair Jones had just vacated.

"I could use a drink," Emily commented.

"Alcohol is against the rules," Alfred said.

"If you can find the tequila, you can confiscate it," Emily said.

"No use. If it was whiskey maybe, but tequila there is not much of a point," Alfred said. Brett walked down the hallway to join them.

"How are they?" Brett asked.

"Fine. No one is going to die," Alfred answered.

"Except maybe you if you don't go and talk to Cynthia," Emily told Brett.

"Why?" Brett asked.

"Because I said so. Now go," Emily told him. Brett looked at Alfred for information but got a blank look. Not getting an explanation, Brett turned and left.

"Cynthia would not kill him," Alfred said.

"No, but I might," Emily said.

"I think I'm going to have to change the various departments and rules," Alfred said.

"Have fun," Emily said.

"You have experience dealing with the rules," Alfred said.

"I'm a doctor. That is what I'm good at, not what you need," Emily said.

"I tried," Alfred said.

"Who else is here?"

"Livia was injected with the same poison as Dr. Grace, though I don't know why. Delilah has a broken arm, and David has some scratches that need stitches."

"How's Robin?" Emily asked.

"Awake and sitting in a prison in department F building with the rest of Schultz's men that we found. Though why you sedated her I do not understand."

"To keep her out of my way. If she woke up and warned Schultz, I might have been in more trouble."

"Travis and I found her, which was how we knew to search for you and Dr. Grace. It took longer than I expected, but I had an outdated map listing the locations Schultz used. We found Brett and he took us to the building where you were."

"He would know, though I really doubt Schultz suspected a spy among his men."

"If he did, Brett might not be here."

"Brett is smarter than that."

"What do you plan to do now?"

"Separate myself from the department so that I can live the rest of my life in peace."

"How soon will this separation occur?"

"Depends."

"Would you be willing to do one last mission for me? It has nothing to do with what I asked before."

"Sure."

"I'll give it to you tomorrow or the next day."

"What time it is?"

"Six thirty ante meridian."

"Then I have something I have to do," Emily stood up.

"See you in one of the next few days," Alfred said.

"Yeah," Emily replied. She left the hospital and headed for Warner's office. Arriving, Emily went passed the secretary and into Warner's office. Warner wasn't there. Emily sat down in his chair and waited. Ten minutes later Warner entered. He sighed when he saw her. He sat down in the chair in front of the desk.

"What do you want?" Warner asked.

"To inform you that I'm going to be leaving the department in two weeks to a month," Emily said, "Alfred already knows."

"Okay, anything else?" Warner asked.

"Don't try to stop me and don't think about trying to call me back once I've left," Emily said.

"Yeah, okay," Warner said. Emily stood up.

"Enjoy your day," Emily said. Emily left the building and headed for Trent's house. She entered and found Daniel and Trent in the kitchen. Trent looked up at her as she entered.

"You look tired," Trent commented.

"I didn't get to sleep last night," Emily replied.

"If you are here to crash, I would suggest you do it before Adriana gets up, which will be soon," Trent said. Emily nodded and went to bed.

Emily got up seven hours later. Trent was sitting at the kitchen table reading. Emily sat down across from him. Trent looked up.

"If you're hungry, there are leftovers in the 'frigerator," Trent said.

"I'm not really hungry," Emily replied.

"Brett showed up at the bar looking for you last night," Trent said.

"He learned about a plot Schultz had to kidnap me and he wanted to warn me," Emily said, "But I was already dealing with it."

"So what happened?"

"I had to rescue Grace, which I succeeded at doing, but Nolan shot Schultz, and Alfred took out most of Schultz's organization. Jones was reunited with his family."

"Sounds like a happily ever after."

"I have one more mission, then I am leaving the department."

"Then what?"

"I'm not sure."

"Daniel has been talking about finding his own place to live."

"That's his choice."

"The discussion, which I'm guessing that I wasn't supposed to hear, was that Jenna would be living with him. Jenna's grandmother hasn't heard that part yet, but I think she will disapprove when she does."

"I hope they don't get into too much trouble."

"Lara was looking for you."

"Why?"

"Something about the house she is currently living in."

"I'll talk to her at some point."

"I have to go to work." Trent got up.

"See you."

Trent left. Emily sat there for a few minutes before getting up and going to the telephone. She dialed a number and waited as it rang.

"Hello?" Lara voice came over the line.

"Hello, Lara. Trent mentioned that you wanted to talk to me," Emily said.

"Yes, I was thinking of moving into an apartment closer to the clinic and I was wondering if you would deal with the house for me," Lara said, "I'll deal with my stuff, all you would be left with is the furniture and the house.'

"Sure, I can deal with that," Emily said.

"Thank you," Lara said.

"You're welcome."

"See you."

"Bye." Emily hung up the receiver. Leaving the kitchen Emily went in the hallway. She dragged the boxes that were sitting there into the living room. Sitting down she started to go through them.

Daniel came home at five post meridian and started supper. Shortly after Jenna brought Adriana home.

"Mom!" Adriana said when she saw Emily. Emily smiled as she looked at Adriana.

"Hello, Adriana," Emily said. Adriana climbed onto Emily's lap. "You must be Jenna." Emily looked up at Jenna.

"Yes," Jenna said.

"I'm Emily," Emily said.

"Nice to meet you," Jenna said, "Daniel said I could stay for supper since my grandmother is out of town visiting relatives."

"You might as well have a seat. It will be a few minutes before it will be ready," Emily told her. Jenna sat down in a chair. Adriana climbed down off Emily's lap and wandered off.

"What do you have training in?" Emily asked Jenna.

"I'm a mid-wife," Jenna answered.

"How do you like it?" Emily asked.

"I enjoy it, but my grandmother thinks I should try and get a medical degree or training to become a nurse," Jenna answered.

"Mid-wives are important and the pay isn't too bad," Emily said.

"I know but Grandmother thinks I could make more money," Jenna said.

"I have two medical degrees and my only source of money is from a restaurant I own," Emily said.

"Supper," Daniel called from the kitchen. Emily and Jenna stood up and went into the kitchen. Adriana was already sitting at the table, waiting.

After they ate, Daniel walked Jenna home. He came back a few minutes later.

When it was Adriana's bedtime, Emily tucked her in. Then Emily went back to sorting through the boxes. Daniel came in and sat down.

"Trent said you were talking about finding a place of your own," Emily said.

"Yeah, I just have to find time to look," Daniel replied.

"Lara is moving, her house will be empty soon," Emily said.

"She probably would like to sell it. I don't have that much money right now."

"She asked me to deal with it. It is fully furnished. She didn't say anything about selling it and it is in my name already. All that is needed is to transfer it into your name and you move in."

Daniel didn't say anything as he mulled it over.

"Okay," Daniel said.

"Good. That gets it out of my hair," Emily said.

"So, do I just need to talk to Lara?"

"Yes. You will need my signature at some point. I will be around."

"Okay."

Silence settled over the room. Daniel went to his room half an hour later. Emily went to bed when she was finished sorting through the boxes.

In the morning Emily got up, ate breakfast and headed for the department. Cynthia greeted her with a smile when she arrived.

"Alfred is waiting for you in his office," Cynthia told Emily.

"How did Brett take the news?" Emily asked.

"He was surprised but seems happy," Cynthia answered.

"That's good" Emily said, as she went to the door of Alfred's office. She knocked before opening it. Alfred looked up.

"Come in," Alfred invited her. Emily entered and sat down. Alfred handed Emily a file folder.

"You won't report to Travis for this one. Just do it, come back and tell me. Dr. Grace is not back yet so you don't have to see her before you go, but I suggest you see her when you get back," Alfred said.

"Okay," Emily said.

"Thank you for doing this," Alfred said.

"No problem." Emily got up and left Alfred's office. In her room Emily read through the file. Once she was finished, she headed out on then mission.

A week later Emily arrived back at the department. She stopped briefly at Alfred's office to tell him that the mission was completed. Then she walked to the medical lab. Grace wasn't there. Emily sat down in front of the computer. A man came in. He was dressed up, sported a white goatee and short white hair. He seemed familiar, but Emily wasn't sure from where.

"I'm looking for Dr. Grace," the man said.

"I don't know where she is, but she'll probably be back soon," Emily replied.

"I'll wait here then," the man said, "You're Emily, right?"

"Last time I checked," Emily answered.

"I'm David," the man said.

"Nice to meet you," Emily replied.

"I have a question for you. Why did you unlock the cell door?"

Emily realized then that this had been the man in the upper level cell.

"I don't know," Emily answered. David was about to say something more when Grace entered the medical lab.

"What do you need?" Grace asked David.

"Your recommendations that Alfred asked for," David answered.

"I'm not finished but I will deliver them to Alfred when I'm done," Grace said.

"Very well," David said then left.

"So they are getting your help with the changes," Emily said.

"Yes," Grace replied.

"I turned down Alfred's offer to help with that," Emily said getting up.

"Why? You are the one who always voices complaints about the rules," Grace asked.

"Because I don't intend to be here that long," Emily answered.

"Where have you been for the last week?"

"On a mission."

"So you're here for the after mission check-up?"

"Yes." Emily went over and sat down on the examining table. Grace pulled the scanner. Emily laid down and Grace used the scanner. When she was finished, Grace put the scanner back in its slot and brought up the results on the computer. Emily sat up. Grace didn't say anything as she studies the results.

"Anything I should know?" Emily asked.

"A few things," Grace answered.

"Like what?" Emily asked.

"Like if you were going to stay at the department I couldn't okay you for a mission," Grace said.

"What are you seeing?" Emily asked.

"First off, you are pregnant," Grace said.

"I was suspecting that," Emily said.

"And the second thing," Grace said, "I've been watching for a while, but it made a jump in the last couple months."

"What did?" Emily asked.

"The cardiopulmonarymentia," Grace answered, "There have been signs of it for years, but always not bad enough to worry about."

"How bad it is now?" Emily asked.

"At this rate, you'll be dead about the time your child is born."

"That would explain some things."

"You are going to see a doctor at the hospital about this right?"

"Yes."

"Good. Leave Trent's address."

"So that you can come and bug me?"

"So that I can get out of here occasionally."

Emily got up and wrote the address on a piece of paper that was on the desk.

"There."

"See you."

"Bye," Emily left the medical lab. She went to her room. Emily packed her clothes into a backpack and her magazines in a box. Everything else was stuffed into a bag that Emily clipped onto her backpack. She slung her backpack over one shoulder, picked up the box and left her room. Cynthia wasn't at her desk when Emily stopped by to drop off her ID cards on her way out. Exiting the building Emily headed for Trent's house. Upon arrival Emily went inside. She dumped her stuff by the door and went into the kitchen. Trent was at the kitchen table eating lunch. Emily sat down.

"Hungry?" Trent asked.

"Not if the revolting feeling in my stomach is any indication," Emily replied.

"Finished with your mission?"

"Finished with the department too."

"Daniel and Jenna moved into Lara's house and Lara moved into an apartment. They were looking for you."

"I figured that."

"Well, what now?"

"I'm pregnant and I'm dying of the same thing that killed my father. Grace figured that the child would arrive and then I would die. Other than that I don't know."

"So, have we hit happily ever after yet?"

"Happily ever after isn't until after the wedding."

"As in close but not close enough. Sounds about right."

EPILOGUE

Daniel was getting ready to head to work. Jenna had left before he had gotten up to tend to a woman in labour. Daniel had finished breakfast and was about to do the dishes, when there was a knock at the door. He went to the door and opened it. Professor Abbott stood there.

"Hello," Daniel said.

"I thought I would stop by and tell you that your prototype has been returned," Professor Abbott said, "And Alfred would like to talk to you about coming back."

"I need to know a few things before I could even think about coming back," Daniel said.

"Alfred has finished reorganizing department H and is currently willing to listen to suggestions about how to improve department C."

"I'll call my boss and tell him that I'll be late," Daniel said, "Then I come by department C and talk to Alfred."

"It would nice to have you back," Professor Abbott said. When he left, Daniel went back inside to call his boss.

A week later, Daniel found himself with his own office in department C, was getting paid to work there and could go home to Jenna every night.

Grace studied the room numbers as she walked by. Finally reaching the room number the nurse had told her, Grace entered. Emily looked pale and exhausted lying on the bed with her eyes closed. Grace sat down in the chair beside the bed. Emily opened her eyes.

"Back to sitting there, are you?" Emily's voice was soft.

"I got the phone call that you were here," Grace said.

"I'm fine. Chandra is healthy," Emily said.

"That's good."

"Trent is with her. He left so that I could get some rest."

"Sorry to disturb you."

"That is okay. Carbrat has found a cure for cardiopulmonarymentia. They've had it for months, but I didn't want anything that would affect Chandra. I got the injection after Chandra was born."

"So you won't be dying."

"Not yet, anyway."

"Going to marry Trent then? Or are you staying engaged forever?"

"We got married when Carbrat sent the news that they had a cure. My mother would like a formal wedding, so I said we would do that after Chandra was born."

"So anytime now."

"Give it a month or two."

"Understandable."

"It will be a double ceremony. Trent and I, so my mother can get her pictures and Daniel and Jenna."

"Sounds like a lot is going on."

"Add two job offers … yeah, a lot is going on."

"Two job offers?"

"One for Carbrat to create medical equipment and the other from the clinic my mother works at, to be a pediatrician."

"I better let you rest then. You'll need your energy. I'll visit another time," Grace got up.

"Okay," Emily closed her eyes again. Grace watched as Emily drifted off the sleep before leaving the hospital room.

ABOUT THE AUTHOR

Heather Mantler has six shelves of books organized by author and genre. She lives in Prince George, British Columbia. She is always working on another story. Heather encourages all her readers to post their reviews on amazon.com.

www.ingramcontent.com/pod-product-compliance
Lightning Source LLC
Chambersburg PA
CBHW071642260626
47170CB00001B/200

* 9 7 8 0 9 8 6 8 7 5 9 2 2 *